Ambush

S. Dietrich

ISBN:9781097508624

DEDICATION

This book is dedicated to those who put everything on the line, every day, to protect society.

CONTENTS

ACKNOWLEDGMENTS

I would like to thank my beloved wife for her support. I would also like to acknowledge my new friend, Vic, who provided some invaluable insights.

Chapter 1

Friday

Captain Jim Churchill was staring out the window of his office, through the rain, at the roof of City Hall. A garden had been installed on the roof when it was built and Jim was wondering if anyone ever maintained it. There was a knock at his door. He turned as his lieutenant, Rebekah Naes, said, "Lloyd's here. You wanted to talk to him sir?"

Jim nodded as Lloyd entered the office. They shook hands and Jim gestured to a chair at a round conference table.

"Rebekah says you've put in your papers."

"Yes sir. I figured after thirty-five years it's time."

"Why now?"

"OK, Jim," Lloyd said with a smile, "I guess after Fred passed, I figured it was time."

Fred Henderson was working a case with another detective when he had a massive heart attack. His partner had found him in the passenger seat of their patrol car.

"We were all worried about him," said Jim.

"Must have been the three cheeseburgers a day diet," replied Lloyd.

"It's too bad. It seemed like he was getting his act back together and starting to come back into form."

"Well it kinda woke me up. I want to be around for my grandkids."

"Well I guess after thirty-five years, you've earned it. What are you going to do now?"

"I thought maybe I'd be a ski instructor."

"You don't ski."

"I don't. Do you think that would be a problem?"

Jim smiled and laughed.

"How's Marianne?" Marianne Wilson was Jim's girlfriend and was currently on tour on the east coast.

"She was in Charleston last night. They have a concert tonight in Charlotte. I'm flying out after work tonight and I'm going to meet them in Roanoke tomorrow."

"Are you coming right back?"

"No," Jim said, "I'm going with them when she plays Washington DC, then I'll fly back on Monday from there. She's going to fly back to Nashville and check on her ranch, then she's coming back on Friday and we'll have next weekend together."

"At least it's not boring."

Jim looked at Lloyd for a minute then said, "can you keep something under your hat?"

Lloyd nodded and said, "Sure."

"I'm going to propose to her in Roanoke."

Lloyd smiled, "Good for you. If she has any sense at all she'll say no."

Jim smiled, "I know. That's why I'm so nervous. I'm leaving early to pick up the ring at that place in the north end, Stuart's?"

"You must be using TW's money," said Lloyd. TW Griffin was the pseudonym Jim Churchill used as a writer.

"You got that straight."

"Well good luck Jim. I wish both of you well."

"Stay in touch Lloyd. If this goes well, I want you to stand up for me."

Lloyd was touched. "Of course I will."

They shook hands at the door.

"Once it's official, don't even think about this place," said Jim, "enjoy your retirement."

"Oh, I will. Good luck again," Lloyd said as he headed back to his desk.

Jim looked at his watch and decided to call it a day. He grabbed his coat and headed out the door. As he passed his admin, Dionne Barrone, she handed him a box of business cards.

"They finally came in? Must mean I'm being transferred."

Dionne smiled, "We can't lose you sir."

Dionne was a holdover from his predecessor. Jim didn't quite trust her but she was efficient and competent.

Jim strolled out to the parking garage and found his car. He jumped into the Explorer and headed down the ramp to the exit. It was just past two and while traffic was building, he was still ahead of the rush.

Jim was thinking about the ring, and what he was going to say to Marianne in Roanoke. Maybe that was why he missed the tail. He got on the freeway headed north, whistling as he went. He was early, but he knew that Stuart wouldn't mind. He got off the freeway and drove east on Northgate Way until he crossed Eighth Avenue Northeast, then turned left into a strip mall. In his rear-view mirror, Jim saw a brown Volvo drive past him on the street, but didn't think anything of it. He pulled in front of Stuart's Jewelry and found a spot to park in the center aisle. The brown Volvo was pulling to a stop in back of the post office on Tenth Avenue. Jim paid no attention to it as he walked into Stuart's Fine Jewelry.

Stuart Hillman was behind the counter. "You're early," he said by way of greeting.

"I decided I didn't want to wait. I still have to get to the airport."

"Well this little beauty should get locked in a safe."

"I got it covered, Stuart," said Jim.

Stuart unlocked a drawer behind the counter and produced a sparkling diamond ring. It was a princess cut of eight and a half carats.

"That looks gorgeous, Stuart."

"Thank you, Jim." He placed it into a box, then slid the receipt over for Jim to sign. Jim signed it and slid it back. He took the box from Stuart and looked at the ring one more time before slipping it into a zippered pocket in the lining of his suit jacket.

"You think that's secure?"

"Close to my heart, Stuart."

"Jesus you're sappy."

Jim smiled, and shook hands with Stuart. "No matter what happens, I promise to let you know how it goes."

"You better Jim. It's a pleasure doing business with you."

Jim walked out of the store and up the sidewalk towards the teriyaki restaurant next door. From between a pair of parked cars a man appeared, holding a cigarette in his left hand. "Got a light," he asked.

Jim's radar finally went off. The man was shorter than Jim, brown hair, thinning on the top. He was wearing a Members Only jacket and jeans, but Jim couldn't see his right hand. Jim closed the distance rapidly, without saying anything. Startled, the man started pulling his right hand out from behind his back.

Jim shouted, "Police, let me see your hands," as he swept his jacket aside to clear his Glock.

He knew he was already behind the eight ball but Jim kept moving in. The mans hand swept up, but he rushed his shot. It felt like Jims thigh had been stabbed by a hot poker but Jim kept moving. His right hand came up and Jim got off two quick shots just as he felt another hot poker hit his left shoulder. The brown Volvo pulled up alongside the man as he ran out to the parking lot. Jim went down on one knee but was aiming squarely between the mans shoulder blades when a shot came from inside the car.

The back of the mans head came off and he collapsed in a heap. The Volvo spun its wheels as it left the parking lot.

Jim realized he was sitting on the ground and blood was pooling under his thigh. Stuart came running out of the store.

"Jim, I called 911, holy shit, let me see that."

"Give me your belt," said Jim.

Stuart pulled his belt out of his pants and handed it to Jim.

"Sorry about this Stuart," said Jim.

Jim slid Stuart's belt under his thigh and as high on his leg as it would go. He ran the belt through the buckle to the last notch and then took the small flashlight off his own waist. Jim slipped the flashlight under the buckle and proceeded to twist until he couldn't twist it anymore. He laid the excess on top of his thigh.

"Hold that right there," Jim said. Stuart held the makeshift tourniquet as the first patrol car arrived. The officer got out, looked around and saw the body, then made a call on his radio.

"Jim Churchill, Seattle PD Homicide," shouted Jim, "Brown Volvo, white male driver, left westbound." The officer grabbed his shoulder mic and made another broadcast before reaching into the car and grabbing a black bag, which he brought to Jim.

"I just had the Care Under Fire training," he explained to Jim.

"Glove up," said Jim, "and pack this wound." Jim was pointing to his left shoulder.

The officer put on blue rubber gloves and told Jim to lay down. He pulled Jims jacket aside and ripped open his shirt.

"Shit sir, you can barely see it." He rolled Jim onto his right side. "No exit wound."

The officer grabbed a roll of gauze from the black bag and held it to the hole, putting pressure on the wound as other cars started to arrive.

"Sir, we got this under control," said the officer.

"Tell them to look for the brown Volvo, white male driver."

"It's under control sir, I already told radio."

"OK, good. I'm going to pass out now," said Jim as he closed his eyes.

Chapter 2

Friday afternoon

Lloyd Murray and Jason King arrived together, in Jasons battered Crown Victoria. Lloyds regular partner was on vacation and they had not replaced Fred Henderson yet.

Lloyd swept his eyes across the parking lot. Jason knew that when asked to recall the scene later, Lloyd would do so accurately and in detail. In the parking lot in front of Stuart's Fine Jewelry was a shapeless lump covered in a yellow blanket. A small pistol lay next to the blanket. A medic unit was in the parking lot and another form lay on the gurney inside, an IV bag hooked to his arm. An officer waved the detectives over. Lloyd was once again reminded of how old he was by the youth of the officer.

"Why are they still here," asked Lloyd.

"He insisted on waiting until you got here," said the officer, "he said he wanted Lloyd Murray."

"I better see what he wants," Lloyd said as he hoisted his bulk into the back of the medic unit.

Lloyd stood over Jim's still form, taking it all in. The medics had cut his shirt off and cut his right pants leg from the ankle until the cut terminated at a makeshift tourniquet at Jims hip.

"Jim?"

Jim Churchill opened his eyes.

"Hey Lloyd. Can you call Marianne?"

"OK Jim. Anything else?"

"Yeah. Check my files. This looks like a robbery but it could have been something else."

"OK Jim. Someone will be searching your desk and locker later."

Jim nodded, then said, "One more thing. Call Sheridan Johnston. Have him meet me at Harborview."

"I will. You take it easy."

One of the medics looked up. "Who is Sheridan Johnston?"

Lloyd looked at him. "One of the top five orthopedic surgeons in the country. Tell Harborview to call him."

"What if he doesn't have privileges?"

Lloyd looked at him like he had spontaneously grown another head. "Never mind. I'll call him." Lloyd opened his phone, found the contact he wanted and made the call. Jason listened to his side of the conversation.

"Sheridan, Jim's been shot."

"Harborview. They should be expecting you."

"The gun's still here. It looks like a twenty two."

"I'll call Marianne. You go work your magic."

Jason said, "Nice to have your own doc on speed dial."

"Yeah, well I'm not looking forward to the next call."

"You sure you want to?"

"No. But he's my boss, and he told me to."

"Do her a favor, call her after her show's over."

"Good idea. Let's start the canvas. Sgt. Worthy and Lt. Naes should be here soon."

Jason went to talk to Stuart Hillman. Lloyd started walking to the Teriyaki restaurant next door. Two doors down was a bank. Lloyd made the executive decision to go there first. He went in and spoke with the manager.

"As soon as we heard the shots, we locked the front door. I don't think anyone saw anything."

"OK, thanks. Oh, do you have video of the parking lot?"

The manager, a portly gentleman in his forties, said, "Of course. Let me call corporate and see if they can get it for you."

Lloyd had worked bank jobs before. This branch was part of a corporation. All the video was digitally recorded and the only people with access were some nameless IT types in another state. Lloyd passed him a business card.

"IT can email it or send me a video."

"Oh they'll do both, no problem."

Lloyd thanked him and went back to the Teriyaki joint. As soon as he walked in, the lone proprietor looked at him and said, "The special today is spicy chicken."

Lloyd said, "how about the beef?"

"Out of beef. Spicy chicken?"

Lloyd nodded and handed him a bill to cover it.

"What can you tell me about what happened in the parking lot?"

"You the police?"

Lloyd lifted his jacket to show his badge on his belt and said, "Uh huh."

"Oh very bad. That guy, he was in here."

"Which one?"

"The dead one. He came in here, didn't say anything. I tell him paying customer only. He gave me a dollar."

"Anything else?"

"He got dropped off. A brown Volvo. I didn't see who the driver was, but the dead guy got out of the passenger side."

"How long was he here?"

"About ten minutes. He was watching out the window, then went out into the parking lot and I didn't see him until the shooting started."

Lloyd noticed the owners English had improved as they started talking. His name was Ken Matsushita and he had been born in Seattle. Lloyd thanked him and went outside with his spicy chicken. Between Stuart's Jewelry and Teriyaki Express there was a trash can. Lloyd made sure that Ken wasn't watching him before tossing the chicken in the trash.

Jason came out of Stuart's and met up with Lloyd near where Jim had fallen, to compare notes.

"This is interesting. Bad guy gets shot and runs to a brown Volvo. When he opens the door he gets shot from inside the car."

"What? Is he sure?"

Jason nodded in the affirmative. Together they walked out to the parking lot where the body lay. Lloyd put gloves on and peeled the blanket back. The body was laying on his back, his knees bent under him. They could see two holes in his shirt, about a hands width apart, even with where his navel should be. In the middle of his forehead, just above his left eye was a neat round hole.

"What do you think," asked Jason.

"Looks like a nine millimeter in his forehead," replied Lloyd, "what does Jim carry?"

"Last time we were at the range, he was carrying a forty."

Lloyd stood about where the car had stopped, and looked past the body.

7

"There." Lloyd was looking just left of the teriyaki joint. There was a scuff mark on the brick wall. Lloyd and Jason walked over and found the spent round laying on the ground behind the trash can containing Lloyd's spicy chicken. The impact with the wall had flattened the round.

"There it is. Ballistics is fucked but that's the round."

"Yep."

Chapter 3

Friday Night
Spectrum Center
Charlotte NC

It was just after ten that night. Marianne and her band had just wrapped up their last set with an encore performance of one of her favorite songs. As usual she was shaking hands and waving to her fans before she followed the band off the stage. She had on a sequined jacket over a purple dress and black cowboy boots. As she came around the corner Mariannes back up singer, Jenny Vacca, was facing her. Behind her were two Charlotte police officers, one wearing a white shirt with lieutenant's bars on the collar points.

Marianne was looking at the officers and said, "What's going on?"

The lieutenant handed her a slip of paper as he said, "I was told to ask you to call this number. That's all I can tell you."

Marianne looked at the number and saw the 206 area code. Her knees suddenly felt weak and her head started swimming. Jenny slid a folding chair under her and Marianne sat down heavily as Jenny handed her a cell phone. She tried to dial the number but her hands were shaking too hard.

Without saying a word, Jenny took the phone from Marianne and dialed the number, then handed it back to Marianne. The phone rang once and a voice on the other end said, "hello?"

"Lloyd, is that you?" Mariannes voice was shaking.

"Marianne?"

"Lloyd, how bad is it?"

"He's going to be ok, Marianne."

"Lloyd, don't bullshit me. I need to know what happened and how bad he is."

"He got ambushed Marianne. He was shot twice but he got off a couple of rounds of his own. The shooter is dead but his partner is on the run."

Knowing Jim had fought back gave her a surge of pride.

"What's his injury?"

"I called Sheridan. He's in surgery right now. These officers are going to take you to the airport. Hank arranged for a plane for you there. The officers are going to stay with you until you get on the plane. Jason and I will arrange for someone to meet you when you land."

Marianne hung up. "Let's go," she said as she stood up.

"Marianne, I'm coming with you," said Jenny.

Marianne nodded, "We need our bags. Shit, I'm not packed."

Ted Bruski, her bass player said, "What do you need?"

Marianne had a moment of clarity. "I need my makeup kit. I have clothes at Jim's. Jenny, how about you?"

"Ted my bag is under my bunk. Just grab it for me ok?"

"I'll meet you at the bus." He sprinted down the corridor.

Jenny took Mariannes arm and followed the officers out to their car. It was a newer Ford Explorer that they had parked near the busses. Ted came running up with Jenny's bag and Mariannes makeup case.

"I couldn't find everything," he explained.

Marianne nodded. She was finding words were harder to come by.

As it turned out, they barely had room for the two bags, as the rear of the car was filled with computer equipment. The officer got behind the wheel as the women got in the backseat. When everyone was settled, he turned on the lights and began forcing his way through traffic towards the exit. Officers directing traffic hurried to clear the way. Once clear of the immediate area of the arena, he mashed his foot to the floor.

Marianne found her smart phone in her makeup bag, and hit her speed dial.

"Hank, thank you for the plane. I'm on my way."

"Honey it's ok. I've cancelled the last three dates and I'm working on makeup dates. Don't worry about a thing, I've got it covered."

"Thank you Hank. What have you heard?"

"I got a phone call from Lloyd Murray, one of the detectives. He wasn't forthcoming. I've been working phones so I haven't gone online yet."

"Thank you Hank, you're a godsend."

They hung up as the police car reached the perimeter road of the airport and headed for the private planes. A guard at the gate saw them coming and opened it for them. The car drove up to a waiting Gulfstream and stopped at the bottom of the ramp. The lieutenant let them out and wished them luck. Marianne hugged him and said thank you. Jenny guided Marianne up the ramp where the pilot introduced himself and had them sit down and buckle up. He wasted no time in firing up the engines and rolling out to the runway. They sat on the threshold for a moment as the engines revved before the pilot let off the brakes, and then they were airborne.   As the plane reached cruising altitude, Marianne looked at Jenny.

"You didn't have to come."

"Do you really think I could let you come by yourself?"

"Thank you," Marianne said, before her face dissolved in tears.

Ted Cysinski had been sitting at his desk when word came in that an officer had been shot. He cradled the phone, grabbed his jacket and raced to the scene. The incident commander was an older patrol lieutenant. He told Ted that the victim was Jim Churchill and it appeared to be an ambush attack. Ted was shocked. He knew Jim didn't like Ted because of their history, but he had always felt a certain respect for Jim. He never thought someone could hurt him. He wrote a brief outline for the media that were on the scene, then found Lieutenant Naes to clear it with her.

"No names for now. We'll release those later."

"OK. What about family?"

"That's being taken care of."

That was good enough for Ted. He spoke briefly to the assembled media, emphasizing that they were attempting to locate an older model brown Volvo and that if one was seen to call 911. When they had enough, he checked in with Lieutenant Naes again.

"Is anyone at the hospital?"

"Patrol is guarding him and they're taking his clothes as evidence."

"How can I help?"

"Ted, that's nice of you, but just doing your job is help enough."

Rebekah Naes had made her bones as a sexual assault detective. She was a stocky, medium height woman who had once fought a rapist for ten minutes before he submitted to being arrested. Her nose bore testimony to that struggle.

"OK. I'll do my best to keep a lid on things here for as long as I can."

Rebekah thanked him and turned to another detective. Ted noticed things were starting to break down, so he went back to his car. Then he started thinking like a cop. Just west and south of the crime scene was the cities oldest shopping mall and just south of that was a park and ride, where commuters would catch the bus to downtown. You could park a car at either one and it might be days before anyone noticed. Both lots had easy access to the freeway.

Ted drove to the park and ride, simply because it was smaller. He drove down each lane slowly. Traffic was at times held up by his slow pace, but Ted didn't care. He found three brown Volvos, rejecting each one for being too new. On the last aisle, he found one he thought might be right. He stopped in the middle of the lane and got out. Behind him a car honked. Ted pulled his wallet out of his coat pocket and flashed a badge at the car. The driver looked annoyed and crossed his arms and slipped down in his seat. Ted eased up to the Volvo and looked in the back seat. Empty. Then he saw a shoe on the front seat. He eased the strap off his Glock, and peeked in. Laying across the front seat was a man. Ted noticed a members only jacket and jeans. But he also noticed that his right hand held a nine millimeter Browning pistol. That hand was laying on the floor. In the mans left temple was a neat round hole, surrounded by bluish black skin.

The horn honked again. "You're not going this way," Ted shouted, "it's a crime scene now." In the confines of his mind he added, "Asshole."

11

Chapter Four

Saturday Morning

When it was just after midnight, Marianne pulled her phone out of her pocket and called Lloyd to tell him they were about a half hour out of Boeing field in Seattle.

"Marianne, we've got some leads up here. Do you know Lieutenant Naes?"

"Who is he?"

"She. Mike is bringing her and they are going to pick you up. How are you holding up?"

"I'm fine Lloyd. How's Jim doing?"

"Sheridan said he'd call when they got out of surgery and he hasn't called yet. But that doesn't mean anything."

"Thank you Lloyd," Marianne said as she hung up.

Jenny looked at her with concern etched on her face.

"I'm done crying. It won't do Jim any good," Marianne said. Earlier in the flight she had washed off her stage makeup. Now she opened her case and began touching up her lips.

"Thank you for coming with me."

"That's maybe the thousandth time you've said that. You'd do the same for me."

"Oh honey, I hope you never have to find out."

The crime scene investigators were working around the body. Ray had found prints in the door handles, the mirrors and on the steering wheel. They had photographed the scene and boxed the gun for prints. Lloyd and Jason were talking with Ted. Lieutenant Naes and Sergeant Worthy were standing nearby.

Jason said to Ted, "Nice work. You single handedly wrapped this case up."

Ted smiled and said, "Well you guys are the experts. I'm just a media nerd. But why are you so sure it's a suicide?"

Jason said, "What makes you think it isn't?"

Ted pointed to the body. "The gun was in his right hand."

"So?"

"His watch is on his right wrist. This guy was left handed. And he's shot in his left temple."

Jason smiled. "Very good. Never assume anything on a scene."

Lloyd grunted.

Ted said, "So what happened?"

Lloyd said, "You tell us."

"Ok. That other guy shoots Captain Churchill. This guy shoots the guy that shot Jim. He comes here to switch cars and someone shoots him."

"How do we prove it?"

Ted thought for a moment. "Video. Print the gun. Ballistics. DNA."

"How will DNA help?"

"If his DNA is at the first scene it'll prove he was there. DNA will prove who else was in the car."

"A lot of times DNA will verify what we already know. In homicides the suspect usually knows the victims but a lot of times they don't have a record so DNA is not on file," said Jason.

Lloyd spoke up, "The case we had last spring, the suspect had no criminal history, and had been off the grid most of his life. The only reason we caught him was because he knew the victim. Once we had him the DNA verified what we already knew."

Ted nodded. "Thanks guys. Maybe I can use that somehow."

Lieutenant Naes spoke up. "Maybe you will, Detective."

Ted looked at her and raised an eyebrow. "What do you mean?"

"That was nice work finding this car. It showed some insight and initiative. Lloyd and Jason were testing you and you passed. As of right now, you are on a thirty day loan to homicide, with an option to stay longer if this case drags out. As soon as you can, get whatever you need out of media and we will find you a desk in the bullpen at Homicide."

Ted stammered out, "Thank you."

Lloyd said to him, "First order of business, get a hold of King County Metro. They run the buses here, and see if they have video of the lot."

"Yes sir," said Ted.

Ted moved off to make some calls. Lloyd said to Lieutenant Naes, "I've never seen him so happy."

Jason asked, "What's Jim going to think?"

"If Captain Churchill doesn't like the idea, then he shouldn't have allowed himself to get shot. He left me in charge, so its my call. Is that a problem?"

"No ma'am."

It was shortly before one in the morning when the Gulfstream touched down. It taxied to the terminal. The co-pilot opened the door and lowered the ramp to the tarmac. Marianne stood at the top for a moment, as a familiar Ford Explorer approached the base of the ramp. For a moment she thought it would be Jim, but then remembered he had a new car issued to him when he was promoted. She brushed her hair out of her eyes and walked unsteadily down the stairs as Rebekah Naes and Mike Worthy got out of the car. Mike scanned the tarmac before he approached Marianne. Rebekah was right behind, continuing to scan the area. Mike and Marianne exchanged hugs before Marianne introduced Jenny. Mike in turn introduced them to Rebekah.

"You look a lot like that singer," said Rebekah.

"I get that a lot," said Marianne, "tell me, how's Jim?"

"Last I heard he's still in surgery," said Mike, "so no news is good news."

"Tell me," said Rebekah, "how do you know Captain Churchill?" Rebekah Naes was the first of Jim's subordinates that Marianne had met that was clearly uncomfortable calling him by his first name.

"We've been living together for a while now."

"So you're not married?"

They were getting into the Explorer when Marianne stopped and looked at Rebekah. "Is that a problem for you?"

"Not for me. But the hospital is very strict. They don't count domestic partners as immediate family."

"Are you sure?" Mike started the car and they were starting to pull out of the airport.

Rebekah pointed at her nose. "When this happened, they wouldn't let my partner in to see me. One of the other detectives in my squad was able to sneak her in on the second day. So when we get there, if anyone asks, let me do the talking."

Marianne nodded. "What about Jenny?"

"We'll figure it out."

Mike drove rapidly and competently through the very early traffic. He didn't bother with using his lights until he got off the freeway at James street and was going up the hill against a red light at 8th. Even then he flicked them off as soon as he cleared the intersection. Rebekah's phone rang and she listened for a moment.

"Good news. He's out of surgery. They are moving him to a private room."

Mike parked the car at the front of the hospital. Marianne realized she was still wearing her sequined jacket from Charlotte.

"Did Sheridan say how he is?"

Rebekah didn't answer right away as they were getting out of the car. She hustled them into the entry. A bored security guard was staffing a metal detector. Rebekah laid her badge on his podium and said, "these people are with me." He nodded and waved them through. Rebekah set off the metal detector as did Mike. She looked sideways at Marianne when she caused it to beep, and raised an eyebrow at Jenny when it beeped at her. Jenny winked at Rebekah as they walked to the elevators.

Mike pushed the button and the doors opened. They stepped aboard, and Rebekah pushed the button to the seventh floor. When they got off the elevator, Marianne noticed that they turned in the direction of Intensive Care. Rebekah approached the nurses station and showed her badge again.

"Jim Churchills room please."

"Who are these people?"

"This is his wife."

"OK. He's in room seven C eleven. It's the one with the cop by the door."

"Thanks." Rebekah turned on her heel and stepped purposely down the hallway. At 7C11, there sure enough was a police officer at the door. An older officer was standing up, sipping a cup of coffee. He recognized Marianne immediately and said, "oh hey."

Marianne managed a smile and patted him on the shoulder. Then Rebekah opened the door and they went in.

Sheridan was going over a chart with a nurse. She looked past them and saw Jim laying in the bed. His eyes were closed and an oxygen mask covered his face. A heavy looking bandage covered his left shoulder and his right leg was propped up with another bandage over his thigh. Both of his hands were lashed to the bed rails.

"Sheridan, why are his hands tied?"

Sheridan looked up from the chart with tired eyes.

"Hi honey. The last time I did surgery on him, when he came out of anesthesia it took six nurses to keep him from pulling his stitches and the tube out."

"Is that normal?"

"With some people yes. But one thing you have to understand, Marianne. Your boy here is a fighter."

"I know." Marianne felt another surge of pride while fighting back tears.

"I won't lie, it was touch and go for a while. He lost a lot of blood. But he was smart. He used a belt from a bystander as a tourniquet and stopped the major bleed in his thigh. The bullet tore the femoral artery and I had to use a Dacron sleeve to repair it."

Marianne had her hand to her mouth but asked, "Will he recover?"

"I think so. But he could be out for a while. I'll know more after he wakes up."

Marianne nodded. "When will that be?"

"I'm letting him sleep tonight. We'll take him off the drugs in the morning and he should come out of it fairly soon after that. "

"So what happens now?"

"He's sleeping. He had a rough day. He got a lot of blood and fluids in the OR and he won't be awake until after I come back to unhook him in the morning. Why don't I take you and Jenny home so you can get some rest and a change of clothes?"

Marianne thought, "What would Jim do," and said, "I'm staying here. Jenny, you go with Sheridan. In the morning you can swing by the house and bring me some clothes."

Sheridan tried to argue, but Marianne walked over to the recliner and plopped down. She crossed her arms and stared evenly at Sheridan. He opened his mouth and closed it, then said, "Ok. Jenny, You can sleep in the guest room."

Marianne said to Jenny, "You might want to leave your purse with me."

Jenny nodded and said, "Well not the whole purse." She reached into the bag and pulled out a small pink revolver, and handed it to Marianne. She took it and slid it into her purse. Rebekah started to open her mouth but Mike looked at her and shook his head. Rebekah's face flashed a look of anger, then it was gone.

Rebekah said, "If she's staying and Jenny's going with Doctor Johnston, there's nothing more for us here."

Mike followed her out of the room and down the hallway. When they got on the elevator she turned to Mike and said, "She was carrying the entire time. In our car and into this hospital. Why did you shut me down?"

Mike chose his words carefully. "Captain Churchill took Marianne to get her carry permit after she moved in with him. Jenny handed hers off. Ma'am they flew across the country on a moments notice so I doubt they had time to stash their guns. And yes, Marianne has a .380 in her purse as well."

Rebekah softened her tone. "When did you know they were armed?"

"Marianne always carries. Jenny I didn't know for sure until they went through the metal detectors downstairs. I suggest we just assume they're legal and leave it at that."

The doors opened and Rebekah said, "Ok then. Just between us."

Sheridan and Jenny left shortly after Lieutenant Naes and Sergeant Worthy. Marianne went to the door and thanked the officer there.

"I'm going to close the door and try to sleep for a bit, ok hon?"

"That's fine by me, Ms Wilson. I'm reading a book by TW Griffin."

"Oh, thank you," she said. Then she closed the door.

Marianne found a spare blanket in the closet, then moved the reclining chair to a spot where she could see Jim. Beneath the mask he looked pale and she was worried. She leaned back in the chair, then suddenly sat up. She took her phone from her purse and checked her internet connection. She found a media story she was looking for on an entertainment web site.

"No word yet on what the family emergency was that forced Marianne Wilson to cancel the last three dates of her tour. Word is they're trying to reschedule. Meanwhile no word yet on why Ms Wilson left Spectrum Center in the back seat of a police car. Witnesses say she didn't appear to be under arrest, and her backup singer, Jenny Vacca, went with her. A Charlotte police spokesperson had no comment."

"Huh. Didn't think of that," Marianne thought. Then she leaned back in her chair, and much to her surprise, fell asleep.

7AM.

Paul Churchill approached the nurses station. He was sixty four years old but looked younger. He wore a corduroy jacket and boots, and concealed under the jacket he wore a Beretta pistol and a chiefs badge for the city of Prescott Arizona. He asked at the desk for Jim Churchill's room, and when he told the nurse he was Jims dad, she said, "Oh! I think they weren't expecting you until later. His wife is in there with him."

Paul raised an eyebrow but said nothing. Instead he walked down the hall to Jim's room. A Seattle Police officer was leaning back in a chair, reading a book. He looked up at the sound of Paul's boots, then stood and said, "Good morning chief."

"Up here I'm still retired, Bob. Call me Paul."

"It's good to see you sir."

"How is he?"

"He's still sleeping. The doc should be back in a couple hours. They had him in surgery a long time."

"I heard he improvised a tourniquet?"

"Yeah, I'm not sure I would have thought of it."

"I'm glad he did. I'm going in now." Paul had retired as an assistant chief several years earlier before taking the chiefs job in Prescott Arizona.

Paul eased the door open and slipped into the room. Facing him was Jim's bed. Jims eyes were closed but he was breathing regularly. On a reclining chair was a head of blonde hair. The rest of her was covered by a blanket and a sequined jacket. As he watched, her eyes opened and she sat up. He watched as she looked at him, then at the man sleeping in bed, then back at Paul.

"You must be Paul."

"I am."

"I'm Marianne."

"Imagine my surprise to learn my son is married again."

"We aren't..oh, the nurse told you."

"You're pretty quick for someone that just woke up."

Marianne sighed. He was a lot like Jim, maybe even more intense.

"We live together. We've been splitting time between his place here and mine in Nashville. Plus also, I travel a lot."

"You are Marianne Wilson."

"You're pretty quick yourself."

"How did you meet?"

"We met at a party last spring," she began.

When she finished Paul said, "I'm surprised I haven't heard about any of this before now."

"We've been trying to find a time to come to Prescott. We were hoping we could come down on one of the holidays."

"He could have called or something."

"And said what?" Marianne's face flushed with anger. "Dad, I have a new girlfriend? He's an adult now, he doesn't need your permission."

Paul's eyes went black for a moment, but then he softened. He found himself liking this woman.

"I suppose you're right. We've all been busy but it would be nice to hear from him."

"His eyes do that," Marianne said softly.

"What?"

"Just now. When Jim gets angry his eyes go black."

Paul nodded. "We're alike in a lot more ways than we're different, I guess."

Paul stepped around the bed and shook Mariannes hand. "Nice to meet you, ma'am."

Marianne smiled and said, "nice to meet you."

Jason and Ted were standing in Jims office. The computer sat on the desk, dark and silent.

"OK. How can we legally search his office," asked Jason.

Ted thought a moment.

"The office is city property. The desk, the locker, the file cabinet, the files, they are all city property. So we don't need a warrant."

"OK. What if it's locked?"

"There's no expectation of privacy."

"Au contrar, mon ami." Jason held up a piece of paper. "Which is why we have this."

"It seems odd that we have to get a warrant to search a police captains office."

"It does. There is no expectation of privacy on the part of the criminal for information developed from someone else's property. But what if what we need is in a personnel file? That might be considered privileged.

19

Besides, you are always better off getting a warrant. If Jim were here he'd tell you the same thing."

"Wait a minute. Are you saying the suspect is a cop?"

"No. But I'm not ruling it out. Which is one reason you're here."

"What do you mean?"

"Jim's been a cop for a long time, and supervised a bunch of guys. He's had to discipline a few. So yeah, it could be someone with a disciplinary history that has an axe to grind with Jim."

"Like say a DUI?"

"Could be something like that."

Ted sat down at the conference table. "This could be the shortest stint ever in Homicide."

"What do you mean?"

"Right about the time he got shot by that auto thief, maybe ten twelve years ago. I was working for Jim as a detective in the auto theft unit. He was my sergeant. One day, we got off work and I went to my favorite watering hole. They were cop friendly and I guess I drank a little too much. I left there and tried to drive home. I fell asleep at the wheel and ran into a telephone pole on the highway."

Jason said, "The troopers took you in and you blew a .12 on the breathalyzer. Jim talked to the lieutenant at the time and had you moved out of auto theft."

"You know about this?"

"I saw the file. Lieutenant Naes asked me to look at it."

"They moved me to the Telephone Reporting Unit so I wouldn't have to drive anywhere. When it came time to deal with the chief, I took my day off without pay and went back to patrol for a few years. And I haven't had a drop to drink since."

"I know. And Jim knew. He kept an eye on you, and was asked to go to media relations. He turned it down but told them they ought to look at you."

"Really? I knew he hated me." Ted was smiling, "He's kicked me out of his office more than once, just for doing my job."

"He was hard on you. On all of us, really. But he looks out for us. You do your job you won't have anything to worry about."

"OK."

"Incidentally, what kind of gun do you carry?"

"Glock 19, .40 caliber."

"OK. You ready to get back to work?"

"Yes sir!"

Jason went back to the large Manila envelope in his hand and pulled out a ring of keys.

"Where did you get those?"

"These are Jims personal effects. We went through his clothing and separated anything out that we won't need for evidence. We took pictures of everything to document it, and signed it out. Once Jim wakes up we'll go to the hospital and give it to Marianne."

"Who?"

"His girlfriend. She flew in from North Carolina this morning."

Realization dawned on Ted, and he shook his head. "I knew it."

"That's one thing that will get you bounced. All the way back to a uniform. If that leaks out...," Jason was suddenly very serious.

"I get it. One thing I've learned over the years is how to keep a secret."

"OK," Jason said, "Let's start with his desk."

He unlocked it, and started going through the drawers. Ted was making an inventory of what they found. The upper compartments had mostly office stuff, paper clips, staples, rubber bands, pens and such. On the right side were miscellaneous memos, purchase orders, and other items related to the day to day operation of a homicide unit. Jason pulled the purchase orders and set them on top of the desk.

In the left side, he found personnel files dating back to Jim's time as a lieutenant in the unit. Jason split the stack, then pulled his own file and set it on top of the other stack.

"That's mine. You'll go through it to eliminate me as a suspect."

Ted nodded.

Jason moved to the file cabinet and unlocked it. In the top drawer were a half dozen files of open cases dating back almost twenty years. He pulled them. In the next drawer was a single file. It was marked "Miscellaneous." Jason tossed it on top of the others. Then he moved to Jim's locker.

Inside, Jason saw Jim's dress uniform. He patted the pockets and found nothing. Jim maintained a class a and a class b uniform, but there was nothing unusual about them. Jason noted that there was nothing in the locker that did not belong.

"Alright, this should give us enough to start."

Ted was staring at the pile of information on the desk.

"This seems overwhelming. Are we going to get help on this?"

"From who? The unit's short staffed, and this is really a one person job. It probably won't amount to much but it's a place to start."

"Seems like a dead end."

"Last spring I flew to Tennessee to check on a possible murder suspect. We all knew it was a dead end, and it was. But while I was there we discovered a video of the suspect buying the murder weapon. It helped to break the case and all because I went on a wild goose chase. There's no telling what going through these files could mean to the investigation."

"Ok, ok. It has been a long time since I did any detecting and it wasn't nearly as involved as a homicide."

"Sometimes we have to prioritize. You gotta decide what needs to be done right now, and what can wait. For instance," Jason put his hand on top of the personnel files, "I think we should start with these, unless you have another idea."

"It's as good a place as any," said Ted, as he scooped up his stack and went back to his desk.

Jason stayed in the office for a minute after Ted left. He looked around the office, then turned in the direction of Harborview Hospital. "Talk to me Jim," he whispered. He waited another minute, and when there was no answer grabbed his stack of files and went back to his desk.

Lloyd was watching the video from the park and ride. Ted had used his contacts with the county and found someone to make a CD from the time of Jims shooting until Ted found the car. Then he went on his own and asked for two hours before and after. All told there was about nine hours of video to review. Plus it had been raining for most of that time so watching the video was like watching a movie through a sheet of tissue paper. Not to mention that at some point Lloyd would have to watch all the video from patrol's body worn video and in car video. He had asked the lieutenant for help. She said she would see what she could do. Lloyd was feeling frustrated and his head hurt.

He opened the video and found a view that covered the last row. Like he had thought there was nothing there. He fast forwarded until he saw the Volvo parked in the stall. He checked the time and saw it was thirty minutes after the shooting. He scrolled back until he found it pull into the lot. It had found a spot along the back row. Lloyd fast forwarded until, about forty five minutes later, a black sedan pulled in and stopped behind it.

"Well this is interesting," thought Lloyd.

He watched it in real time. The rain was cascading over whatever was covering the lens. A man got out of the drivers seat of the black car and approached the Volvo. His hood was up and Lloyd couldn't see the face. He walked up to the drivers window as it rolled down. The driver handed something to him and the man looked at it for a moment, then a flash of light and the driver walked around to the passenger side of the Volvo. He reached into the car for a moment, then straightened. Without looking he walked back to the black car and got in before driving away.

Lloyd made a copy of the video on his computer before packaging the CD to send it to the video unit. Then he stood and stretched, cracking his neck, before moving to the white board on the wall behind him. Lloyd thought it might help him organize his thoughts. He wrote "Jim Churchill" in the corner, then drew an arrow and wrote, "John Doe #1." He drew another arrow and wrote, "Brown Volvo, John Doe #2." Then he drew an arrow down and wrote, "Black car, unknown Doe." Then went back to his computer and sent Lieutenant Naes an email. Picking up his cell phone, he called her.

"Hello?"

"Lieutenant, where are you?"

"Sergeant Worthy and I are just leaving Harborview."

"How's Jim?"

"The surgeon is going to try to wake him up tomorrow morning. I guess, actually, that'll be this morning."

"OK. I found something on the park and ride video. I want to try to run it down but I need help watching the other video."

"I can talk to HR and get someone on light duty."

Lloyd waited until the anger passed. "Can I get a couple guys? This is important and it's always useful to bounce opinions off each other."

"I'll check. I won't make promises."

"OK. How's Marianne holding up?"

"She's doing better than I would be in her place."

"She's a strong woman. Oh, I'm still waiting on the prints to come back on our suspects. I have to drop the CD off at the video unit anyway, so I'll stop by there and see if they have anything yet."

"Sounds good. Let me know if you need anything."

Lloyd rang off, then cursed. The light duty officers would be officers that were recovering from an injury or illness. They could be placed in positions that would allow an able bodied officer to be freed up, but they couldn't work overtime and most of them couldn't do any physical labor. Lloyd's experience with light duty officers was that they tended to be not very motivated, and the ones that were motivated tended to want to get back to their regular jobs. He grabbed his jacket and stood. He looked at Ted and Jason and said, "I'm about tapped out guys. I'm running down to the prints section and the video unit to see if they can clean it up." He explained about the black sedan. "If we can get a clear picture that might be our best lead yet."

"Are you going to get any help with that video," asked Jason as he looked up from a file.

"Naes is being a bean counter. She's maybe going to get me a couple light duty guys."

"Shit. OK. Hey are you going to be here in the morning?"

"I don't think I'm going home for a couple days, I don't give a shit what the lieutenant thinks."

"Why isn't she bringing in some guys from intel?" The intelligence unit had assisted them before.

23

"What she told me is that we have the guy that shot Jim, and we have the guy that shot the guy that shot Jim. She doesn't want to spend overtime on what she thinks should be a closed case. But fuck it, they were going to kill Jim, and I want to know why."

Jason nodded his agreement, while Ted kept quiet. After Lloyd left, Ted asked, "What's going on?"

Jason looked at the lieutenants office then said, "homicides are expensive. To do them right you have to do them right and it costs money. Lieutenant Naes came from special assault. It's an important job and needs to be done right but their investigations are usually not as complicated as ours. There usually aren't any witnesses to interview other than the victim so they rely on physical evidence. We do too, but we still have to talk to witnesses, look at video, all that stuff. It's labor intensive and Jim understands that. Naes is a good Lieutenant but she's going to have to learn that."

Ted nodded. "So you're training her and me."

Jason grinned. "You bet your ass."

Chapter 5

Saturday 7:58

Having made their peace, Marianne and Paul were chatting quietly over bad coffee donated by the nurses station.

"Why did you tell the nurses you were married?"

"I didn't. Rebekah did, but I went along with it. She told me that if I said we weren't married, they might not let me in."

"That's stupid. You flew on a moments notice from the east coast, still wearing the outfit you sing in. It's pretty clear how you feel about Jim."

"Jim told me once that there are some people that enforce stupid rules because they can. It helped that Rebekah and Mike brought me in. They got me past the battle axe at the front desk."

At that moment the door to the room opened and Jenny walked in, wearing jeans and sweatshirt, followed by Sheridan, who was wearing a long white lab coat over a sweater and slacks.

"Who you calling a battle axe," Jenny said.

Marianne looked behind them, then said, "we were discussing taxes. You know how hard it is to pay taxes on income from forty different states?"

Paul looked thoughtful. Sheridan raised an eyebrow and turned around to the nurse that had followed him in.

"I need you to swap out the IV. He should come out of it fairly quickly but he's going to need fluids."

She nodded and said, "yes doctor." She moved past the knot of people by the bed and began replacing the bag. Jenny handed Marianne a leather satchel with the monogram "TWG" on the flap. Marianne hugged Jenny and took the bag, setting it by her chair.

"Sheridan, how's Jane doing?"

"Sick as a dog every morning and getting bigger by the hour," he said. Jane Johnston, MBA, JD, was normally a tall, thin, athletic woman. She had become pregnant with their first child some seven months earlier. Her pregnancy was complicated by the fact that she was nearing forty and had been confined to bed rest during the third trimester. She could continue to work from home, but could not do any heavy lifting.

"Tell her as soon as I can, I'll be over to see her."

"She knows you will. And Jane knows where your priorities need to be right now," said Sheridan, "don't worry about her. She has one of the best doctors in the country on speed dial."

"Oh? Who would that be," asked Marianne sweetly.

Sheridan shot her a look.

"By the way, have you met Jim's dad, Paul?"

They shook hands.

"Hey, careful there," said Sheridan, "I have to operate with that hand."

Marianne introduced Jenny to Paul and they shook hands. Paul thought her eyes were intense and her manner friendly.

The nurse said, "he's coming out of it, doctor."

Marianne flew to the head of the bed as Paul came up behind her. Sheridan stood on the other side and watched Jim thrash against his restraints for a minute.

Sheridan looked at the monitor next to the bed. No one noticed the look of concern on his face.

Then, Jim's eyes opened. "Hi honey," he croaked through his oxygen mask. "Someone want to untie my hands?"

9:02AM

"OK, things are looking good," said Sheridan, "but we're going to keep you here for a few more days just to be sure."

Jim nodded.

"For now, you're on a clear liquid diet. Broth, ice chips, you know the routine."

"I'd kill for a sandwich," Jim rasped.

"Maybe by tomorrow, if you do exactly what I say," said Sheridan.

Jim started to open his mouth but Marianne placed a spoonful of ice chips in it.

"Jim, I know you think you're fine and you don't need to listen to me on this, but your femoral artery was torn. Your shoulder will be fine but it has stitches in it. Do not overdo things. You're going to be fine and you'll be back to being yourself but you must take it easy for the next several weeks. Now as much as I'd like to be your own personal physician, I do have other patients to attend to. If you need anything call the nurse or tell one of these guys."

"OK, doc."

"I mean it Jim."

"I know doc."

"You always call me doc when you're shining me on. Marianne, can I count on you?"

"I will make sure he stays in bed. He's not going anywhere."

"OK. I'll be back later today. Get some sleep Jim."

Sheridan left the room and closed the door.

"I'm starving," said Jenny. "Anyone want to run to the cafeteria with me?"

"I'll come," said Marianne, "just let me change first." She picked up the satchel and slid into the bathroom. Jenny sat down in the recliner and looked straight at Jim.

"You better do something really nice for her when this is over," she said, "she's put everything on hold for you."

"I know," Jim managed to scratch out.

Paul looked at Jenny, his eyes black. "He would have done the same for her. This isn't the time to kick him when he's down."

"You're right, that was out of line. I just want you to know when she got the news she dropped everything to come here. She's my friend, as well as my boss."

Paul started to say something when Marianne came out of the bathroom, wearing a leather motorcycle jacket over a peasant blouse and pinstriped slacks. She had kept her cowboy boots and allowed her pants to flow over the top. Her hair was brushed back into a pony tail and Marianne was wearing a pair of large glasses.

She looked at Paul, then at Jenny, then at Jim.

"Can I talk to the two of you in the hallway please?"

Jenny stood and walked to the door. Paul took one look at Marianne's face and followed Jenny.

"I'll be right back," she said to Jim before going outside.

In the hallway she looked at a Paul and Jenny and said, "I don't know what the two of you are arguing about, but if you hurt him," she pointed at the room door, "I will hunt you both down." She looked at Jenny, "I love the music, and I love you guys in our band, but that man in there has done more for me than anyone else ever has. He would do anything for me. You are here to support him. I'm not leaving until he can fend for himself." Marianne turned to Paul. "You are his father. You had better start acting like it. Now the two of us, the three of us if you are willing to stick around, need to be a team. You heard what Sheridan said, he needs rest for a while. We need to work together and if you can't be positive and supportive in front of him you better get out now."

Marianne turned and went back to the door. There was a new policeman sitting outside, a fresh faced kid with a pink face. He stood as Marianne approached but didn't say anything. Marianne ignored him as she paused at the door and collected herself. Then she pushed the door open and stepped in.

Paul turned to Jenny and said, "Fresh start?"

"Agreed," said Jenny as she took Paul's offered hand.

Inside the room Marianne approached the bed, bent and kissed Jim on the forehead. "I'm glad you're back," she whispered.

Jim took his good arm and wrapped it around her waist, the IV line whipping against the pole.

"Did you straighten them out?"

"I don't know. We'll see. Honey, did you listen to Sheridan?"

"He's Sheridan. When he's right, he's right."

"You better do as he said. I've got my eye on you."

She bent and kissed his lips, then said, "I'm taking Jenny down to the cafeteria. Your dad is staying here. I'll be right back."

"Be careful," Jim rasped, "put your back to the wall. And bring me back something, OK?"

"Maybe a sprite."

"How about a donut?"

27

Marianne kissed him again, then walked to the door. She paused a moment to collect herself and stepped out. The young policeman was still outside. Jenny and Paul were on the other side of the door.

"Paul, do you want anything from the cafeteria?"

"If they have like a breakfast burrito, something like that, and coffee. Whatever they have at the nurses station is well past its prime."

Marianne smiled and turned to the officer, "how about you, can I get you something?"

"Oh, no thank you ma'am."

"Do you drink coffee?"

"No ma'am."

"Ok." She shook hands with the young officer and said, "Thank you for being here. I appreciate it, and he does too."

His face was visibly red, but he was able to compose himself enough to say, "Thank you."

Marianne turned on her heel and said, "Jenny, lets find the cafeteria."

Paul watched them walk down the hall towards the elevator. Before he went back into the room he told the officer, "If you ever meet a woman like that, marry her."

Jim was sitting up in bed still, although he looked pale. There was a small table on wheels that was designed to fit over the bed. Paul wheeled it into place and put Jims ice water on top, so he could reach it.

"So, you didn't duck," said Paul.

"No I guess I didn't," Jim replied as he sipped at the water.

"You did good son."

"Really? I felt like I screwed up."

"How so?"

"I was so wrapped up in what I was doing, I wasn't alert to what was going on around me until it was too late."

"What were you doing?"

"That place is a strip mall. There's a shop there called Stuart's. It's a jeweler."

"So?"

"So that's where I was going."

It took Paul a moment to realize what Jim was saying. He sat down on the edge of the recliner and said, "oh."

When Jim didn't say anything, Paul said, "Jim are you sure?"

"Dad, when I was waiting for the medic I passed out. When I was down, I spoke to Heather." Heather had been Jims first wife and had died in an accident.

Jim went on, "she told me there were people here that loved me and that my work wasn't finished yet. Then I came to in the back of the medic unit. Just now when I was coming up from the anesthetic I felt Marianne was there and I reached out for her."

Paul nodded. "I know son."

Jim leaned back on the bed. Paul realized he was asleep.

Chapter 6

Ted and Jason knocked at the door before they walked into Jim's room. Jim was sitting up in bed, his face pale. His left arm was in a sling across his chest and his right leg was resting on a pillow. There was a napkin tucked under his chin. Marianne had a spoonful of broth and was feeding Jim while making airplane noises. Jim was laughing until he saw Jason. Then he quickly took a mouthful of broth, swallowed and said, "Hello gentlemen."

"Sorry to interrupt," said Jason.

Ted was hanging back.

Jason went on, "We heard you were back from the dead." Jason saw Mariannes face and immediately regretted his choice of words before plowing ahead. "I thought we'd swing by and see if you were up for giving a statement."

"Why are you here Ted? I don't see a camera anywhere."

Ted stepped forward, cleared his throat and said, "I'm on a thirty day to homicide, with an option to buy."

"Excuse me?"

"Jim," Marianne cautioned.

"It's ok honey. Ted was just leaving."

"Actually sir, I'm not. With all due respect I've been asked to assist in this investigation and I intend to do my job."

Jim looked at Ted for a moment. Ted held his gaze. Jim finally said, "Alright. Ted, what's your first question?"

Jason nodded at Ted.

"Alright sir. Tell me what happened."

"I was running a quick errand before I went home. My plan was to grab my bag, switch cars and head to the airport. I was going to meet my girlfriend in Roanoke Virginia."

"What happened next?"

"I came out of the store and a guy came out from between two of the parked cars. He was holding a cigarette in his left hand and was asking me for a light. His right hand was behind his back."

"Could you see anything in his hand?"

"Not right then. But it seemed suspicious to me. So I told him I was the police and said to show me his hands."

"OK, what did he do?"

"When he brought his right hand out he had a gun in it."

"Did you have your gun out?"

"No, but I was working on that."

"OK. What happened next?"

"He got off a shot and hit me in the thigh. His next shot got me in my shoulder. By then I had my gun out, and I got off a shot."

"How many rounds did you fire?"

"Two I think."

"How many rounds do you keep in your gun?"

"Fifteen, plus one in the pipe."

"By 'one in the pipe,' I assume you mean one in the chamber?"

"Yes Ted, one in the chamber."

Jim glanced at Marianne. Her face was white. "There isn't much more honey."

Marianne nodded and swallowed. "Ok," she said.

"Honey, this next part gets a little rough."

"Jim, I need to hear it."

Jim nodded.

"OK, Ted. This is the part that gets interesting."

"Go ahead sir. I'm listening."

"I remember going down on one knee. A car pulled up, a brown one. This guy turns and runs to it. I mean I just shot him twice, and he's still on his feet running. So I lined up on the middle of his back and I'm thinking 'this son of a bitch has killed me and I'm not going to let him get away.' But before I could crank off another round, the back of his head came off."

"Wait, did you shoot him in the head?"

"No Ted, whoever was in the car shot him in the head."

Ted nodded. "Got it. What did the car look like?"

"It was a brown car. Maybe a Volvo. An older one, like maybe from the eighties."

"So why did the driver of the Volvo shoot the guy that shot you?"

"I don't know Ted. Find him and you can ask him. Or better yet, I'll ask him."

Ted nodded. He took Jim through the rest of it, even drawing out how he had used Stuart's belt to make a tourniquet. When Ted felt there wasn't anything else Jim could give him he said, "Do the names 'Mario Fortunato or Edward Lazzari mean anything to you?"

Jim thought for a minute. "Not really. Why?"

"Fortunato was the shooter. Lazzari was the driver." Ted let that sink in a little. "Fortunato got out of prison two months ago. Lazzari a month before that. They never reported to their probation officer after they got out."

"What were they in for?" Jim was curious.

Ted looked at Jason who nodded back at him.

"Fortunato was in prison for manslaughter. It was a plea bargain from second degree murder. Apparently he got a sweetheart deal. Lazzari was in for an assault. They were supposedly enforcers for a gang in Tacoma."

"A couple of sweethearts," said Jason.

Jim grimaced.

"Are you okay honey," Marianne asked as concern etched on her face.

"I'm ok, just moved funny I guess," Jim said. "So did you find Lazzari?"

"He was found dead in a car in the park and ride at Northgate. It looks like a self inflicted gunshot wound, but we're not sure yet."

Jim nodded.

"Jason do you have anything," asked Ted.

"If I think of anything I'll let you know," said Jason.

"OK sir, I think I'm done."

"How did you find Lazzari," Jim asked.

Jason said, "Actually Jim, Ted found him."

Jim looked at Ted and said, "Tell me about it."

"I went to the scene to be the press liaison. When I was done, I figured if they were going to be that obvious with the car, they had to ditch it someplace. So I figured the park and ride by the freeway would be as good as any to start."

Jim nodded but kept quiet.

"Hey sir," said Jason, holding up a large Manila envelope, "I have your personal effects. This is the stuff that's not needed for evidence." He placed the envelope on the table. Jim looked at it and left it sitting there.

Marianne picked it up and said, "Jason you should know better. How do you expect him to open this with one hand?"

She ripped the envelope open and shook the contents out onto the bed. Jim's wallet, ID holder and badge lay on the bed alongside both of his smart phones. A small velvet covered box lay amid the debris. Marianne looked at it for a minute, then picked it up. She looked at Jim and back at the box, then back at Jim.

"Jim, honey, what is this?"

Jim said simply, "open it."

Marianne slowly opened the box and gasped when she saw the diamond ring inside.

Jim said, "I was going to ask you in Roanoke, but there's no point in waiting. Honey, will you marry me?"

Marianne looked at Jim and simply said, "yes" before she hugged him around the neck and kissed him hard on the mouth. Ted and Jason looked at each other. Jason nodded at the door and they quietly left the room. Outside Jason said to no one in particular, "well that was unexpected."

Ted was looking at the door and said, "yeah." Than he turned to Jason and said, "he was at the jewelers wasn't he? Was this a robbery after all?"

"That's a theory worth looking into. One thing you'll find is that sometimes you have to run theories down if for no other reason than to eliminate them as possibilities."

"I get that. He has pretty good recall."

"Have you ever been in a shooting?"

"No."

"What you see is sometimes they have great recall. Sometimes it's really bad. Jim is a detail guy. As time goes by he may remember more details."

The door behind them opened. Marianne stood in the entry, her left ring finger glittering with her new diamond.

"He wants to see you," she said.

Jason started for the door, but she put her hand on his chest and said, "Not you." She pointed to Ted. "You."

Ted swallowed and followed Marianne back into the room.

"Ted," Jim said.

"Captain Churchill."

"That was a good interview. You showed me something when you didn't back down. If you're going to stick with this unit you cannot be intimidated."

"Yes sir."

"Finding the car was huge."

"Thank you, sir."

"Jason is a good teacher. So is Lloyd. You listen to those guys and if you are half as good as either of them, you'll still be pretty good."

"Thank you sir."

"And for the record, call me Jim."

He held out his hand. Ted took it and they shook hands. Jim lay back in the bed for a moment and closed his eyes. A moment later Ted realized he was asleep.

Marianne walked him out. Jason was waiting outside, along with Paul and Jenny.

"He's sleeping. Jason, thank you for bringing his things. Thank God his phone is dead."

Jason smiled, "he will stick it on the charger first chance he gets. I suggest hiding them."

"I will, I promise."

"Oh and congratulations," said Jason.

"Congratulations on what," said Jenny.

Marianne held up her hand and showed off her ring.

"Oh my God," she said softly. Then she hugged Marianne.

When they parted, Marianne looked at Paul.

"Can't say I'm surprised. Congratulations Marianne, welcome to the family," said Paul.

Jason said to Jenny, "I didn't know you were back in town."

"I flew in with Marianne," she said, "and we've been busy."

"You want to get together tonight? Say around five."

"Sure," she said, "I'll be ready."

Ted turned and said, "Marianne, there's security camera footage of the shooting. The department is going to release some of it tomorrow afternoon, in time for the five o clock news."

"OK."

"I'm telling you so you can make sure the television is off for him. He doesn't need to see it."

Marianne was touched. "Thank you Ted."

She watched the two detectives walk down the hall towards the elevators. Then she turned and went back into the room, followed by Paul and Jenny.

Lloyd was shaving at his desk when he heard a familiar voice say, "Did you pull another all nighter?"

"The latest in a long string of all nighters. Are you back from vacation?"

"I was watching the news last night and saw a piece on an officer involved shooting," said Ross Nolan, Lloyd's partner. "So I called the North precinct and they told me who the officer was. How's he doing?"

"He lost some blood, but Sheridan Johnston came in and patched him up. He's going to be out for a while."

"Who's running the shop?"

"Lieutenant Naes."

Ross sat in his chair, opposite of Lloyd's. "How's that going?"

"She's brand freakin' new. How do you think it's going?"

Ross smiled. "You've had your hands full."

"I can't get any help with watching video. I need to look at body worn and in car video and I've been so busy I haven't even started yet."

Ross reached over and picked up the file. "Let me get caught up, and I'll give you a hand," he said.

"Jason's the lead," Lloyd said, "I'm just helping out."

"Who else is on it?"

"You aren't going to believe it. She brought in Ted Cysinski."

"What the hell?"

"Believe it or not he's doing OK. She brought him in because he showed some initiative and found the suspects car."

Lloyd related the story. When he was done Ross nodded approvingly.

"Tell me from the beginning."

"I had just finished talking to Jim about retiring. I went back to my desk and he left for the day. He told me he was going to Stuart's to get Mariannes engagement ring."

"They're engaged?"

"Not yet. Anyway, he comes out and Furtunato ambushes him. Jim gets hit but he gets a couple shots off."

"Did he hit him?"

Lloyd said, "two shots in the abdomen. I could have covered the entry holes with my hand."

"Not bad," said Ross.

"Anyway, Lazzari drives up in the car. As Fortunato runs to it, Lazzari shoots him in the forehead and drives off."

"Ouch."

"Not for long. He's dead before he hits the ground. So we're all up at the scene, and Ted shows up to do the media thing. When he's done, he drives over to the park and ride by Northgate and finds the car. He creeps up on it and lo and behold, Lazzari is laying in the front seat."

"Suicide?"

"Look at the pictures."

Ross opened the folder and began leafing through the pictures. When he got to Lazzari he stopped for a minute.

"Lazzari was left handed."

"Yep. What else?"

"The gun is in his right hand, but the bullet went in the left side. That doesn't make sense."

"No it doesn't. So three big questions."

Ross looked up and into Lloyd's eyes. "Why did Lazzari shoot Fortunato, and who shot Lazzari."

"Why did Fortunato shoot Jim?"

"That, my friend, is the sixty four dollar question."

Chapter 7

Saturday
5pm

Jason came down the hospital hallway to discover a small knot of people in front of Jim's room. Paul, Marianne and Jenny were standing in a cluster along with the current uniformed officer that had been assigned to guard Jim.

"Everything ok," Jason asked.

"Sheridan's in there," said Marianne.

"He's taking out the catheter," Paul said.

"Really Paul," said Marianne, "you didn't have to say that."

"Why should I be the only one to suffer," said Paul.

"It does hurt to think about," said Jason.

"You are no help at all," said Marianne.

Jenny's eyes were twinkling. "I'm ready if you are," she said.

The door opened and Sheridan came out. "All set," he said, "You can go in now."

Jason said, "I just want to say hello."

Jenny nodded as Marianne led the group back into the room. Jim was leaning back in bed, his left arm still slung and his right leg on a pillow.

Jim saw Jason and said, "I understand you have a date."

Jason glanced at Jenny and said, "Yes sir," with a smile.

"Don't let me keep you from getting started."

"You're not sir. Just a quick question."

Jim started to make a go ahead gesture with his left hand, winced, then said, "Ask away."

"Do you have any thought as to who would want to kill you?"

"I dunno. Have you looked at my case files?"

"I went back two years. Anyone you had a hand in arresting is either dead or in prison."

"Then you got me. Why don't you bring me the files and I'll see if any stand out to me."

"Will do, next time I come by."

"Where are you two going tonight?"

Jason asked Jenny, "Do you like seafood?"

Jenny looked doubtful but said, "Sure."

"I think Elliotts then."

"Stay away from the Oysters," Jim said.

"Jim," Marianne admonished.

Jim shrugged his good shoulder.

"I think we should go now," said Jenny.

She took Jason's arm and he led her out of the door.

Once in the hallway Jenny let go of his arm and they walked down the hall together.

"Are you in a rush," Jason asked.

"Not really. I need a break," Jenny said, "and I don't have a curfew."

Jason raised an eyebrow but didn't say anything. They got on the elevator and talked amicably until they reached the ground floor.

As Jason put the car in gear and pulled away from the curb he asked, "What's going on?"

"It's nothing really. I don't want you to think I'm complaining."

"Hey, you flew across the country on a moments notice," said Jason, "just because your friend needed you. If you've got something to say I think you have the right to say it."

Jenny thought for a minute before she spoke. "Don't get me wrong. I love Marianne. I'm still in the field because of her."

Jason nodded.

"She was so upset when she got the news, I knew she'd need a shoulder to lean on. Now that we're here, though, she's just become so controlling."

"How so?"

"She just took charge. She's making schedules, but she never leaves. It's like she doesn't trust us. Now she's trying to get him to retire."

"You've seen them together, right?"

"Of Course. He's been flying out on the weekends just to spend some time with her between concerts."

"You ever pay attention to how they look at each other?"

"Well it's clear they love each other."

"Right. She almost lost that. It's a new reality for her."

"So what do I do," Jenny asked.

Jason parked at the curb on the waterfront, in front of Elliotts Oyster house. "Have dinner with me," he smiled, "and let's leave them alone for a bit."

Marianne was fussing over Jim to the point that Paul felt embarrassed. He excused himself and stepped out of the room. The officer on guard had just arrived and was reading a magazine.

"What do you have there," Paul asked.

"It's a golf magazine," the officer said, showing Paul the cover.

"Oh cool. We have a couple nice courses back home," he said.

Jim was laying back on the bed, flexing the fingers on his right hand. Marianne was on his left watching him.

"So," Jim said, "Jason and Jenny?"

"They met when the band came out for rehearsals. What do you think?"

"I don't know, dating a singer? Not everyone can handle that."

"Hey now. Actually, it does bother me a little."

"Why?"

"She's gotta have ten years on him."

"Well," Jim said, "Jason is in his thirties. They're both adults. Why don't we let it play out and see what happens? Hell it's not like we really have a choice."

Marianne walked over to the window. Jim sat up and tried to swing his legs over the side. Marianne was right there.

"Don't you dare. You're not ready yet."

"Honey,"

"Jim.."

"Honey, he said rest. He didn't say confined to the bed. I'll be right back."

Jim stood and hung onto the IV pole. He used it to support his weight and wheeled it into the bathroom. When he was done, Marianne was waiting for him.

"Are you alright?"

"It hurt a bit," Jim acknowledged, "but I am ok."

"Jim…"

"It's fine honey."

Lloyd and Ross were watching video.

"Hey Lloyd, look at this."

Ross played back the surveillance video he had been watching. Lloyd watched as Jims Explorer pulled into the parking lot of the strip mall. Behind him a brown Volvo drove past.

"Now look at this one," Ross said.

It was a different camera, looking towards the east end of the lot. A brown Volvo drove past on tenth avenue, then a moment later it parked behind the post office, facing back south. Ross fast forwarded about ten minutes until it pulled into the lot and disappeared from view under the camera.

"That's the suspect car. I forwarded past the passenger getting out but that's the car."

"So it was following Jim. Where did they pick him up," asked Lloyd.

"Think about it a minute. Jim parks his car in the garage. He pulls out, and sometimes cuts through the parking lot under the freeway."

"Right."

"That has to be it. Do they have cameras?"

"Let's take a walk," said Ross.

The duo walked out of the bullpen, grabbing their coats as they went. It was shorter to cut through the garage to the ground floor. They walked across the street and under the highway. It was raining again, but the parking lot was covered by the interstate. It was a favorite sleeping spot of transients and there were a half dozen tents pitched.

Ross walked up to one of the tents and said, "Hey Elmer."

A voice from inside said, "Shit, just a minute man."

Ross and Lloyd waited patiently until a rail thin African man opened the tent flap and peered out.

"Officer Nolan."

"You were here yesterday, right?"

"Every day man. They feed us right over there," Elmer pointed across the street, "I don't even have to leave my tent."

"Good deal, man. Who was here around three yesterday?"

"AM or PM man. You know this crowd changes."

"PM man."

"I was here. I was buying some product, ya know."

"OK. Was there a brown Volvo parked in here?"

"Let me think." Elmer tilted his head and stared at the underside of the interstate. "Yeah man. Right behind that column over there." He pointed to a wide cement column just up the hill from them.

"Did you see who was in it?"

"A couple of white guys. I stayed away from them man. They looked rough."

"Thanks Elmer." Ross handed him a folded bill. Elmer smiled a toothless smile. "There's programs I can help you with," Ross added.

"No thanks man. I'm good," Elmer said.

Elmer went back into his tent. Lloyd and Ross walked up the hill to the column Elmer had pointed out. They stood in the parking space next to the column and took in what they could see.

"What do you think," said Ross.

"From here you could keep tabs on the exit gate and be ready to fall in behind once he went by."

"You think they followed him all the way up north and he didn't notice?"

"I do. We are not going to ask him that, by the way. We'll just keep that here," Lloyd tapped the side of his head.

"Jim wouldn't care. But she might."

Lloyd nodded in agreement. "But it's the only thing that makes sense. So we'll talk to Jason when we see him next."

As they strolled across the street, Lloyd asked Ross, "how do you know Elmer?"

"Known him a long time," said Ross.

"Yeah, but how did you meet."

Ross was reflective a minute.

"You know how sometimes you look back and you see that if you took a certain path things would be different?"

"Sure," said Lloyd, "Like joining the Marines instead of the army. Or going to WSU instead of Udub."

"Man, you got no idea. Elmer's not his real name. But he and I were friends in high school. He had NFL style speed on the field. He coulda been a hell of a wide receiver. But he got started in crack, while I was hitting the weights he was smoking shit would kill a horse."

Lloyd nodded, and stayed quiet as they went into the building.

Jason was telling Jenny about the case over dinner. She had been hungry but was picking at her food, listening curiously.

"You think it was a hit," she asked.

"I wouldn't say we're a hundred per cent on that, but it's definitely the way we're leaning."

"When will you know?"

"We're going to start running them down on Monday. That's when the guy from Corrections will be in his office."

"It's cold blooded. Does this happen a lot?"

"A hit on a cop? Not very often," Jason said, "even in this day and age most bad guys know we'll pull all the stops."

"So cops deserve more attention than us ordinary folk?" Jenny hid a half smile behind a cocktail napkin.

"It's not like that," replied Jason, "if someone would go after a cop they could go after anyone. No one is safe if the cops are getting taken out."

"I guess that's true," Jenny said. "I never thought of it like that before."

"Most people don't," said Jason, "nobody wants to think of what cops do while the 'ordinary folk' are safe in their beds." He spoke without rancor.

"Tell me, why did you ask me to dinner?"

"Since I met you, I enjoyed being around you. Then you dropped everything to help out your friend. Someone like that, I'd like to get to know better. Why did you agree?"

"I'll tell you later," she said, a twinkle in her eye.

"When?"

"Maybe over breakfast," she said.

Chapter 8

Sunday 7AM

Jason awoke to the sound of his phone ringing. He looked at the screen and saw who it was. He pushed the button and said, "Shouldn't you be sleeping, captain?"

"Jason," Jim said, "I hate to bother you but Jenny didn't come back last night and Marianne is worried sick."

Jason looked at the lump next to him and said, "I'm sure she's fine skipper. Did you try her phone?"

"Seems it's off."

Jason said, "ok. I'll tell her."

"OK, well if you hear from her, tell her to call Marianne."

"Right. Thanks for the call skipper."

Jason rang off. Jenny opened one eye and said, "I gather that was Marianne looking for me."

"Actually it was Jim."

"Did you tell him I was here?"

"Yes and no. He doesn't want to have to lie to Marianne, and I think he senses what's happening there. So he was careful what he asked me."

"Shit. I better call her," Jenny said, sitting up in bed.

Jason admired her body for a moment before saying, "hold on."

"What?"

Jason sat up and put an arm around her shoulders.

"If you call her back now, then a) she will know you are here and b) she will blame Jim for not telling her."

"Got it. Let me find my phone."

"Maybe in a minute," Jason said pulling her back into bed.

Ted was sitting at his desk looking at the video logs. He saw the note that Lloyd had made about the black sedan and pondered that for a minute. He pulled the video up and watched it for the first time. He made a couple of notes, before Ross Nolan walked in.

"Good morning Ted. I heard you were over here now."

"We'll see. Beats the heck out of dealing with the media wolves."

"I heard. Wouldn't know myself. How long you been here?"

"About ten minutes. I thought Jason was coming in this morning."

"You know on a case like this he generally doesn't go home."

"Well," Ted hesitated for a minute, "he did have a date last night."

"Anyone we know?"

"Maybe. That Hispanic chick that came in with Marianne."

"Well good for him," Ross said.

Ross was looking over Teds notes and saw pictures from the video, frozen on the black sedan.

"Does that car look familiar to you?"

"Not really. Might be a Ford Taurus. Why?"

"I can't place it. Probably nothing."

Lloyd walked in and said, "who wants to run up to the 'zoo?"

"Where," asked Ted.

"Harborview. Rhymes with zoo. And also, quite often what it's like in the ER."

"Got it. I'll go."

"Me too," said Ross.

About an hour later, Ross, Ted and Lloyd knocked on the door to Jims room and entered. Paul was standing by the window. Jim was sitting up in bed. Marianne was standing on his right, her arms crossed, crying.

"Is this a bad time," Lloyd asked.

Marianne turned and faced away. Jim opened his mouth but Paul spoke first.

"Timing couldn't be better. Let's go downstairs so you can buy me coffee."

The four of them left the room. Marianne turned back to Jim.

"Do you think I'm overreacting?"

"I think you've been through a lot in the last couple of days and it hasn't been easy."

"Damn right it hasn't. What the hell is she thinking? She is so much older than he is and..."

Jim interrupted, "That's not what this is about is it?"

Marianne stopped and wiped her eyes. "What do you mean?"

"Honey, you've been working your ass off for six weeks. I know, I've been there and seen it. Then this happened," he gestured around the room with his right hand, "and suddenly everything changes."

Marianne was crying again, "you have no idea what it has been like."

"This isn't my first rodeo," Jim said. "Dad got pegged a time or two. I know what it's like for the family. Mom tried to take control of everything and everyone around us. It doesn't work. Jenny and Jason are a couple of adults that seem to like each other. Maybe it'll work out for them, maybe it won't, but that's up to them."

Marianne was crying again, "I just want you to be better."

"I don't want you to worry. Sheridan is the best at what he does and he got me patched up pretty good. I'll be good as new in no time, and you can finish your tour."

"What about the next time? What if it happens again?"

43

"I can't make any guarantees. But I can tell you the odds of it happening again are minimal. I'm a captain. This kind of thing just doesn't happen to captains."

She smiled through the tears. "It better not. I can't take it if it does."

"Honey, you'll have friends like Jenny and me for life. You don't have to take this walk alone."

Somewhere he had taken hold of her hand. He pulled her down close and kissed her. Marianne stood and said, "I must look a fright."

"No honey, you look as beautiful as ever."

She wiped her eyes again, then went into the bathroom and washed her face. When she came out a moment later, Jenny and Jason were standing in the doorway.

"Jenny," she began.

"Marianne."

Marianne pulled her shoulders back. "I'm sorry about what I said on the phone. You didn't deserve it."

"I know. I'm your friend, and I'll always be there for you. I just needed a little break last night and it stretched out to this morning."

Marianne looked at Jim, "well I know what that's like. Please forgive me?"

Jenny nodded. "OK, you're forgiven. Jason and I might go out again tonight."

Marianne nodded. "You don't need my permission."

Jenny said, "I know. Jim, is it going to be a problem for you if I'm dating one of your detectives?"

"Well, not for the next few weeks."

"Marianne," Jenny said, "from now on, when we're working you are my boss. But when we're not, I'm your friend. Agreed?"

"Agreed," said Marianne.

Jason walked into the cafeteria and found Lloyd, Ted, Ross and assistant chief Paul Churchill (retired) and current Chief of Police for the city of Prescott Arizona. They were sitting around a circular table. Ross and Paul were enjoying eggs and bacon. Ted had a bagel and Lloyd was sipping at his coffee.

"Well the wandering Lothario comes," said Lloyd as he spotted Jason.

Jason's cheeks turned pink but he grabbed a chair and spun it around to sit backwards and face the table.

"What did I miss?"

"First," said Ross, "how much trouble are you in with the boss?"

"Whatever do you mean?"

"Come on," Ted said, "Jenny goes out with you and doesn't come back until this morning."

"Aw, you know," Jason replied, "I'm like a son to him."

Everyone turned to look at Paul, who burst into laughter.

"I'm sorry sir, I seem to be putting my foot in my mouth a lot lately," said Jason.

"It's ok, son. We were just talking about the possibility that Jim and Marianne might have kids. I was just pointing out that I'd given up on grandchildren when you walked in."

"Still," said Lloyd, "You've been socially awkward lately. What's up with that?"

"I don't know. Yesterday I walked into Jims room and really embarrassed myself."

"That wasn't too bad," said Ted, "Jim didn't seem to mind."

"Marianne did," said Jason.

"Guys talk like that. We've known her long enough for her to understand that. But maybe it is a little soon to joke around her, after her betrothed got himself shot," said Lloyd.

"Did you really say 'betrothed,'" asked Ross, "damn you are old."

Lloyd displayed his middle finger towards his partner, then turned to Jason.

"Shouldn't you be out detecting, instead of indulging in hedonistic fantasies?"

"Sue me. I decided to take a night off. I gotta do some background on Fortunato and Lazzari. Which means when you are done making fun of me, I'm going in front of a computer for probably eight or nine hours."

"Well Ross and I figured out where they picked up Jim."

"I'm gonna guess the parking lot under the freeway."

"You have been thinking on this. Very good."

Jason stood, "I'm going to get started. Ted, do you want to help?"

"You bet," said Ted.

The two shook hands with Paul and said goodbye before going back to work.

After they left, Paul said to Lloyd, "He's the lead. I'm a little concerned that he's not focused on his investigation."

"Jason is one of the best. I guarantee he would have been available last night. I think he ran into too many dead ends and needed a reset."

"How does he get along with Jim?"

"Jim trusts him."

"OK, that's good enough I guess," said Paul.

"I want to check in on Jim before we go," said Ross.

"I suppose," said Paul, "I just hope there's still a wedding in the future."

Lloyd and Ross and Paul slipped quietly into the room. Jim was laying back on the bed, his eyes open. Jenny was sitting in the recliner, reading a magazine she had borrowed from the cop at the door. Marianne was sitting in another recliner on Jims right side, her feet towards Jims head and holding his right hand. Mariannes left hand lay on her abdomen, the new engagement ring winking in the dim light from the fluorescent bulb. Jim winked at them and gave a thumbs up without moving his left hand. Lloyd and Ross slipped quietly out of the door, Jenny joining them outside.

"Just so you know, she was awake all night."

Lloyd was concerned. "Is she taking anything?"

Jenny looked at Lloyd, a flash of anger across her face.

"Really? Do you really think she's on drugs? You don't think it could have anything to do with her future husband coming this close to getting killed?" She held her first two fingers about a quarter inch apart. "She's under a lot of pressure and a lot of stress. Doctor Johnston gave her something to help her sleep, and that is where she ended up."

Lloyd held his hands up in a gesture of surrender and said, "I'm sorry. You're right."

Jenny locked eyes with Lloyd.

"I think Jim is in a lot more pain than he's letting on. Turns out he did not sleep at all either."

Jenny looked at Lloyd for a minute, and made a noise that sounded like 'harrumph,' spun on her heel and went back in to the room.

"Let's get out of here," said Ross, "before we both piss her off."

Lloyd nodded and they headed for the elevator.

Chapter 9

Sunday
1PM.

Jason was standing behind Ted, showing him how to run a rap sheet. After a moment, the screen blipped and line after line came up. Ted reached for the print button and soon the whirring of the machine behind him started.

"Scroll through this, let's see what we got," said Jason.

Mario Fortunato had a lengthy rap sheet that stopped about six years ago. The majority of crimes included assaults and robberies. There was one kidnapping where he had been acquitted. Like most of his activity, it had been handled by Tacoma police.

"OK, click on LINKs," said Jason. That stood for "Law enforcement Information NetworK." It allowed the detectives to read certain reports written by other agencies.

Ted clicked on the link and typed in Fortunato's name. The kidnapping report was about ten years old and had to do with a girlfriend who later recanted. They quickly realized that the reason there had been a six year break in criminal activity was because of a manslaughter conviction. Ted opened the report. There were no follow up notes, as the only information available was the initial report. Ted printed out what he had and made a note of the case number.

Ted went back and repeated the process with Edward Lazzari. His sheet was similar to Fortunato. Many of the crimes seemed to be related.

"They must have been partners," said Ted.

Jason sat at his desk and pulled up the Tacoma Police department website. There was nothing there about an organized crime bureau. Jason thought for a moment, then dialed the number for their communications section. When someone answered, he identified himself, and said, "I'm trying to find someone who works in organized crime." He was transferred to another number that was answered almost immediately with, "Detective White, gang unit."

"Good afternoon Detective. I'm Jason King, Seattle PD Homicide."

"I saw the news. Looks like you came awfully close to getting a new captain Friday."

"Yeah it was touch and go but he pulled through. Listen, that's kind of why I'm calling."

"You recruiting? Thanks, but I don't have what it takes to be a captain."

Jason found himself liking White. "I don't think it works like that, but I'm investigating the shooting."

"How does that work," asked White, "isn't that a conflict of interest to investigate your boss?"

"Well he's out on the sick lame and lazy roster for now. So technically he's not my boss for the time being. Listen, if I gave you a couple of names, could you see what you got on them?"

Jason could hear the tapping of a keyboard, "sure, go ahead."

"Mario Fortunato and Edward Lazzari." Jason recited their birthdates.

"Shit, I can give you what I know right now. They're a couple of real bad actors. They pulled a lot of stunts together. Did you see the kidnapping charge?"

"I did. Looks like a DV thing?"

"You could call it that. Because it was that. She and Fortunato lived together off and on. She had…" Jason heard the keyboard clicking, "two kids with him. He seemed to enjoy knocking the shit out of her from time to time."

"I'm not surprised to hear he's an asshole. What was the kidnapping thing?"

"She wanted him out. He came home one day and his stuff is out on the lawn and the locks are changed. He didn't say anything to her. Didn't pick up his stuff. He went and got Lazzari. They waited until she was leaving for work that night, she had a job as a cocktail waitress."

"OK. What happened?"

White went on. "She went out to her car and they grabbed her. Duct taped her mouth, tied her hand and foot and threw her in the trunk of Lazzari's car. They drove down to the waterfront and carried her into a shipping container down there. Fortunato and Lazzari took turns beating her. When they were done, Fortunato tied her up again and they locked her in the container, telling her they were going to ship her to Japan."

"Shit. How did they find her?"

"Fortunato comes back four hours later, opens the container and tells her that if she doesn't want to go to Japan, she will never try to get him to move out again. She went along with it until after they got home. She calls work and they called us. We popped him down by the car museum."

"Why the hell is he not still in prison?"

"At first she cooperated. But we couldn't find Lazzari. We kept an eye on her, but we think Lazzari paid her a visit. She came in to the prosecutors office and said she didn't want to press charges and she'd made the whole thing up. She said it was all BS."

"And that was it?"

"No. The prosecutor tried to talk her out of it but no way. So he threatened her with false reporting. She said she'd rather go to jail than testify against him. So he gave up."

"So he dropped it."

"It wasn't winnable. Uncooperative victim, no independent witnesses, etcetera. He couldn't put her in jail when he knew she'd been telling the truth."

"So it got dropped and she went back to him."

"She's still around."

"What's her name," asked Jason.

"Alaina Miller. When do you want to talk to her?"

"Is today too early?"

"She works at a bar on the waterfront. She's graduated to bartender now. She's probably at work."

"My partner and I can meet you be there in an hour. What's the name of the place."

"It's called Quinns."

"An Italian girl working an Irish pub?"

"I know, right?"

"Hey, I don't want to forget about the manslaughter conviction."

White said, "I thought you'd never ask. Homicide brought me in on that. We had him cold on second degree murder, then a witness went missing. The prosecutor got nervous, so he offered a plea to manslaughter. Ten to fifteen years, he was out in six."

White paused, then went on. "The theory is that the two of them went to collect a debt. Their method of persuasion was overly enthusiastic and dude wound up dying."

"OK. We'll meet you in an hour at Quinns?"

"See you then."

Jim was alone in the room when there was a knock at the door. The tray table in front of him was littered with the detritus from his lunch. The door opened slowly and a tall thin brunette came in. She was wearing a sleeveless dress and high heels which exaggerated her height. Jim was watching Russell Wilson get sacked yet again as he turned the television off and said, "hello Gretchen."

Gretchen Henderson moved with the elegant grace of a model. She approached Jim's bed and laid a hand on his thigh.

"I heard what happened, Jim. I'm so sorry," she said.

"Thank you Gretchen," Jim said. She was Fred Henderson's widow and he had always wondered why he didn't like the woman. Her hand being where it was made him uncomfortable.

"You were so kind when Fred died. Your girlfriend, too, what was her name?"

"Marianne. She should be back soon."

"Oh." Gretchen lifted her hand. "Can I get you anything? Are you thirsty?"

Before he could say anything, Gretchen picked up the cup from Jims tray and took it to the sink. As she filled it, she said, "Where is your girlfriend anyway? If I was with you, I'd never leave."

"She's been here since Friday night. I figured she needed a break, so I asked her to bring me some clothes from home."

Gretchen handed him the cup. Jim set it on the tray.

"That's sweet of her," she said.

"How have you been holding up," asked Jim.

"Oh you know. Every day is a challenge. We had our differences, but he took care of his family."

"A good detective, too. Always willing to lend a hand."

The door swung open and Paul and Marianne came into the room.

"Hello Gretchen." Mariannes voice was ice cold. "What are you doing here?"

"I just came by to say hello. The two of you were so nice to me when Fred passed." Gretchen said mechanically.

Paul asked, "who are you?"

"Dad, this is Gretchen Henderson. Her husband was one of my detectives."

"Oh. I heard what happened. I'm sorry for your loss ma'am."

Gretchen put her hand on Paul's chest and said, "thank you. You don't look old enough to be Jim's father." Her voice dropped an octave.

"I've been working out."

Marianne reached for the cup of water on the tray at the same time as Jim. The cup tipped over and water flowed off the tray onto the blanket.

"Oh damn honey, I'm sorry," said Marianne.

"My fault entirely," said Jim as he hit the call button for the nurse.

"Anything I can do to help," said Gretchen.

"No, thanks." To Marianne, Jim said, "I'll have to change out of this hospital gown honey."

Gretchen said, "I had better get going. I hope you feel better Jim."

Gretchen passed the nurse going out.

"Dad, get the door," said Jim.

Paul caught the door. A quick glance down the hall showed him that Mrs. Henderson was headed for the elevator.

"I do not like that woman," said Marianne.

"There's a lot not to like," said Jim.

Gretchen Henderson came out of the stairwell in the parking garage and walked directly to a black Buick sedan. She slid into the passenger seat and kissed the driver.

Tom Meeker was younger then Gretchen and had a vacant look in his eyes. "How did it go," he asked.

"That idiot girlfriend of his spilled it everywhere."

"Shit," he said as he started the car.

"We have to put everything on hold for now," Gretchen said, "if we try again people are going to talk."

"I could do it," he said.

"Not right now, precious," she said giving him a squeeze, "it would be too soon."

He nodded as they drove out of the unstaffed gate.

Chapter 10

Sunday 3pm

Jason and Ted took longer than expected to find Quinn's. They were to meet detective White in the parking lot of an electrical supply company on Port of Tacoma road. Jason and Ted pulled into the parking lot and spotted an old battered El Camino. A tall, skinny black man was inside. He got out when the Crown Victoria pulled into the lot. Jason and Ted noticed that his denim jacket just missed completely covering the holster on his hip. He was wearing a Hawaiian shirt and cowboy boots with his jeans to complete the ensemble.

"The uniform of undercover cops everywhere," said Ted.

Jason suppressed a chuckle. They stopped behind the El Camino.

Jason got out and White said, "Jason King?"

"That's right, you must be Daniel White."

"Call me Danny. Who's your partner?"

"Ted. Ted Cysinski," Ted said extending his hand.

"Aren't you the media guy in Seattle?"

"I've been temporarily paroled," Ted said.

"What do you have for us," asked Jason.

Danny reached into his car and produced an expanding file folder. He pulled out a Manila folder and opened it on the hood of the Crown Victoria.

"Alaina Miller, white female aged forty five. Two children. Both taken into custody of child protective services and are now adults. Common law wife of the recently departed Mario Fortunato. Former exotic dancer, cocktail waitress and currently the bartender at Quinns. She got a DUI about ten years ago. Other than a couple shoplifts, nothing in her history that really stands out."

"Got a picture?"

Danny pulled a printout of a drivers license photo.

"It's about three years old. If anything she looks older."

Jason saw young eyes in an old face. Her nose twisted first in one direction, then back to another.

"Can I keep this?"

"Sure. You gonna do this now?"

"Any reason why not?"

"This time of day on a Sunday, it's probably not gonna be too crowded. Probably as good a time as any. You guys go in first, then I'll come in a minute or so later and sit near the front."

"Sounds good," said Jason.

They got into their respective cars, and Jason followed Danny to the bar. Danny parked on the street, but Jason pulled into the tiny parking lot and parked near the door. There was an old Harley that had seen better days parked near the entrance. A black Ford Taurus was sitting at the end of the lot. Ted pointed out that the rims on the tires were different colors and it was missing the passenger side mirror. The building itself was tarpaper. A neon sign advertising various local brands of beers did not lend much hope. There was a short walkway leading to a glass door.

"Place looks like a dump," muttered Ted.

"I've been in worse."

They got out of the car. Someone had hot topped the parking lot and it had actual painted lines for parking spaces.

"Urban renewal," said Jason.

They made their way to the door and Jason pushed it open. They gave themselves a moment to adjust to the light inside, and Jason saw Alaina Miller standing at the bar. She was pouring a coke into a glass. Sitting in a chair by the front door was a greasy looking biker with his thick forearms crossed. They made their way to the bar and took stools side by side. Jason heard the door bell tinkle a moment later and was conscious of Danny taking a seat in the corner. Jason looked in the mirror and saw that the biker had left. Alaina walked down the bar to them, and set the coke in front of Jason.

"What's this?"

"I figured you're not allowed to drink on duty, officer." Jason noted that Alaina was a medium height woman. He knew she was forty five, but she looked at least sixty. Her dark hair was going to gray. What hadn't been evident in the photo was the scar tissue that had bulked up around her eyes.

"Thank you Alaina." She looked startled for a moment but quickly recovered.

"What do you want with me?" Her voice had dropped.

"I need some background information is all."

"On who?"

"Mario Fortunato and Edward Lazzari."

"Fuck you. Get out."

"It's not like that, Alaina."

"The fuck it is." She dropped her voice. "The last time I talked to you fuckers I god damn near got killed. I'm not going to talk to you again."

"OK Alaina," Jason stood, "just so you know, neither one of them can hurt you anymore."

"Fuck you."

Jason and Ted started for the door. Alaina said, "what do you mean they can't hurt me?"

Jason and Ted looked at each other and headed back to the bar. Jason pulled out his ID holder and displayed his badge and card.

"Alaina, we're from Seattle PD. The homicide unit."

"Who did they kill?"

Jason took a direct approach. "They went after a police officer. There was a gunfight, then it looks like Lazzari killed Fortunato."

"Where's Ed?"

"Later that night, he was found in a parking lot with a gunshot wound to the head. It appears he killed himself."

Alaina nodded. She bent behind the bar and came up with a bottle and three glasses. She poured a measure into each one and handed one to each of the detectives.

"May the good Saint Patrick protect ye," said Alaina.

"And the devil neglect ye," said Jason.

Alaina clinked glasses with the detectives and downed her shot. Jason downed his, so Ted drank the coke.

"What do you want to know," she said. To Jason she suddenly seemed several years younger.

"How long have you been with Mario?"

"I was fifteen when it started. He was easily ten years older than me. I thought I was in love. God what an idiot I was."

"What happened," Jason said, feeling as though he knew the answer.

"Lets sit at a table," she said. They moved to a table near the bar. Jason sat with his back to the wall. Alaina sat where she could watch for customers.

"I was sixteen when he took my virginity. That was also my first taste of alcohol. I was so naïve, I thought I had to stay with him. When I was seventeen he gave me my first joint. A couple months later it was heroin. Then he faked my ID, and got me a job at a 'gentlemen's club.'"

"He had you stripping?"

"I figured out later that he was grooming me the whole time. I was young and pretty, and looked like the girl next door. As soon as he figured he could get away with it, he started making money off me."

"Did the clubs know you were seventeen?"

"Probably. I can't say for sure."

Jason wanted to speed things up, but he knew she had been waiting years to tell someone.

"What happened next?"

"I did that as long as I could. I thought for sure he'd turn me out, but one time he thought I'd cheated on him with a customer. That was the first time he hit me."

Jason nodded.

"I ended up pregnant. They wouldn't like a pregnant stripper, so I went to work as a hostess. Mario knew someone that owned a restaurant. After the baby came I just stayed there. When I came back they had another hostess, so I became a waitress."

"You had another kid?"

"I got pregnant again right away. There was some problems with the pregnancy and it was a cesarean. I told the doc when he went in that I wanted my tubes tied. I couldn't go through that again."

"Mario didn't know?"

"As far as I know he didn't. But that's when the hitting got worse. At first it was a slap or two. It escalated to full scale beatings. Sometimes he'd use a belt or a brush. I'd hurt so bad I could hardly stand up, but he'd make me go back to work the next day."

"Eventually you kicked him out."

"I tried. He and Lazzari were peas in a pod. I came out to my car to go to work, and they jumped me. I think Mario did most of the work but there was a bag over my head and he duct taped me into it. They tied me up and threw me in the trunk of a car."

"I read the report."

"It doesn't tell the half of it. Ed held me down, that's true. But what Mario made me do to him, makes me sick whenever I think about it. They beat me so bad. I had a busted nose, a blown out eye socket, busted ribs, I don't know what else. I kept hoping I would die so I could escape. After he took me home, I called my friend at work to cover for me, she was the one that called the cops. I thought for sure I was free after that."

"What happened?"

"Ed showed up one day. I still don't know how he got in, but I woke up and he was standing next to me. He made me do worse than what I had to do in the container. Then he told me I'd have to tell the prosecutor I made a mistake. If I didn't he'd be back and it would be even worse."

"Did Mario know?"

"He told Ed to do it."

Jason nodded.

"So I thought I'd tough it out. Took whatever drugs I could find to numb the pain. Just tried to make it through day by day. They would pass me back and forth like a toy. The kids got taken away, but Mario didn't care. He figured I could make more money if I didn't have to watch them."

"Did he work? Or was he living off you?"

"You don't know, do you?" Jason raised an eyebrow. "He's an enforcer for a mob that works the waterfront. Both of them are. Or were. That robbery that went bad? That's bullshit. He was picking up protection money."

"When he got out, did he come home?"

"He was in and out. I'm not sure where he was staying but he picked up some of his stuff and left. When Ed got out, they spent more time at the house. It wasn't long before they were back to the same old same old."

"Did they ever talk in front of you?"

"That was the weird thing," said Alaina, "It was like after all they did to me, they trusted me enough to talk in front of me. Maybe they thought I'd be too scared."

"Anything in particular they talked about? Like what they were up to?"

"They were talking about one job. Arguing really. It was the only time I ever saw Mario when he didn't want to do a job."

"What was the job?"

"I wasn't sure. But Ed kept telling Mario that they were going to get ten grand apiece. Mario would get worked up, saying this one might be different, but Ed would tell him he was gonna get ten grand for it."

"When were they talking about it last?"

"Thursday night. They were drinking and doing lines. I quit that shit two years ago, so I was just sitting in the corner. Mario was getting upset. Ed told him to knock it off, that once the job was done he'd have ten grand to blow on whatever he wanted."

"Where was the money coming from," asked Jason.

"Don't know really. Whoever was paying him for the job."

"Does he use a computer or smart phone? Anything like that?"

"He's got a phone, probably with him. He never left home without it. He had a tablet that ran out of battery and he never charged up again. Why?"

"I'd like to go through his stuff. Maybe he wrote some of it down."

"I don't know. There's not that much at the house anymore."

"If it is easier for you, I could get a search warrant."

Alaina brightened at that. "Yeah, that would be good."

"OK. We'll probably be back tomorrow. Who did he report to on the waterfront?"

"Dunno. I never met him."

Jason felt like that was not true, and he wondered why. He thought for a minute. "Ted you got anything?"

"What about the car? Could we search the car?"

"Yeah, I suppose. Why?"

Jason jumped in. "One like it was seen near the murder scene. We're trying to eliminate it."

"Oh sure," she said, "let me get my keys."

Alaina went behind the counter and came back with her purse and a set of keys. Jason pulled a consent to search form out of his folder and filled it out with Alaina, making a note of the license plate and vehicle identification number from the registration Alaina provided. When he was done, he went through the form with her and had her sign it.

"Before we start, did anyone have the car in Seattle on Friday?"

"No. I drive it to and from work. If it's not here it's in my driveway."

Jason nodded and they went outside.

In the parking lot, between the door and Jason's car were two men, one of them the biker from the doorway. On the other end of the parking lot were four more men. All of them, except for the biker, were wearing members only jackets.

"Alaina, go back inside."

She didn't say anything, just turned and went back into the bar.

"We should really call for backup," said Ted.

"Fuck that. I'm sick of this."

Jason walked off the porch, Ted walking behind him. In the time they had, Jason told Ted, "watch the guys in back."

Jason walked up to the two by the car. The biker had large forearms, but was really pretty skinny. Jason surmised he was an addict and his arms were swollen from shooting up. The other guy was about six two, and built like a weightlifter that never showed up for leg day.

"Something I can do for you," said Jason, before the weightlifter could speak.

57

"You a cop?" The tone was clipped. He sounded like a movie tough guy.

"You could say that. But not around here."

"You need to leave Alaina alone."

"Why? You think she knows something?"

"Leave her the hell alone or you'll wish you hadn't."

"Do you want to show me what I have to look forward too? I'm trying to plan my day."

The weightlifter smiled, and cocked his fist. Jason had been balancing on the balls of his feet, letting his arms relax by his side. As soon as the fist went up, Jason pushed off his back foot and struck out with his left foot, catching the inside of the weightlifters left knee. Something popped and the weightlifter slowly turned to his left and collapsed, a look of surprise on his face before the pain hit him. Jason looked at the biker. The guy was staring at Jason in shock, then he threw his hands up, slowly turned and started running. Jason went back to the weightlifter, bent down and took an old, well cared for, revolver off his hip. Jason opened the cylinder and saw there were five loaded cylinders, with the one under the hammer left unloaded. "Idiot," Jason muttered to himself. The weightlifter was holding his knee, a look of anguish on his face. Jason looked to Ted, as Ted looked back at him. Ted had a red mark on his right cheek, that was going to swell and purple up later. What struck Jason was that Ted was smiling and his eyes were bright. On the ground in front of him was one of the members only guys spread eagled on the hot top. Another one was trying to stop his nose from dripping blood while on his hands and knees. There was no sign of the other two.

Danny and Alaina came out of the door.

"Patrol is on the way. I saw the whole thing."

"Cool," said Jason. He bent and handcuffed the weightlifter.

"You'll want to get some ice on that," he said.

Tacoma PD sent a half dozen cars. Medics from Tacoma Fire were called and showed up shortly after. By the time they arrived, Nose Bleed and his friend were sitting on the curb wearing handcuffs. The medics said all three were going to the hospital, which meant they'd need to be guarded. Jason and Ted gave their statements on a recorder to Danny, and Jason got pictures of all three. Jason called Lieutenant Naes and explained the situation to her.

"I'm not coming down for that. If you've got pictures try to get a statement from them and get back to the office. I'll be in tomorrow morning."

Jason and Ted then went and did a careful search of Alaina's car. Jason found a paper sack with some marijuana edibles in the glove box. Since the state had declared marijuana should be legal, they found nothing illegal in the car. By the time they were done, all three of the suspects had been transported to Tacoma General hospital.

"Unless you need something from us, we're going up there. I want to talk to that weightlifter dude," said Jason.

"I'm good here. By the way that gun is coming up stolen. Your guys name is Lawrence Benvenuti. I'll call ahead and let them know you're coming," Danny said, pulling out his phone.

Jason thanked him, then went back to the trunk of his car and retrieved a lap top. Next he tossed the keys to Ted.

"You're driving, Ted."

"I have no idea where this place is. I'm good in Seattle but every time I drive in Tacoma I get lost."

Jason walked him through pulling up a maps application on his department smart phone, and showed him how to turn the sound on so it would give him step by step directions.

"OK, what are you going to be doing?"

"I've got a date tonight. I'm working on my statement so I can get off work on time."

"Rub it in," said Ted.

In the emergency room at Tacoma General, they found Lawrence Benvenuti shackled to a gurney in one of the exam rooms.

"Hi Larry. Remember me," asked Jason.

"Hey asshole, take these handcuffs off and I'll kick your ass."

"You know Larry, you really aren't in any position to demand anything. But since I'm here, what were you thinking trying to jump a couple of cops?"

"You were arresting Alaina."

"We weren't, but why would it be any of your business if we did?"

"Mario told me to keep an eye on her until he got back. That's all."

"Mario Fortunato?"

"If you say so."

"Why would you listen to anything that child molester would say?"

"Hey now, I don't know anything about him messing with kids. He never did that shit around me."

"Because he know's you're a stand up guy, right Larry?"

"Damn straight."

"You know what the age of consent is in this state, Larry?"

"Stop calling me Larry. My mom calls me Larry."

"Age of consent Larry."

"Fine. It's like seventeen or something."

59

"Do you know how old Alaina was when he got with her?"

"He said he met her when she was in college."

"More like high school, Larry." Jason decided to fudge a bit. "She was fifteen when he first got with her."

"Bullshit. No way. Mario isn't like that."

"Larry he is. I guarantee you once Tacoma PD starts looking they are going after anyone that might even have had the slightest clue what he was doing."

Benvenuti paused for a minute. "I. Had. No. Idea."

"Convince me."

"How?"

"What were Mario and Lazzari up to?"

Benvenuti laid back on the bed, his mouth closed. He was shaking his head.

"Larry, I'm going to show you a couple of pictures."

Benvenuti closed his eyes and turned his head away.

"Look at them Larry," Jason held the pictures above his head.

Slowly Benvenuti opened his eyes. Mario Fortunato's lifeless eyes stared back at him from the parking lot. Blood had pooled behind his head.

"What the fuck is that?"

"Fortunato and Lazzari tried to hit a cop. That's what happened. What I want to know is who hired them and why."

"What's in it for me?"

"You took a swing at me. I'll talk to the prosecutor and see if they'll go misdemeanor instead of felony. Less jail time and closer to home. Probably be done in thirty days."

"What about the gun?"

"That depends. How many bodies are on it?"

"None from me, I swear. I bought it off a guy three weeks ago and never fired it."

"If that's true I'll talk to him about that too."

Larry nodded and thought for a minute.

"I never know what the jobs are. Someone calls me and they tell me they need someone special. I call Lazzari. They negotiate their own price and I get a ten percent finders fee."

"Who called for the job on Friday?"

"Some guy. He said he got the number from a friend. I just passed it on. I don't take names or numbers, just transfer the calls. Anything that doesn't sound legit, I tell them to take a hike."

"Ten per cent? What was your cut from this last one?"

"Lazzari told me I'd get a hunnert bucks."

"Lazzari got ten for himself and ten for Fortunato. That's twenty thousand bucks. Your cut should have been two thousand."

Benvenuti sat up, "what? Those assholes. I'm gonna kill Lazzari."
"You won't have to. He's already dead."

5pm.

Jim was staring at the tray of food in front of him. There was a dried up looking hamburger, a green salad and some kind of chocolate pudding thing for dessert. He'd asked for a coke and that was in a tiny glass. Sheridan had strapped Jims left hand to his chest, with instructions to leave it alone for the time being and Jim was trying to figure out how to use the knife.

Marianne and Jenny were playing cards at a small table. Paul was watching the news. Jim was trying to take a bite of his hamburger while holding it one handed.

"Hey son, doesn't that guy work for you?"

Jim looked up and saw Jason and Ted walking into the emergency room of a hospital in Tacoma. Jim put down his burger and turned up the volume to hear, "a Tacoma police spokesperson said that a gun was involved, but that no shots were fired. They would not say why Seattle Police detectives were involved in the investigation. As you may remember, a Seattle Police captain was shot and wounded during a robbery attempt on Friday afternoon. We do not know if these two incidents are related."

Jim turned the volume down.

"Jenny," he said, "Jason's gonna be late picking you up."

Jenny looked up from her hand. "How would you know that?"

"He was just on the news. In Tacoma."

"Well he better have a good explanation."

"I'm sure he does. They said something about busting a string of massage parlors."

Without looking up, Marianne said, "someone is feeling better."

Jenny went back to the cards in her hand. "Bastard," she said, jovially.

There was a knock at the door. Rebekah Naes and Mike Worthy came in. Jim shut off the television and said hello.

Rebekah walked up to Marianne and said, "you are Marianne Wilson."

"Oh honey. You knew it all along."

"Mike explained it to me on the way over. I feel like an idiot."

"I'll make it up to you. When Jim gets out of this place, you come over to the house and we'll have dinner for you. And then we'll let you in on all our secrets."

"That's a deal. Jim, I just got off the phone with Detective King. They got jumped by six guys in Tacoma. Jason said Ted put two of them in the hospital, but the third one all but told him Fortunato and Lazzari were hired to hit you."

"That's interesting."

"Do you have any idea who would do that?"

"Is it because I'm popular?"

"I keep forgetting you're still on painkillers."

"He is, but then again he's always like this," said Marianne. "Tell me, who hired those two?"

"We don't know yet. Jason and Ted are on their way back. They're going to look at this guys phone records and see if they can figure out who made the calls." She was looking at Jim as she spoke.

Jim nodded, "They probably ought to do something with this woman, what's her name, Miller?"

Rebekah confirmed it, "Alaina Miller."

"They went after cops. They won't hesitate to go after her if they think she's helping us."

"Jason gave her fifty bucks and sent her to Seattle. He told her to check into a hotel and not tell anyone where she is. He's got a code word he gave her if he needs to meet with her again."

Jim nodded.

"Skipper, how can you eat that thing," Mike asked.

"It's not bad once you get past the taste and texture," Jim said.

"Jenny, right," Mike said to her.

"Yes."

"Jason said he'd be here as close to seven as he can. Eight at the latest."

Jenny thanked him, then laid a card down and said, "Gin."

"Dammit," said Marianne.

Chapter 11

8pm

Marianne had just finished zipping Jenny into her dress when Jason knocked and came into the room.

"Wow, you look great," he said.

She thanked him. Jim was laying back on his bed, half asleep, but he roused himself enough to say, "tell me about Tacoma."

Jason looked around and said, "we interviewed Fortunato's girlfriend. It wasn't pretty."

Jim raised an eyebrow, and said, "I heard you got jumped."

"Those guys were idiots." Jason launched into the story, leaving out how he had blown out the weightlifters knee, but said, "Ted took out two before the rest started running."

"Really?"

"Yessir. I didn't see it happen, but when I turned around one was unconscious and the other was on his hands and knees. Ted was having the time of his life."

"He used to be a pretty good scrapper. Good to see he still has it in him."

Marianne asked, "what did the girlfriend have to say?"

"Ma'am, with all due respect, you don't need to hear that."

Jim started to open his mouth, but Marianne said, "Jason, what happened?"

Jim looked at Jason's face and said, "honey I wouldn't push it."

Marianne nodded as Jason said, "ma'am, it's ok. I just need to process it."

Jenny brushed her dark hair back and said, "I'm ready if you are."

After they left, Marianne said, "that poor woman."

"It had to be bad for him to act like that."

"What do you think happened?"

"I have no idea," Jim said, "Jason's a good cop, and he'll push through. I hope Jenny can help him forget for a while."

As they got on the elevator, Jenny said, "what are our plans?"

"I was thinking dinner, then who knows?"

"How about dinner at your place, and then who knows?"

An hour later, they were in Jason's living room. Jenny was sitting on the couch, her shoes off and her feet tucked under her, a glass of red wine in her hand. Jason sat on the floor, cross legged, his glass sitting on the coffee table between them, half empty boxes of Chinese food scattered across the surface.

"You haven't talked much," said Jenny.

"I'm still trying to organize my thoughts."

"How bad was it?"

"The way she described it, I know it was bad. She looked like she'd done a few rounds with Buster Douglas and Mike Tyson."

Jenny was quiet for a moment and reflective.

"Do you know," said Jason, "that five out of six victims of rape do not report the crime to the police? Do you know why?"

Jenny rolled her wine glass and shook her head.

"It's because they are afraid. Afraid they won't be believed. Afraid they'll get in trouble. Afraid because they know their attacker and they don't want him to get in trouble."

Jenny nodded wordlessly. A tear, unbidden, rolled down her cheek. Jason did not notice in the dim light.

"This woman, she did everything right. Our side couldn't find the second guy. But he found her and he forced her to recant. So she became a victim all over again."

Jenny's voice was surprisingly steady. "For me, I thought I would get in trouble for drinking and staying out late," she said quietly, "my parents had no idea."

Jason was quiet.

"You're the first person I ever told. I was fifteen when it happened. My grades went from A's to C's. The teachers thought I was on drugs but I couldn't sleep. I was afraid he'd come back."

Jason looked down at the floor, then at her face. He picked a napkin off the table, stood and moved beside her. Gently he wiped her tear.

"I know a guy," he said, "might be of help."

She waved her hand, "that's sweet of you but no."

"I know you're busy, being a world famous musician and all, but he could help."

"I've been through the whole counseling thing," Jenny said wiping a tear, "it helps. If I need to theres a woman in Nashville I can see."

Jason nodded. He took Jenny's hand and hugged her.

An hour later, they lay in bed, Jenny's head on his shoulder. Jason lay on his back, staring at the ceiling. Silently he wondered to himself if he really knew what he was getting into. He enjoyed her company and she seemed to like his. They trusted each other with secrets that no one else would know. He sighed softly.

"Are you awake," she said.

"No. You?"

"Not a bit. You really need to sleep. I have to be back at the hospital by ten. Jim's probably going home at eleven."

"It's nice of you to come out to help a guy you barely know."

"I didn't come here for Jim. I came for Marianne."

Jason nodded in the dark. "How is she doing?"

Jenny raised her head. "I won't mince words. She is stressed the fuck out. She's better now, but man when we first got here."

There was something about her when she swore.

"Are they in love?"

"You ever look at them? They can be in a crowded room, and they always know where the other one is. I've never seen two people that seem to be more in tune with each other."

Jason changed the subject. "Do you want to come to the office with me in the morning?"

"And see where you work? Meet your friends? Umm, let me think about it, ok what time do we have to be there?"

Jason chuckled. "I get there between seven and eight usually."

Jenny crawled onto his chest and kissed him. "Then we have time," she said.

Chapter 12

Monday
10am

Sheridan was examining Jim's injuries while changing the bandages.

"So here's the thing, Jim," he was saying, "I know how relaxing this place is, and if you really want to spend a couple more nights here than I can arrange it. However, things are looking good. There's no sign of infection and I understand you are able to get up and walk around a little."

"Mostly just from here to the bathroom. But if I use the IV pole for support it helps."

"OK, we'll get you a set of crutches. But I think if you feel you're up for it I'd like to send you home."

"OK, quick question. Marianne has to go back and play those dates she cancelled. Dad's got to go back to work, and I'm a bad enough cook with two hands."

Marianne piped up. "Jim, I'm not leaving until you can function by yourself."

"Honey, you can't do that. You have to play those dates."

"I will, I promise."

"You two work that out later," said Sheridan, "but we can arrange for someone to come in and check on you every day."

"I can have Miguel and Rosa come out." Miguel and Rosa were a husband and wife team that formed the main staff at Mariannes Nashville house.

"That works for me," said Sheridan, "but Jim the important thing is to rest your shoulder. I know you and you can be stubborn but what you need now is rest."

Jim nodded. "Miguel still thinks I'm after your money."

"What he doesn't know," said Marianne, "is that I'm after yours."

Jim laughed. "Sheridan, are you still going to kick me out of here by eleven?"

"I thought I'd plop you on the curb and let you take the bus home," smiled Sheridan.

"Sheridan!"

"Marianne, I'm joking," he said, "I think his dad has arranged transportation."

"That's right," said Paul.

"I'll have the nurse bring you some papers to sign. In the meantime why don't you get ready to go?"

"It would be nice to get home," said Jim.

Sheridan shook his hand, then left the room, as Jason, Jenny and Ted came in.

"Any updates," asked Jim.

"TESU is working on a warrant for the phone records," said Jason. TESU stood for 'Telephone and Electronic Surveillance Unit.'

"Any luck with video?"

"That's a make work detail at the moment," said Jason. "Naes got a couple of light duty guys to look at it. Lloyd and Ross caught another case last night but that one is pretty straight forward."

"Good, good. Ted, how's your hand?"

Ted held up his left hand, wrapped in an ace bandage. "Doc said it's jammed a little. Ice, rest, the usual thing no one has time for."

"Get Sheridan to take a look at it. That was some good work."

Ted beamed. "Thank you."

Marianne handed Jim an electric razor. "Guys, I gotta get dressed," he said.

"We'll wait outside," replied Jason as he, Ted and Jenny left the room.

Once Jim was shaved, Marianne pulled a sweatsuit out of the bag and helped him put the pants on. The jacket fit on his right arm, but they finally decided to simply zip it over the left and let the empty sleeve hang. Marianne helped him put on a pair of sneakers.

"Jeezus, I feel like an old man," Jim said.

"Honey, you look fine," said Marianne, "I'm just..." she didn't know how to finish the sentence.

Jim was sitting on the edge of the bed, and pulled her in with his good arm.

"Sweetheart, it's going to be ok," he said as he kissed her forehead.

"What happens if it's not?"

"It will be."

"That's not what I mean. They haven't found these people yet. You are still hurt. I'm beside myself with worry that even after you get better it could happen again."

"I'm a captain. The odds of that are worse than winning the state lottery."

"You say that, but here we are. What if it does happen again? What if it's worse next time? I love you and I don't want to lose you."

"You won't. I won't let it happen again."

"Be serious, Jim. How can you make sure it won't?"

Jim was quiet.

"There are no guarantees are there?"

"No, there aren't. It's a tough call," Jim said, "because that's life. There was no guarantee that you and I would fall in love yet here we are. Part of that for me is accepting that the woman I love is away from home a bunch. I have to trust you to do your best. You just have to trust that I'll do my best." Jim paused and took a deep breath, then said, "I could retire. I'd have to wait to get my pension but I've got my books and I really don't need my pension anyway. But part of our relationship is accepting each other for what we do. I love you and I know you love your job, and I'd never ask you to give it up. You love me, please don't ask me to give up my job. In return I promise I will do my best to make sure this never happens again."

Marianne kissed him. "Honey," she said, "I love you. I promise, I'd never ask you to quit doing what you love, because I know if I did you'd stop. And I'd do the same. But please, be careful."

Jim kissed her back and said, "I will honey, I promise." Then they kissed again.

"None of that," said the nurse, "You'll tear your stitches."

The nurse had entered without making noise and was holding Jim's discharge paperwork.

"It wasn't that kind of surgery," said Jim, his arm still around Mariannes waist.

"I need to go over this with you," she said, and proceeded to discuss keeping the wounds clean, changing bandages twice a day, and emphasized that he get as much rest as he could for the next two weeks.

"Do you understand?"

Jim nodded.

Marianne said, "I will make sure he does."

"Ok," said the nurse, whose nametag said 'Simone,' "sign here."

Jim signed with a flourish as Sheridan came in pushing a wheelchair. Lloyd, Ross, Ted, Jenny and Jason followed him in.

"Shouldn't you be planning out your retirement," Jim asked Lloyd.

"I pulled my papers," said Lloyd.

Jim couldn't say anything.

"Jim, you need to get in the wheelchair," said Sheridan.

"I'm not getting in that thing," Jim replied.

"Suit yourself," said Sheridan," but do you really want to walk out on one leg?"

"Since you put it that way," Jim said as he eased off the bed and into the chair. Lloyd took the handles as Marianne positioned his leg on the rest.

"Try not to run me into the wall," said Jim.

"Relax. It's been at least three weeks since my last accident," said Lloyd.

They wheeled out of the room, and down the hall towards the elevators. Jim looked at Marianne and said, "How are we getting home?"

"It's covered," she said.

They crowded into the elevator and rode to the lobby in silence. When the doors slid open, the dozen or so detectives from the day homicide squad had formed a loose half circle around the elevators. Jim rolled off the elevator and told Lloyd to stop. Slowly he eased out of the chair until he was on his feet, with one crutch under his right arm.

"Jim, sit down," whispered Marianne.

Jim shook his head. He went to each detective and shook their hands as he thanked them for coming. As the detectives realized what was happening they came to him. He didn't sit down again until he had shaken everyone's hand and spoken with all of them.

Once he was seated, Marianne leaned over and whispered, "Don't do that again. You will hurt yourself."

Jim nodded and waved at his officers as they moved towards the lobby exit. Paul was waiting next to a brand new black Yukon. A camera crew from one of the local stations was waiting on the sidewalk. Jim started to get up again, but Marianne shot him a look and put a hand on his shoulder. Jim stayed in his seat. Ted moved up between Jim and the camera.

"Mr. Churchill, Mr Churchill!" A tell slender redheaded reporter was trying to get his attention.

Ted stopped in front of her and spoke to her.

"Captain Churchill is not giving interviews today."

"Ted, right," she said slipping him a business card, "call me later. I can make you famous."

Ted left the card in his pocket. By then Jim was standing with help from Marianne and Jenny, and being helped into the Yukons back seat. Marianne got into the seat behind the driver. Jenny sat in the passenger seat. Lloyd and Ross headed to a shiny unmarked crown Victoria while Jason and Ted got into another one parked in front of the Yukon. By a prearranged signal all three pulled from the curb at the same time. Jim's window rolled down, and he waved to his detectives, then he pulled his arm back in and rolled the window up.

"Home Paul," he said to his dad.

"Yes sir."

When the procession turned onto ninth ave, they passed a black Buick, parked on the curb. Tom Meeker sat in the drivers seat, a baseball cap pulled low over his eyes. He cursed to himself. Tom waited for the procession to pass before he called Gretchen on his smart phone.

"There's too many of them. No way this works."

"Tom, are you sure?" Her voice was soft and low. Sexy yet plaintive.

"There will be another chance," he said, "It's too risky today."

"OK, come home. I know you did your best."

Something about the way she talked to him that made him feel like a third grader. When he passed the intersection of seventh avenue and James street, he saw the last Crown Victoria heading north to the freeway. He drove to sixth avenue and headed south to Kent.

Chapter 13

Noon

Jason and Ted stopped at the gate. Jim called the guard shack on Mariannes phone to tell him to let these three cars in. The gate went up, and the short convoy drove to the right and stopped at Jims house.

As a writer, Jim had done quite well for himself, writing under the nom de guerre of TW Griffin. Jim owned the house in Hunts Point on the shore of Lake Washington.

Jason and Ted parked just past the driveway, while Lloyd and Ross parked just short of it as the Yukon pulled into the drive.

Marianne looked at Jim and said, "you will be careful, right?"

"Of course honey."

Jim felt exhausted. After three days of bed rest, the short time on his feet at the hospital had tired him. He'd slept part of the way home, but rallied when they pulled into the gate. It was good to be home, and he said so to Marianne.

"Yes it is," she said, "although there have been some changes."

Marianne got out of the truck and came around to help Jim. Jenny was on the other side but Jim held the crutch out and gingerly stepped down from the truck, landing on his good leg. Using the crutch for support, and with the help of Paul and Marianne, he started working his way up the sidewalk. The four detectives were watching the street. As Jim got to the front porch, the door swung upon. Rosa, Mariannes caretaker from her ranch in Nashville, was standing in the doorway.

"Welcome home, Mr. Churchill."

"Hello Rosa. Good to see you. Is Miguel here too?"

"He is coming out later. He wants to make sure someone can take care of the horses."

"Where are you sleeping?"

"Marianne found us a nice room on the main floor," she said, "very nice."

"Glad you like it," he said as Rosa stepped aside to let him and his entourage in. Jim introduced his father. Rosa and Jenny conversed rapidly in Spanish for a moment.

Jim said, in English, "nonsense Jenny. You can stay here, there's plenty of room. Dad, you too."

Jenny said, "are you sure it's not any trouble?"

"None at all."

Paul said, "I moved into the guest room next to you. I need my beauty sleep so if you fall out of bed and break a leg, don't come running to me."

Jim groaned.

"Now I know where you get it," said Marianne.

"Lunch is ready," said Rosa.

"Jim is going upstairs first. If you'd be so kind as to make a tray for him, I'll come back and take it to him," said Marianne.

"Honey..," said Jim.

"Don't argue. We are going upstairs."

Jim knew not to argue. He dutifully limped to the bottom of the stairs. Someone had installed a stairlift. Jim's eyes went black for a moment, then he proceeded to limp up the stairs.

"Jim, please use the lift."

"No honey. I'm not a cripple."

It was Mariannes turn not to argue. She shrugged and climbed up on his left side, carefully slipping her arm around his waist and helped guide him up the stairs. By the time they got to the top, Jim was sweating.

"Honey, please use the stairlift next time."

"I'll think about it," Jim said in a tone that Marianne knew meant he had no intention of using the stairlift.

A moment later Jim and Marianne heard a whir as a motor kicked on. Lloyd was sitting on the seat as it ascended the stairs. He had a smile on his face as he raised his arms over his head and stuck his feet out in front of himself. Jim couldn't help himself and let out a laugh at the sight.

"Lloyd, you're a natural," he cried.

"I always wanted to do that," Lloyd said as he reached the top.

"Lloyd, it's not a toy," said Marianne.

"Yes ma'am." Lloyd was not at all contrite.

"Help me get him into bed," she said.

"Come on boss. She's right, you look exhausted."

"Gee Lloyd, thanks."

"I'm here to help," he said as he took a hold of Jims right arm and opened the door to his bedroom.

In the middle of the room was an adjustable bed.

"That's new," said Jim.

"Sheridan said it would help if you could sit up in bed and keep your feet elevated. So I picked this up and had it delivered over the weekend. And yes, I used TW Griffin's name to get it done. So there," said Marianne.

Lloyd guided Jim to the left side of the bed, which was raised. Jim sat on the edge of the bed and tried to gather himself for a minute. Marianne bent and took off his running shoes.

"There's a pair of slippers right here," she said pointing, "if you need to get up for something wear them so you don't fall."

Jim laid back on the pillow and closed his eyes. In a moment his breathing became slow and regular. Marianne put a finger to her lips and pointed towards the door. Lloyd and Marianne went out onto the landing and she kissed Lloyd on the cheek.

"What's that for?"

"That was a nice thing you did, even if you don't know it," she said.

"Hey, I always wanted to ride on one," he said.

"You gave him a good laugh. Are you staying for lunch?"

"Don't know why not," said Lloyd.

In the dark of the bedroom Jim opened his eyes. The door was closed but the room was lit by the ambient light from outside. Jim slid his feet to the floor and stood. He went into his walk in closet and limped to the far end, behind his long rack of suits, minus the one that had been cut off of him three days before. A pistol safe was mounted to the wall. Jim ran his thumb over the sensor and the top popped open. Inside was a government model 1911, originally made by Colt, but this one was made by Kimber.

Jim picked up the gun and checked the chamber. It was empty. Carefully he slid the magazine out of the well and saw it was full. He slipped it back in, popping the magazine against his hip. Then he placed the rear sight against a shelf and pushed down until the slide was all the way back. Then he let the slide fall forward, making an audible click. The first round was now chambered. Jim limped back to the bed and placed the gun into the nightstand.

Lloyd and Ross were having chili. Paul was at the back window, looking through the rain at the lake. Jason and Ted were outside. Jenny was in the kitchen putting together a care package for them. Marianne walked to Paul and stood next to him for a moment before he spoke.

"How is he?"

"Stubborn as hell. I'm worried he's going to hurt himself if he doesn't listen to Sheridan."

"He's always been that way. Once he's told he can't do something it just makes him want to do it even more," said Paul.

Marianne smiled at the thought. Then she asked, "How are you doing?"

"Thank's for asking," he said, "about what you'd expect for a father that came that close to burying his son."

"I know how I felt. I can't imagine that feeling."

Paul looked at her. "You've known him, what, a year?" Marianne nodded. "He's been my son his whole life. He's smart and cocky, arrogant and humble, tough and sensitive. When his first wife died it was like he put a shell on and did not come out for a long time. He threw himself into his work, and he's good at it. The first time he was shot, I was still working. When I got to the hospital he said, 'hi dad, how's it goin?' Like he'd just come home from football practice. When I got back to my office I cried for an hour."

Marianne reached out and put her hand on his arm. "When I got word in Charlotte, I'd just come off stage. A very nice lieutenant handed me a phone number to call. I saw the area code and I just knew. I couldn't make the call, Jenny had to do it for me."

"This one wasn't as bad for me. I don't know why, maybe knowing he'd survived it before, or having the luxury of distance I don't know. I'm sorry I had to meet you the way I did, but I'm glad you were there for him. How long have you been engaged, by the way?"

"Counting today? Two days."

Paul smiled. "That's what he was doing. Picking up the ring."

Marianne paled. "This is my fault?"

"No honey. This was a setup from the get go. If it hadn't happened then it might have happened when he stopped for groceries or in the entry to the neighborhood. Where it did happen was probably the best place for it to happen. He had cover and he was on his home turf."

Marianne nodded, unconvinced. Paul pushed through and changed the subject.

"The first I knew of you was when I met you in the hospital. I was suspicious when I was told his wife was there. I googled you the first chance I got to find out more about you. You are supposed to be dating some guy named T.W. Griffin."

"Oh really?"

"I've got his books. He's a good read, but I always thought it sounded familiar. Jim is T.W. Griffin."

"He never told you."

Paul shrugged. "I never asked."

Marianne said, "And you're still here."

"When he wants to tell me about it he will. It explains the house. That's a hell of a boathouse out there, I'd love to see the boat inside."

"When he's better, we'll all go out on it."

Paul nodded. "That would be good."

"Last summer we took a trip on it. We went out the Ship Canal and cruised up to the San Juans. It was lovely."

"I have to go back to Prescott this week. I'm leaving Wednesday. I'll help out as much as I can until then."

Marianne nodded. "I'll tell Jim. I know he understands."

Paul shrugged again.

"Look, what do you want from us? He hasn't been the perfect son, but how many times have you called him? I'm glad you're here now, but is this what it takes for the two of you to talk?"

"Well," Paul began.

"Even then, you haven't talked. Not meaningfully anyway. You've got two days. Make the most of it."

Marianne turned on her heel and walked into the kitchen. Jenny was on her way out with her care package.

"Jason and Ted are going back to work. I want them to have some chili."

"I'll walk out with you," said Marianne, "I want to see Jane and I need some air."

Jenny nodded as they headed to the door. Marianne stopped to slip into a trench coat and put an umbrella over their heads. They stopped at Jason and Teds car. Jenny handed off the package and kissed Jason.

"If it's not too late," he said, "maybe I can come back."

"I'd like that," she said and they kissed again.

Ted put the car in gear and eased away from the curb. They turned around and headed towards the exit. Jason rolled his window down and stuck a hand out into the rain to wave goodbye.

The two women strolled up the street to Jane and Sheridans house. It was the only other house on the long block. Marianne knocked on the door and Sheridan opened it a moment later.

"Big day ladies. Marianne how's he doing?"

"He's tired. He was sleeping when I left and his dads there now. Why don't they ever really talk?"

Sheridan stepped back and let them in. "That's a topic that I've never been able to broach. I think it's a guy thing. If you get too deep into your conversation you expose too much."

Jane was resting on the sofa, watching television.

"Marianne, hi! Is he getting settled in?"

"He didn't like the stair lift. I think it was a waste of money."

Jenny asked, "How are things with the baby?"

Sheridan excused himself and went into his office.

2PM.

Marianne and Jenny came back into the house, shaking the rain from their jackets. Ross was in the living room. He pointed upstairs and said, "You'd better get up there."

"Dammit. Paul had better not be upsetting him."

Marianne ran up the stairs. Jim was sitting up in bed. Paul was pressing a gauze pad to Jim's shoulder. Lloyd was holding his cell and scrolling through his contacts.

"What happened," she asked.

"I came upstairs and he was on the floor," said Paul, "he fell."

"I was going to the bathroom and my leg went out from under me. I tried to catch myself with my bad wing," said Jim.

"What were you thinking? Dammit," Marianne said as she pulled her phone from her pocket.

Marianne dialed a number from memory, and when it was answered she said, "Sheridan he pulled out his stitches."

"That didn't take long. I'll be right there," he responded.

Three minutes later Sheridan came into the room with a black leather doctors bag.

"You've got to be kidding," said Lloyd.

"I know," Sheridan said, "I'm a stereotype."

He stepped in and lifted up the bandage. He took a towel out of his bag and arranged it under Jim and around the wound. Then he irrigated the wound with a bottle of distilled water and pulled the edges back together.

"Everyone out. Except you, Marianne. You are going to assist me."

Marianne nodded. At Sheridan's direction she found the suture kit. She arranged the instruments on another towel in Jims lap. Sheridan selected a needle and thread and told Jim to look away. Carefully he trimmed and replaced the torn stitching and added a series of butterfly bandages.

"Sorry doc."

"Sorry my ass," said Sheridan. "I dropped everything for your call. I left my pregnant, bedridden wife to answer that call. I drove like a madman. I worked for hours to save your leg and this shoulder. Some of my best work is in there. You ever pull a stunt like this again I'll leave you in the hands of a third year medical student."

Sheridan snapped his case shut.

"I mean it. If you're going to kill yourself, I won't stand by to watch it."

"I promise doc, it won't happen again."

"It better not." Sheridan glared at him.

"How's Jane," said Jim.

"Fine, thanks for asking. Her OB says everything is going well, given her age and all. Have you guys set a date yet?"

"Not yet. Honey, have you told your parents yet?"

"Unbelievable," Marianne said, "did you hear a word he said?"

"Believe me honey, I heard every word. I'm on my best behavior."

"And for the record, I sent a text to my dad. He's very happy for us." Marianne pulled her phone from her purse and said, "damn. It's dead as a door nail."

Marianne went to her side of the bed to plug it into the charger. Sheridan picked up his bag.

"I've got to get back. If you're up to it, we'd like to have the two of you over before the baby comes."

"We'd like that. Sheridan, I'll walk you out," said Marianne.

She took Sheridan by the arm and they worked their way down the stairs together. When they got to the door, Marianne said, "Sheridan, thank you. I can't believe he did that."

"He's not used to being laid up like this. He'll be ok, he just wants to be better. I'm sorry if I was too harsh."

"I'm worried you weren't harsh enough," Marianne said.

"He's tough. Did you notice not so much as a whimper when I sewed him back up?"

"I didn't think about it until just now."

"He's going to be just fine, so long as he doesn't go for any more gymnastics."

Sheridan hugged Marianne and left. Marianne went into the kitchen and asked Rosa to bring up something for Jim to eat, then went upstairs.

Jim was silent as Marianne knelt on her side of the bed.

"Honey," she began, "did you listen to Sheridan?"

"I learned my lesson."

"Good. One thing I learned today is how much your people look up to you. You can't let them down."

Jim nodded.

Marianne leaned over to pick up her phone. Jim leaned back but kept his eye on her.

"Oh shit," she said quietly.

"What is it?"

Instead of answering, she dialed a number. Jim listened to her side of the conversation.

"Hi daddy." "No, I'm fine." "Dad, there is seriously no need for that. Jim got hurt and I flew back to be with him." "Yes daddy, my fiancé," she said smiling at Jim.

When she hung up she said, "apparently it's all over the television that I've disappeared, and was last seen in the company of the Charlotte police department. There's been a bunch of conspiracy theorists that seem to think I'm a) an alien and have been pirated away to area fifty one, or b) I've been kidnapped by the government for experiments."

"Well doesn't that beat all. How do we handle this?"

"Dad says he's been getting phone calls from all over wanting to know where I am. He hasn't told anyone what's happening. But, I'm going to have to say something."

"Call Hank, let him deal with it."

"He already put out a statement, but that hasn't been enough. I have an idea though."

"What's that?"

In response she reached across and picked up Jims phone. She found an app for satellite radio, tuned into a station, and then plugged a set of headphones into the phone. Jim dutifully plugged the earpieces into his ears. He found himself listening to something called the "Hunt and Hunt show." The music was good but he didn't care for the banter.

He pulled one of the ear buds out of his right ear and said, "is this a good idea?"

"Trust me honey, I know what I'm doing."

Jim plugged back in and heard one of the DJ's say, "I understand we have someone very special calling into the show."

"That's right Jeff, let's go straight to the phones. Hi you're on the air."

Jim saw Marianne's lips move, and then about eight seconds later he heard her voice over his ear buds.

"Hi y'all."

"I understand that this is Marianne Wilson, is that right?"

"Yes it is. I realized all the hubbub going on, and I figured I'd talk to the most popular show on radio."

"Well thank you!"

"Unfortunately, I couldn't get on through to them so I called you instead," she continued.

Jim heard about five seconds of laughter and then, "you got us Marianne. So we hear that you were kidnapped by aliens and are hiding inside area fifty one. Any truth to that rumor?"

"Oh my, y'all will believe anything. No, so here's what happened. After my show in Charlotte, there were two Charlotte police officers waiting for me back stage."

"Uh oh, someone forgot to pay their parking tickets." More laughter.

"Oh, you two. No, they told me my boyfriend had been seriously injured in an accident. They took me to the airport and I flew straight out to be with him."

"Isn't your boyfriend TW Griffin? How did he get hurt, paper cut?"

"No no, it was a rogue paper clip." More laughter.

"Now bless your heart. No, it was pretty serious, but I can't go into that right now. But he is recovering at home, and I'm with him for now. Now here's the reason I called. I still owe my fans three concerts. I promised Roanoke, Columbus and Washington DC. Now anyone who still has their tickets should hang onto them and we'll honor those tickets. As soon as my manager can get new dates, we'll let y'all know."

"Hey great, thanks Marianne."

"Thank you, now I gotta go. You boys be good now."

Jim unplugged before he had to listen to any more of their chatter.

"Well that ought to hold them," he said.

"For now. But it should also get Hank moving on setting up the dates."

Rosa knocked at the doorway, and came in with a tray, holding a large bowl of chili and two sourdough rolls.

"I thought you might be hungry, Mister Jim."

"Rosa, just Jim. Please."

"I will try Mister Jim."

Rosa went back downstairs. Lloyd leaned in the doorway. "Ross and I gotta run. Your dad's still here, but we got a call."

79

"Go. Work before whatever this is," said Jim.

Marianne rolled off the bed and closed the door. "I'm taking a shower," she said, "I'm somewhat desperate for one."

Lloyd stepped off the stairs and headed for the door. Ross was waiting for him in the car. Lloyd consulted his notes and said, "the Airplane motel, off East Marginal way."

"Got it." It would not be their first trip.

Ross got onto the floating bridge before he felt compelled to hit his lights and siren. They were going against the commute, so traffic was only medium bad until the headed south on the interstate. Once they got through the city center, traffic backed up again and forced them to slow down, in spite of the emergency equipment. They picked up speed again when they got off the freeway and took Corson Ave to E Marginal. As soon as they turned the corner, they could see the lights on the street. The motel itself was 'U' shaped. The office formed the head of one side of the U, and the rooms were numbered in sequence from right to left. It was known for low rents and high levels of criminal activity.

A sergeant was running the scene. He was rolling a toothpick around in his mouth, but his eyes showed a certain intelligence. He was thick muscled and bald, and was wearing a well cared for but worn leather jacket.

"Pete," said Lloyd as a way of greeting. Peter Walsh was a senior sergeant. He knew almost everyone on the department.

"Lloyd," Pete said, "She's in room seven, right there in the corner."

Pete indicated the left side of the U.

"Anyone else here yet?" Pete understood that to mean other detectives.

"Naw, you're the first."

Lloyd, Ross and Pete walked over to room seven. A patrol officer stood outside, his body camera glowing red.

"Tell your guys they can turn those things off," said Ross.

Pete spoke into his radio and shut down his own camera, as the officer did the same.

"We've kept everyone out of the parking lot. The tenants were all identified, but only three of the rooms were occupied," he said.

The officer stepped aside and Pete carefully opened the door with a gloved hand. It was a basic one room motel room, with an attached bathroom, and a small shelf with a sink just outside the bath. A chair had been knocked over and broken. A lamp on the nightstand was missing the shade. The lampshade lay torn on the floor. The television screen was smashed. The mattress on the bed was askew, and on top of the mattress was the body of a woman. She looked to be in her forties, or maybe older. Her nose had been broken and healed, but was still at an angle. In the middle of her forehead was a neat round hole.

Ross looked around the room and saw her purse on top of the dresser. "Not a robbery," he said.

"Are you thinking domestic?"

"I think she knew her attacker," said Ross.

They backed out of the room. "Did CSI give an ETA?"

Sergeant Walsh consulted his watch. "Probably twenty minutes," he said.

"Did you guys do a canvas?"

"We got contact cards from three other rooms." Pete pulled the cards from his pocket. "Three, five and eleven. The rest are unoccupied."

"OK. Do we have a name on the victim?"

"Yeah. Alaina Miller. She lives in Tacoma."

"Alright then. Ross, let's go talk to the other tenants."

Chapter 14

Monday
6pm

Jason and Ted were standing in the lobby of the medical examiners office, going over their notes. They had sat in on both autopsies, and had noted no surprises. The medical examiner had made a note that Lazzaris bullet wound was on the left side of his head, consistent with being left handed, but the gun had been in his right. Fortunato had two rounds in his abdomen that should have killed him. The head wound was a 'through and through.'

"I take it the captain is a pretty good shot," said Ted.

"You're only saying that because after getting shot twice and essentially being one handed, Jim put two rounds on target that you could cover with a smart phone. Yeah, he's a pretty good shot," said Jason.

The phone in Jason's pocket went off. He glanced at the phone, and said, "its Lloyd," before putting the phone to his ear.

"Jason?"

"Yeah, I'm here. Ted's with me too. What's up?"

"CSI found your card at my scene."

Jason got a sick feeling in his stomach.

"Lloyd, who is it?"

"Do you know Alaina Miller?"

"Shit. I just talked to her. She was Fortunato's girlfriend. I take it she's the victim?"

"What did she tell you?"

"Lloyd, is she dead?"

"I'm sorry, yes."

"Dammit. I gave her fifty bucks and told her to go to a motel in Seattle and not to call anyone. She had to have called our suspect. Is her phone there?"

"We haven't found it yet. Did she give you anything?"

"Fortunato and Lazzari would take turns abusing her. When I told her they were dead she was glad. Looks like she didn't have much time to enjoy her freedom."

"No, it doesn't. We're about wrapped up here. Why don't we meet in the office?"

"Sounds good. By the way, no surprises in autopsy. Both are dead by gunshot wounds."

"Shock. Ok, see you in a half hour."

Jason hung up and said, "Alaina was murdered. That's the call Lloyd caught."

"That's messed up. I heard we're going back to the office."

"Yeah, I better call Jenny. We're supposed to go out tonight."

"Call her when we get to the office. That way you'll have a better idea when you'll be done here," said Ted.

They got to the car and headed down the hill to headquarters. As they pulled into the parking garage, Ted's phone went off.

"Who is this?"

Jason was focused on driving the car when he heard Ted say, "Can you hang on for a second? I'm going to put you on speaker while I'm driving."

Jason raised an eyebrow as Ted hit the speaker button, and said, "who is this again?"

"Maria Sorensen, news 5." She was a reporter for one of the local stations.

Jason glanced right, but said nothing.

"Maria, I'm on loan to detectives. I'm not in media right now."

"I know Ted, but I wanted to talk to you. Do you still have my card?"

Ted pulled the card out of the pocket of his trench coat. "Yes I do."

"Well, you didn't call so I figured I better call you."

"You got me. I'll ask again, what can I do for you?"

"Do you know who Marianne Wilson is?"

"She's an actress or something, right?" Ted looked at Jason, feeling shell shocked.

"A singer. Anyway, no one has seen or heard from her since she did a concert in Charlotte Friday night and then abruptly cancelled her last three dates."

"Charlotte is a long way from here," said Ted, "what's that got to do with me?"

"Something like twenty two hundred miles. Anyway, she called a radio station and said she went to be with her boyfriend after he got seriously hurt in an accident."

"He's a writer. I think I heard he lives in Hunts Point. Medina covers them, did you call over there?"

"Well here's the thing Ted. I didn't think anything of it until I watched the video, but Marianne Wilson was walking out of Harborview Monday morning, with Jim Churchill."

"Hey, I was there. What makes you think that was Marianne Wilson?"

"I compared her side to side with shots from the concert in Charlotte. It's the same woman."

"I think I'd know."

"Ted. Marianne Wilson is Jim Campbells girlfriend. And I want to talk to her. Actually both of them."

Ted looked at Jason. Jason shrugged.

"Maria, let me make some phone calls and see what I can find out. I'll call you back."

"Ted, thank you. I'll owe you one."

Ted disconnected and laid his head back on the seat while Jason maneuvered into a parking spot.

"Now what do I do," said Ted.

"You tried. You were covering your tracks but I think you gotta call him."

"I'm so screwed. If I call him he's gonna be pissed. If I don't call him and she puts that on the air, he's gonna be more pissed. And to be honest, I don't know if I'm more afraid of him or Marianne."

"Yeah, you won't get any help from the rest of us either. Just call him. He'll probably think of something."

"I gotta think about this."

"I don't think you have a lot of time. Call from inside."

Ted nodded, as they got out of the car to go into the building.

Twenty minutes later, Lloyd and Ross came in.

"What's going on," asked Ross.

"First things first. I gotta work up the courage to call Jenny and tell her I'm gonna be late. Ted has to call Jim and explain-just what the hell is it you have to explain?"

"There's a reporter that wants to interview Marianne and Jim," Ted explained.

"Better you than me," sad Ross.

Lloyd spoke up, "first and foremost, Jason call Jenny before it gets too late. Ted, you're screwed. But I think you are better off making that call than not."

"What do you have at the Airplane," asked Jason.

"Ross thinks it was someone she knows."

"Ted, we should talk to that weightlifter dude. What's his name?"

Ted flipped through his notes., "Lawrence Benvenuti."

"I'll call Danny White and see if we can talk to him tomorrow morning."

Jason pulled up his contacts, then used his desk phone to call Detective White. He answered on the third ring.

"Hey Danny, you busy?"

"Just had to get up and answer the phone. What's up?"

"Hey we got some more questions for Mister Benvenuti. Is he still at Tacoma General?"

"Yah, he got admitted. We have a guard on him until Wednesday, then the Pierce County jail takes over."

"Could we meet you there at say, eight am?"

"I'll call ahead so they know you're coming and walk you in. Just don't blow out his other knee."

"No worries. Thanks bud."

Marianne was sitting on a stool, dressed in a t shirt and shorts, strumming softly on a guitar and singing quietly. Jim was leaning back in bed, his eyes closed but his good foot keeping time to the music. Jenny came to the doorway and watched quietly. She was also wearing a t shirt but had on a pair of tight jeans. When Marianne finished, Jenny knocked quietly on the door frame.

"What's up, hon?" Marianne swung her feet to the floor and rested her guitar in its stand.

"Can I ask you something?" Jenny was clearly nervous. Jim had opened his eyes and was watching her, but said nothing.

"Anything," said Marianne.

"I guess I'm a little confused about Jason."

"What happened?"

"He just called. He said they're working and he expects to be here about eight."

"What's the problem?"

Jenny looked at Marianne strangely. "It just seems to me that if he was interested in me he'd make me the priority."

Marianne looked at Jim, and saw his eyes go black. She shook her head and turned back to Jenny.

"That's his job honey. Do you have any idea how many date nights we've had screwed up because that damn phone of his goes off at midnight?" Jenny shook her head. "He likes you or he wouldn't have called. If you think it's worth it to you, you will have to learn to deal with him being on call."

"How do you handle it?"

"We talked about it fairly early, and some since then. Jim gets called out and he goes. I had to accept that. But he makes it up to me as soon as he

85

can. To me it's worth the effort. You have to decide if Jason is worth yours."

Jim's cell phone went off. He rejected the call and it went to voicemail.

"Like that," said Marianne, "although that's the first time I've seen him reject a call."

"If I can interject something," Jim said. Marianne made a go ahead gesture. "Jason is good at what he does because he is dedicated. I think you guys make a great couple and he already knows that you're going to be on the road, what four months a year? Maybe six? So he thinks you are worth it. Relationships are not fifty fifty. Right now, Marianne is putting in about ninety eight percent while I achieve cauliflower status. Sometimes it's sixty-forty. Sometimes it's seventy-ten. But sometimes it's about eighty eighty, and when you can do that, something wonderful happens."

Jenny nodded, but she seemed a little confused.

Marianne said, "he's on painkillers. But he has a point. Sometimes you have to make the effort, sometimes he does."

"So this isn't his way of trying to blow me off?"

"No Jenny, it's not. If he says he'll be here by eight he will. Sometimes stuff happens. Stuff you and I do not ever want to know about."

Jenny nodded. "OK," she said, "thanks. I think I just needed a boost."

Marianne said, "he's a good guy. Just let things take their course."

Jenny nodded, and went downstairs to the living room. Paul was brooding in a recliner, watching the news, a drink in one hand. Jenny nodded, and sat down on the couch to wait.

Upstairs, Marianne said, "who called?"

"Ted. He left a voice mail."

"Am I really giving ninety eight percent?"

"More like a hundred and ten, but I wanted it to seem like I was contributing something."

"Oh you are," she said, and bent to kiss him. The phone rang again.

"You better answer it. I know you're not going anywhere."

Jim nodded, and hit the answer button.

"Hello Ted."

A moment passed, and then he said, "Hang on, she's right here. Let me put it on speaker."

Marianne was curious. After a moment Ted's voice said, "Marianne are you there?"

"Yes Ted, both of us are here."

"We have a problem." Ted explained the best he could about Maria's phone call, then said, "The bottom line is she wants an exclusive interview, I think with both of you. I didn't tell her anything, but she knows."

Marianne said, "well we knew we'd have to deal with this sooner or later."

Jim said, "any way you can stonewall her?"

"Maybe. But if you don't talk to her she'll put out what she wants to put out. And in this case, it's pretty close to the truth anyway. In my opinion you ought to get in front of it."

"Ted, you did that job for a long time. Is that your professional opinion?"

Ted swallowed and said, "yes sir, it is. And I think the sooner the better."

"I'll call you back," Jim said and ended the call without waiting for a reply.

Ted looked at his phone and said, "I'm so screwed."

"Why," asked Jason.

"He just hung up on me. I could tell he's pissed."

"Hey man," said Lloyd, "You were looking for a job when you got this one, right?"

Ted chuckled. "I guess."

A moment later the phone rang. Ted answered.

"Jim here. OK, we'll do it. Wednesday, eleven AM. You bring her here, just her and her camera. No crew."

"I'll pass it on," Ted replied.

"See, not so bad after all," said Jason as Ted closed his phone.

8:30pm.

Rosa answered the knock at the door.

"Hello Rosa," said Jason, "I'm here for Jenny."

"Mister Jason, come in. I will get her."

Jason stepped into the foyer. He touched briefly on that night last spring when he stood shoulder to shoulder with a Bellevue cop in this very spot.

Jenny came down the stairs, still wearing a pair of Levis that were skin tight, and a black t shirt with a red heart on the front.

"Hi honey," Jason said, before Jenny put her arms around his neck and kissed him. It was a long moment before they broke away from one another. Jason had his arms around her waist.

"You're late," she said.

"I'm sorry," he said.

"It's ok. I have never dated a homicide cop before."

Jason laughed, "mostly it's like dating any other cop."

Marianne came off the stairs, saw them and said, "hey you two. Get a room."

Jenny and Jason stepped away from each other, but they were smiling like they were guilty. Jason had a sudden thought.

"Marianne, is he up? I'd like to talk to him if he is."

"Go ahead. I'll be up in a minute."

The couple went upstairs and Jason knocked on the open door. Jim was sitting up in bed, a laptop in front of him, typing one handed. He looked up and waved them in.

"Hey Jason. What brings you upstairs?"

"Tell me you aren't working."

"Well, since I can't do my regular job, I thought I'd see if I could still write. It's a struggle but it keeps me from being too bored." Jim closed the laptop. "What's on your mind?"

Jason looked at Jenny and then asked, "I'd like to brief you on how your case is going."

Jim said, "Jenny, Marianne just went downstairs. Can you see if she needs any help?"

Jenny nodded, and went down to the kitchen.

"How are things with her?"

"I don't know, but she's fascinating to me."

"So what's on your mind?"

Jason briefed him on the case. When he got done telling him about the interview with Alaina he paused.

"That's a rough life for anyone," Jim said.

"You told me once that no one ever tells you everything. So I wonder what else is there she didn't say?"

"You could ask her."

"No, I can't. Lloyd and Ross caught a case at the Airplane on East Marginal."

"I'm familiar with it," said Jim.

"Alaina was beaten and executed in room seven."

"Damn."

"Yah. How much do you share with Marianne?"

"We talk. She asks questions, I tell her what I can. She's smart enough to know what to ask and what not to."

Jason nodded.

Jim asked, "what's your theory?"

Instead of answering, Jason said, "have you given any thought as to why they targeted you?"

"Some. And outside the usual I have nothing. I've got a couple side projects, but they are at dead ends. I considered Mariannes ex but it just doesn't seem like him. He's a pain in the ass but he's totally involved with another woman now."

"What are the side projects?"

"Nothing major. I'm waiting on test results on something. But honestly I doubt it's going anywhere."

"OK. You got any theories?"

"Check phone records. It seems like someone was trying to sever a connection. If you can splice that back together, you'll have your killer."

Jason nodded and said, "thanks."

Jim changed the subject. "What are you two up to tonight?"

"I thought we'd go to the Lime. It's getting late though, so I'm not sure."

"Well, you're welcome to stay here. The couch in my office folds out, so if you need to you could sleep there. But you should go, have fun."

Jason smiled and said, "thanks."

Jenny came in to the kitchen. Marianne was putting a water glass and a banana on a tray table.

"What's that?"

"Jim has some meds he's supposed to take, and he's supposed to eat something with them. So he gets the banana, then he takes his pills. And then he's likely to sleep through the night."

"Must be frustrating."

"I'll deal with it. What's important is that he gets better. What's wrong with you?"

Jenny was scowling.

"I think something bad happened and he doesn't want to tell me."

"Oh boy. Honey let me tell you, some of the things those guys see you don't want to know about."

"So Jim keeps secrets from you?"

"Sort of. I just don't ask questions when I don't want to know the answers."

"How did you learn that?"

"Experience and patience. If you stick with him long enough, you'll learn."

"What if he's really bothered by something?"

"I tell him I'm there for him. If he needs to talk he will. There's a fine line between letting him open up to you and prying."

"What does Jim do to handle the stress?"

Marianne turned and leaned her butt against the counter. "One day he came home from work. I was downstairs in the music room. The door was open, but he walked right past without a word. He went into the gym, and started punching the bag in there. I waited a few minutes, then went in. By the time I got in there, he was working up a good sweat. So I just went and held the bag for him." Marianne paused for a moment. "That was the

89

day Fred Henderson died. He was clearly upset, but he couldn't let his people see it. It may be the only time he brought work home, and even then he worked it out before he ever said a word to me."

Jenny nodded.

"Come on," Marianne said, "I have to put him to bed."

Marianne grabbed the tray and they trooped upstairs.

When they came into the bedroom, Jason smiled at Jenny and said, "Jim offered to let me sleep on the couch."

"Ohh. That sounds uncomfortable."

"You guys better get going. What time do you have to be in Tacoma," asked Jim.

"Eight. Yah, let's get going," Jason said.

After they left, Marianne gave Jim his pills, an antibiotic and a Vicodin.

"What's going on with the case," she asked.

"What makes you think we were talking about the case?"

"Jason sent Jenny out of the room. What else could it be?"

Jim smiled, "You should have been a detective."

"There's no money in it. Come on, spill."

Jim said, "Jason interviewed the girlfriend of one of the guys that ambushed me. Turns out she was pretty badly abused throughout the relationship. Pretty tragic really. When Jason told her the guy was dead, she toasted his demise."

Marianne was quiet.

"So the kicker is," continued Jim, "Jason gives her fifty bucks and tells her to get to Seattle. He wanted her to be someplace that no one would know. So Lloyd and Ross get called out, and it turns out it's her. She'd been executed."

"Oh God. Why?"

"Probably the people that hired Fortunato and Lazzari. Jason thinks she knew more than she told him and she apparently told him a lot."

"That's sad."

"I know. She finally gets some peace in her life, and it gets taken away from her. Can you imagine?"

"Yes, Jim I can."

"That's right. I'm sorry, I didn't mean…"

"Not that. Jim you have no idea what it's like to be a woman in this day and age."

"I'm sure I don't. But honey, you don't need to worry about getting groped all the time."

"Maybe not when you're around, but I can give you an example of what it's like for women on a daily basis."

Jim cocked an eyebrow.

"Do you remember our first date?"

Jim smiled at the memory. "I do. We took the boat out, and got dinner at Ivars. Then you fell asleep on the way back."

"That's right. You put me to bed on the sofa at the back of the boat and covered me in blankets so I'd be warm. Which was very sweet of you by the way."

"Thank you."

"Anyway, do you know the first thing I did when I woke up?"

"No idea. I was down below."

Marianne nodded. "It was so long ago. But the first thing I did was to lift up the blanket and make sure everything was where it should be."

"Honey, I'd never..."

"No, you wouldn't. But I didn't know that for sure until I checked. But for women, that's got to be the first thought. For me it wasn't even an annoyance. For this woman, Alaina?" Jim nodded. "For Alaina it was a certainty. If not that day than another. I just hope she found peace."

Jim nodded. "Honey, me too."

Marianne said, "change of subject. Guess what?"

"What?"

"I got my first Brides Magazine today!" Marianne held it up from where she'd been concealing it under the tray.

"That's great. We have got to set the date."

"You know, we could just dispense with all this, what do you call it? 'Bravo sierra?' You probably know a judge that would come here and marry us right now."

"The proper term is bullshit. But here's the thing honey. I don't want to marry you until I can walk you down the aisle. Not with a cane or a crutch. On my own two legs."

"I know Jim," Marianne said, easing close to his face, "I know." She kissed him, deeply and passionately. Then she pulled back.

"I cant wait," she said.

Jim was already asleep. Marianne laid down next to him. She laid her head on his shoulder, keeping her body well away from his injured right leg.

Paul was in Tacoma. He'd parked the Yukon in the empty parking lot of the electrical supply company. Carefully he took the cash out of his wallet and dropped the wallet into the center console, along with his badge. He unclipped the Beretta from his waistband and slid it under the front seat. He had an old policeman's sap in his back pocket. Down the street he could see the lights from Quinn's. Paul was wearing a leather jacket and he placed a baseball cap on his head. He hoped he looked like an old man. Surprise would be key.

He made sure the dome light was off, and slid out of the car, closing the door carefully. As he stepped out to the sidewalk, a car on the street opened a door. Paul stopped and watched carefully, regretting leaving the Beretta in the car.

"Paul." Lloyd Murray stepped in front of the car, his hands in his pockets.

Paul relaxed a little. "Lloyd."

"What's your plan, Paul?"

"I want to find out who tried to kill my son."

"Is this the best way?"

"Probably not. But this has got to stop. What are we at, three dead now? I'm lucky it wasn't four."

"Paul, what if you get down there and it's loaded with bikers?"

"There's only one Harley in the lot. One other car, looks like a Volkswagen."

"You aren't as young as you once were."

"Neither are you, Lloyd. Didn't you put your papers in?"

"I pulled them. But I can put them in again tomorrow if I want. Are you determined to do this?"

"Lloyd I haven't been much of a father to him. But he's my son."

"You taught him to control his emotions Paul. Jim would not be here, he'd leave it to his detectives."

Paul stood there for a moment, looking down the street.

"I'm not much of a boss, am I?"

"Paul, you're the best assistant chief I ever worked for. I looked you up in Arizona. Your department respects you. But you're human. You told me when he got shot the first time, that you felt like you let him down. You didn't though. It's the same thing here. You came, you helped. He's getting better and you have a glimpse into his life now. Take credit for the way he turned out. You had a great career in Seattle. You're a great chief in Prescott. Don't throw it all away for some misguided attempt at revenge. I doubt the people here have any idea who hired Fortunato and Lazzari. Leave it to us to handle."

Paul nodded. "Why are you here?"

"We've got some questions to ask. We were hanging out to see if anyone else showed up when we saw you pull in."

Paul realized that Ross was still in the car.

"Mind if I tag along?"

"Are you heeled?"

"It's in the car."

"Leave it there and get in the back."

They got into the car. Ross said, "hello chief," as Lloyd pulled away from the curb and they drove to the end of the block.

"Ground rules, Paul," said Lloyd, "You can come in, but you stay back and let us do the talking. If you think of something to ask, keep it to yourself."

"Got it."

Lloyd parked on the street, facing back the way they had come. They got out and assembled on the sidewalk near the front of the car. They crossed the hot top parking lot. Lloyd led the way in the door. The biker that Jason had described was sitting in the chair by the front door. The bartender was a cute little redhead. Lloyd put her age at somewhere between seventeen and twenty five. The biker started to get out of his chair, but Lloyd shoved him back down. Ross stepped behind the bar with his badge in his left hand and showed it to the girl. He put a finger to his lips and pulled the curtain aside. Three men, all wearing members only jackets were sitting around a table, playing cards.

"The eighties called, they want their coats back," said Ross.

"No darkies allowed," said the closest, as he started to stand.

Ross punched him once in the throat. He fell back into the chair gasping for breath. The other two sat in their chairs as though frozen, not daring to move.

"That is no way to greet a potential customer," said Ross, "I want to ask you boys, who hired y'all to kill my boss?"

No one said anything. The guy in the chair was the only one making noise.

"Y'all know why you have a new bartender tonight?"

One of the other guys said, "Alaina went missing, so we brought the new kid in. She's Vinnies daughter."

"You have no idea why Alaina isn't here?"

"She talked to those cops yesterday. When we came back she was gone."

"She went to a shitty little motel in Seattle. While she was there someone put a bullet in her forehead. We think it's the same people that hired you to kill a cop."

The first guy said, "Lawrence set that up. We had nothing to do with it."

"Lawrence? The weightlifter guy?"

"Yeah. He'd get a call for a job and he'd tell those two idiots who to talk to. He never said anything about names. Lazzari would call or meet the buyer and get the particulars. I doubt Lawrence would even know it was a hit."

Ross nodded. He glanced over his shoulder, and saw Paul behind him, a little five shot revolver in his right hand.

93

"You fellas stay right there for a minute, will you? Say about ten minutes. Don't come out before then. I'd hate for my friend here to startle."

They nodded. Ross stepped out of the room, then grabbed Paul's belt and guided him out from behind the bar.

"He give you anything?"

"If anyone knows anything it's the Benvenuti dude. This guy's shot up way too much smack,"said Lloyd.

The biker nodded, and Ross noticed his eyes dilated wide open.

"Alright, lets get out of here," Ross said.

When they were back in the Crown Victoria, driving back to Paul's car, Lloyd said, "I thought you told me you weren't armed."

Paul grinned. "I said I left it in the car. You asked if I was heeled. I thought you meant was I wearing boots."

"Like father, like son," said Ross.

Chapter 15

Tuesday
1AM

She spotted the room by seeing the young Tacoma Police officer sitting in a chair outside. His name tag said 'D. Johansson.' She smiled at him as she pushed the door open. She knew what she looked like, and she was wearing nurses scrubs so she was confident she would get past him. When she went in the room, she went straight to the bed.

"How are we today, Mr..." she looked at his chart, "Benvenuti. Am I saying that right?"

"Yes ma'am," he said.

"Looks like they want you to have a little shot. It goes right into your IV, so you won't feel a thing," she said.

She took a needle from the pocket of her scrubs, and slipped off the cap. She pushed the tip into the injection port, and when it had gone through depressed the plunger, emptying the contents.

"Now it might feel a little cold going in, but that's normal."

"Where do I know you from," he said.

"I don't think we've ever met before," she said.

"I swear I know you," he said. "Oh, hey, there's the cold."

"It won't be long now, Lawrence."

"Am I supposed to feel like this?"

"Like how, Lawrence?" Her voice was low and soothing.

"Like someone sitting on my chest," he said gasping, "it's getting hard to breath."

"That's because you're having a heart attack, Lawrence. Don't worry though. They'll think it's because of all the steroids you took."

"You...the....phone..."

"Shh, Lawrence. That's right we talked on the phone. You're almost there now."

He tried to push the call button, but she moved the cord out of reach.

"You.." he started but did not finish. His eyes were still open. She looked into the hallway to see the officer had gone back to reading his magazine. She reached up and with two fingers closed his eyes.

"It's all over now," she whispered.

She straightened and slid the needle into a pocket on her scrubs before turning and leaving the room.

The officer glanced up, and said, "how's he doing?"

"I gave him something to help him sleep. I think he'll be ready to leave tomorrow."

"Great news. I'll pass that on."

He watched her walk down the hall past the nurses station. Then he went back to reading.

Jim awoke in the dark. Marianne had rolled off his shoulder and had her back to him. Carefully he swung his feet over the side. Using his crutch for support he slowly stood. Jim limped to the door. As soon as he opened it, he could hear giggling coming from two rooms down.

"Shit," he thought. He looked at the stair lift with disdain, then looked at the stairs. Reluctantly he sat in the machine and pushed the button. It whirred and slid smoothly down the rail to the bottom of the stairs.

Jim limped into the living room to the bar. He found a bottle underneath and stood just as the front door opened. Jim slid a drawer open with his right hand and wrapped it around a snub nose .38. Then he heard a thump, and Paul's voice saying, "crap."

"Keep it down, Dad."

Paul came into the living room as Jim was setting two shot glasses on the bar.

"Not bad for a one handed gimp."

Jim poured a measure into each glass and handed one to Paul as he walked up to the bar. Jim picked up the other, and they silently touched glasses and drank.

"Where were you," Jim asked.

"I took a little drive. Found myself in Tacoma outside a place called Quinn's. Ever hear of it?"

"It's come up in conversation."

"Well, before I could do anything too stupid, Lloyd and Ross showed up. Instead of just me, all three of us went in."

"Dad, that was a really dumb idea."

"Don't I know it. Sort of like someone else I know."

"Water under the bridge, dad."

"Well, we aren't having this conversation."

"OK," said Jim, misunderstanding.

"Son, those guys really care about you. I watched one of them throat punch a guy just to make a point."

"Aw no. Dad,.."

"It's all hypothetical son. But when Jason goes to Tacoma to talk to that guy, that guy will talk. Jeez, you should have seen them."

"No dad, I shouldn't. You know better. Why would you even go there?"

"I was gonna get answers or burn the place to the ground. You are my son and no one gets away with what they tried to do."

"I gotta sit down," Jim said wearily. "Come on into the living room."

"I'm coming. I like those two. They get things done."

Jim sat heavily in the recliner and eased it back. "Dad, what if those guys file a complaint? You could lose your chiefs job."

"Not those guys. They'd have to admit they're mobbed up. But I think Jason broke them up. They seemed more scared than anything."

"Of the three of you?"

"No, something else. Lloyd and Ross noticed it too. It wouldn't surprise me if they're on the way to Florida."

"So why did you go?"

"Honestly? I didn't want to let you down. I know you. You put it all on the line for someone you love, I guess I wanted you to know I would too."

"Thanks dad."

"You better get back in bed before Marianne realizes you're up."

"Or what?"

There was a light foot fall at the bottom of the stairs. Jim knew the sound well.

"In here, honey."

Marianne came in looking sleepy, her hair pushed up on one side. She was wearing a long, silky nightgown. Jim thought she was adorable.

"At least you're sitting down. Why are you awake?"

"Cabin fever honey. Then dad came in and we're sharing a drink."

"And you rode the stair lift."

"Why are you awake?"

"I woke up the minute you got out of bed."

Marianne had worked her way next to his chair. "Paul, why are you up?"

Paul told her.

"So what happens now?"

Jim said, "I figured I'd tell Jason to find the owner of Quinn's. At this rate, I was thinking of just knocking on their door."

Marianne sat on the arm of the chair, leaning against Jims shoulder.

"You are going nowhere," she said, wrapping her arms around his neck. His good arm found its way around her waist.

"Uh, I'm right here," said Paul.

"He's still going nowhere unless it's straight to bed. Paul, could you make me one of what you're having?"

Paul stood and went to the bar. As soon as his back was turned, Marianne said, "you sir are supposed to be taking it easy."

"I know. But the pill wore off and I was sick of being in bed."

She kissed him on the cheek. "I'm glad you're feeling better," she said, "but slow it down. There's no rush."

5am.

Jason and Jenny came down the stairs holding hands. Jason was wearing the same suit he'd had on the day before, but the necktie was stuffed into a pocket. Jenny was wearing slacks with a sleeveless t shirt. They could smell bacon frying from the kitchen. As they walked past the living room, they could see Jim and Marianne stretched out in the recliner. She had her back to them. Jims eyes were closed.

"Isn't that just the cutest thing," asked Jenny.

"Jason before you answer that, I'm still your boss," Jim said, his eyes closed.

Jason grinned, and led Jenny by the hand into the kitchen.

"Hello Jenny," said Rosa, giving Jason a nod, "help yourselves."

There were scrambled eggs and bacon and sourdough biscuits with butter and jam. All of this mingled with the smell of freshly brewed coffee. The couple picked up plates, and Jason suddenly realized just how hungry he was.

Jim and Marianne came in from the living room, Jim still using a crutch. Jim sat at the breakfast counter. Rosa set a cup of coffee in front of him, a smile on her face.

"It is good to see you up, mister Jim."

"Just Jim, Rosa. It's good to be upright."

"What do you want to eat, Jim."

"Just hand me one of those biscuits and maybe some bacon," he said sipping at his coffee.

"Shouldn't you have your feet up, Jim," asked Jason.

"They've been up for four days. I think they can handle being down for a bit."

Jason took a seat at the counter next to Jim, Jenny on his left. Marianne filled a plate and sat next to Jim on the other side.

"What's on the agenda for today," Jim asked as Marianne buttered a sourdough biscuit.

"We're meeting at eight this morning at Tacoma General. Ted and I are going to interview Benvenuti. Mostly because we got nowhere else to go," said Jason.

"You think he'll turn on whoever did the hires?"

"No idea. But it's pretty much all we got at this point. How about you?"

"Well Marianne and I thought we'd start off with a nice jog into town, then who knows."

Jason smiled. Marianne gave him an elbow.

"I better get going," Jason said, "I'm picking up Ted in the office."

"You might see who owns that bar, Quinns," said Jim, "seems like they might have some answers."

"Thanks skipper, it's worth a shot."

"I'll walk you out," said Jenny.

They got up and headed for the foyer. Rosa swept up their plates and slid them into the dishwasher.

When they got to the door, Jenny wrapped her arms around his neck, and kissed Jason on the mouth.

"When will you be back," she whispered.

"Not sure, I'll call you," he whispered back.

She nodded and they embraced. He kissed her again, and then was gone.

Jenny took a minute to compose herself before she went back to the kitchen. When she walked in, Marianne was refilling Jims coffee cup as Jim nibbled on a piece of bacon. Rosa was scrubbing pans in the sink.

Marianne set the coffee in front of Jim, took one look at Jenny and said, "what's wrong with you?"

Jenny shrugged. Jim sat still, silently chewing.

"It's been so long since I've had a real-I dunno, relationship? If that's what it is. I'm not sure what's normal and what isn't."

Marianne poured her own cup, and said, "who knows from normal. What happened?"

"I asked when he would see me again, and he said he'd call. I'm wondering what I did wrong?"

Jim swallowed. "That's guy speak for 'I can't wait to see you again.'"

"Really?"

"He's spent most of the last four days with you. I'd say he's pretty infatuated. But he's also got a job to do, which by the way I've got a personal stake in him doing it right. This thing could break anytime and he knows it and the only way to make it break is by working the problems. He knows it and that's why he didn't commit right now."

"What if it doesn't break? How long does he work it?"

"These things have their own weight. I'd give it another week, maybe two."

"And then what? Something else happens? Another couple weeks?"

"It isn't always easy," said Marianne, "when I first moved in, his phone was going off at midnight every night and this one would be gone like the wind. Then I'd lay awake worrying about him."

"How did you deal with it?"

"He told me he's a commander now. That the odds of something happening to him were worse than winning the lottery. Seems a little hollow now," Marianne glanced at Jim, "but for a while it made me feel better."

"Well, there are even worse odds of it happening again," Jim said, then, "hey Rosa, what are your thoughts?"

"Jim, do you want the truth?" Rosa cocked an eyebrow.

"And nothing but," Jim said.

"Oh God," said Marianne.

"I think people are too quick to jump into relationships now. Look at you. One day you don't know each other, then the next you're living together. And you," she pointed at Jenny, "you're as bad as they are. Get to know him."

Jim smiled. "In my defense, she took advantage of me."

"Jim!"

"I'm sorry if I overstep," said Rosa, "but you asked for the truth."

"Thank you, if I didn't want it I wouldn't have asked."

Jenny said, "so you think we're moving too fast?"

"No," said Jim, "each relationship has it's own rhythm and moves at it's own pace."

"So you don't think we're moving too fast?"

"I'm no judge. Just understand that Jason's job is murder. Some days are longer than others. It's no reflection on you, it's just his job."

Jenny looked thoughtful.

Rosa said, "excuse me."

Marianne nodded at her.

"Miguel is arriving this afternoon, at the airport. Is there a way you could arrange for him to be brought here?"

"Do you want to pick him up?"

"I have no car. I could use that, what is it? Uber?"

Jim said, "do you have a license?"

"From Tennessee."

"Why don't you take my car. It has a GPS so you won't get lost."

"Oh no, I couldn't."

"Marianne, is she a decent driver?"

"She's very good. Never had an accident."

"Then it's settled. The keys are by the door to the garage. Marianne can show you how to use the GPS."

"His flight arrives at two. When should I leave?"

"I'd say noon to give you plenty of time."

"I don't know. I can drive around Nashville pretty good. But my English-when I drive I translate the road sign to Spanish, sometimes before I realize it I miss the exit."

"Hey Jenny," said Marianne, "maybe you could drive Rosa."

"Yah, sure," said Jenny, "let's leave at say eleven, just to be sure."

"Jim, I think you need to get upstairs," said Marianne, "you've been upright long enough."

Jim nodded, and with Mariannes help he walked up the stairs, ignoring the lift.

8 AM.

Jason and Ted stepped off the elevator and walked down the hallway to Benvenutis room. There were two Tacoma PD officers standing guard outside. Jason flashed his badge and one of them said, "you can't go in just yet, sir."

"Is Detective White here?"

"He's inside."

"We're supposed to meet him here."

"We've been told to have you wait here sir."

Jason looked at his watch.

"Well crap. If I hadn't stopped at home we could have got coffee on the way. Is there a coffee stand in the building?"

"There's one by the gift shop. Sir."

"You guys want anything?"

"Sir, I've been told to ask you not to leave."

Ted had been looking bored, now he was curious. "What the hell is going on? This is supposed to be a quick interview, why the stall?"

Danny White stuck his head out of the door, a scowl on his face. "You're here," he said.

"Thanks Danny, nice to see you too," said Jason.

"Where did you go last night?"

"Why?"

"Dammit Jason, this is serious!"

"OK, what happened?"

Danny sighed. "Benvenuti died last night. You want to tell me where you were now?"

101

"We attended an autopsy yesterday afternoon. Got out around six, then got word that our witness was found murdered in one of our fleabag hotels. We met up with the primary around, what, six thirty maybe. We compared notes with the primary on that call, and decided to come here this morning."

"When did you leave work?"

"I think around eight. Ted stayed to get caught up on paper."

"Did you go home?"

"No, I had a date."

"Rub it in," said Ted.

Jason shot him a look, then said, "dinner at the Lime, then back to her place."

"When did you leave there?"

"A little before six this morning. What killed him?"

"Probably a heart attack. But it's possible he got a blood clot from blowing out his knee, and that traveled to his heart causing a heart attack. But we got to be sure."

Jason nodded.

"What's your dates name."

"Jennifer Vacca." Jason gave Jennys phone number.

"Where does she live?"

"Nashville Tennessee," said Jason.

"So is she in a hotel?"

"No, she's staying with friends in Hunts Point."

"What's she doing in Seattle?"

"Taking care of a sick friend," said Jason. "Can we look at the body?"

"Why not," said Danny, and led them into the room. There were two other detectives in the room. Danny carefully peeled back the sheet from Benvenutis face. The pillow around his head was stained and yellow. The face was convulsed in anguish.

"Did he get any medication last night," Jason asked.

"Not that we know of. The kid that was guarding him last night got relieved and went home. Now he's not answering his phone."

"Where does he live?"

"Gig Harbor. Why?"

"Benvenuti looks like he had a convulsion when he died. And look at the pillow. That stain is probably Diaphoresis. Both of those are signs of Lidocaine poisoning. I suggest you send someone to that officers house and bring him back here, pronto."

"What are you saying?"

"I'm saying he was murdered."

"Dammit. That's what I thought you said."

It took an hour for a sergeant to locate the address of Officer Johansson in Gig Harbor, and to send an officer out to wake him up when he did not answer his phone. By the time he got back to the hospital it was almost ten in the morning. Jason and Ted had bought coffee for the detectives, and Danny had apologized to Jason after he called Jenny to verify his alibi.

Officer Johansson came in, escorted by an older sergeant. Johansson was wearing a gray t shirt and black jeans. The handle of a small revolver stuck out above the waistband next to a badge clipped to his belt.

White started in. "You had the shift here from midnight to four. Anything unusual happen?"

"Not really," he replied, "pretty quiet. He had one visit from a nurse, I think."

"What time was that?"

Johansson thought for a minute. "Maybe a little after one. I was reading a magazine and she walked in."

"Did you get her name?"

"Shit. I didn't even look for one."

"Why not?"

"If you'd seen her, you'd understand. She was beautiful man."

"That's detective. Think carefully officer. What did she look like?"

"She was tall, white but tanned. Thin but you could tell she was well built."

"What was she wearing?"

"Those things nurses wear. What are they called, scrubs? Yeah, scrubs. Kind of a light blue. She had one of those caps on too, like the surgeons wear, so I have no idea what her hair looks like."

"Eyes?"

"Brown eyes to die for. Did she do something?"

"Yeah. She may have murdered your prisoner. Anything else you can think of?"

"Man no way. After she left, he might have moved around some."

"Detective King here thinks she injected him with lidocaine. Do you know what that does?"

"That's for heart patients right? Helps fix the heart?"

"Sort of. But if you take too much it can give convulsions and diaphoresis. That's excessive sweating. What you heard was him going into convulsions. But the worst part is it mimics a heart attack. So your new girlfriend was literally giving your guy a heart attack."

"How much trouble am I in."

Jason stepped in. "I personally don't give a shit how much trouble you are in." To Danny he said, "do you guys have a sketch artist? If he was able to look above her neck maybe we can get a sketch of her."

103

"Worth a plan. Sergeant, take this young man to headquarters. In the ID section is Detective Andersons office. I'll call ahead and maybe she can work with him." To Johansson he said, "I don't need pictures of her chest son. I need to know what this woman looks like. And if the only thing you're worried about is how much trouble you're in, just remember this prisoner died on your watch. Focus on helping us find this woman."

"Yessir." The officer followed his sergeant back down the hallway.

Detective White made the phone call and tucked his phone back in his pocket.

"What if it turns out to be a blood clot after all?"

"I don't think blood clots cause convulsions like that."

Ted was looking at the body.

"He was our best hope," said Ted.

"Don't think like that. What does this tell you?"

Ted shrugged. "That we were on to something?"

"Exactly."

"But he can't tell us anything now," Ted replied.

"But someone can."

"Who is going to talk to us now?"

"We'll find someone. I'm thinking we should go back to Quinns."

Ted smiled. "I can't wait."

11AM

Ted and Jason were parked up the street from Quinns when the Harley rolled past and turned into the hot top parking lot. They waited until he got off the bike and was unlocking the front door before they pulled into the lot. He looked at them and started to push the door open as Ted jumped from the car while it was still moving. Ted reached the biker as he started to go through the door, and pulled him back outside, shoving him against the wall. The biker put both his hands on the wall and said, "you ain't got shit on me."

Jason leaned against the wall to his left. "Don't know about that, Gilbert."

Gilbert turned his head to look at Jason. "How do you know my name?"

"It's tattooed on the side of your neck," said Jason, pointing out the script lettering.

"What do you want?"

"Hey Gil, be nice. We're all friends here. Maybe we can help you out."

"What the fuck can you help me with?"

"First, never finish a sentence with a preposition." Jason reached into the pocket of his trench coat and pulled out his cell phone. "Next, take a look at this picture."

"Fuck you," Gilbert said, but he looked at the picture. "That's Larry. What did you do to him?"

"You were there, Gil, but that's not what's happening here."

"What's wrong with him?"

"Do you know what Lidocaine is Gil?"

"Is it a type of beer?"

"Not even close. It's a heart medicine. If you take too much you can get convulsions. Do you know what convulsions are Gil?"

"They're like seizures?"

"Very good. Plus also they're painful. Do you know what else happens without medical intervention?"

"No."

"You get a heart attack. Look at this picture, Gil." Jason held up the picture.

"He's having a heart attack?"

"Had Gil. He had a heart attack. He's dead Gil."

"Shit."

"Gil, we think the person that did this is the same one that tried to kill my captain. We also think they killed Alaina."

"Wait, what? Alaina is dead?"

"No one told you?" Jason spoke softly.

"Oh God," Gil said and started to sob. Gil's knees buckled and Ted let him go as Gil slid to the ground. He turned over and sat on his butt, burying his face in his hands.

Jason and Ted looked at each other. Jason crouched down onto his ankles and looked at Gil for a long moment.

"You were in love with her." It was a statement, not a question.

"That's why I worked here, just so I could spend time with her. Aw man. This place has almost no business. Plus it doesn't open until two. I'd get here at eleven, and help her with setup. When her old man was in prison, she'd set up the bar, and I'd make sure everything else was ready. No one showed up until after it was open anyway, because those guys aren't technically employed here. So once the place was set up, we'd go in back and, well…"

"Yeah, I get the idea. Why'd you run the other day?"

"I looked in your eyes. I knew if I stuck around you'd kick my ass too. And I could tell you weren't going to hurt her. So I left."

Jason nodded. "What happened when her boyfriend got out of prison?"

"He came by the bar. It was his and Lazzari's before they left. They signed it over to her and she just took over man. She ran the place like you wouldn't believe."

"This dump?"

"It's not what it looks like."

"That's good. Because it looks like a dump."

Gil looked at Jason oddly, and said, "You have no idea."

Ted said, "lets go inside. Do you have coffee?"

Gil said, "Yeah, sure."

Jason helped Gil to his feet. They followed him inside. Ted went behind the bar and found the coffee machine and started a pot. Gil sat heavily in a chair at a table. Jason sat on his left where he could watch the door.

"Tell me a story, Gil."

"Alright. You ain't gonna like it."

"Try me."

"You know what he did to her, right?"

"I've seen the file. She got hurt pretty bad."

"After that it was weird. It was like they trusted her. They'd talk in front of her about what they did. The shakedowns, ripping off containers, all that. She kept her mouth shut and just listened. Then they got popped for a robbery gone bad. Fortunato was supposed to get ten years, but they both did six. Turns out he was a model prisoner."

Jason snorted. Ted set a coffee in front of him, and one in front of Gil.

"I know, he's a dick, but hey he knocked four years off his sentence. So before they go off, they both sign over the bar to her, on the promise that she'll give it back when they get out. Turns out she lied about that. When they came home, she was running the whole show. She'd tell the crew which containers to target, who hadn't paid protection, who needed an attitude adjustment. All of it."

"They went along with it?"

"She'd brought in Larry and those other guys, and Larry had a chat with them. So they agreed, they worked for Alaina. She told me though, that she knew she was going to have to get rid of them. They were gonna knock her over and get the shop back. She didn't know when."

"So she made them her enforcers?"

"I guess we're all enforcers. Except maybe I'm more of a bouncer. But we all watched out for her. She was fair with us and made sure we all got our cuts."

"So she assigned the jobs?"

"Her and Larry. Sometimes he'd take the phone, sometimes she'd have it. Larry got the call for your boss."

"Did Alaina know about it?"

"Yeah man. No one made a move around here without her knowing about it. I guarantee you she knew all about that job. I'm pretty sure that's why she gave it to Mario and Ed."

"Tell me about that."

"I think she was hoping they'd be killed. She told me she had a bad job and she was gonna give it to them."

"What was bad about it?"

"When she had a bad job, that was one where they might not come back from. So Alaina calls Fortunato and Lazzari and gives them the job. Lazzari actually talks to the customer to get the specs, and then they plan the job. But man, they were scared. I mean they couldn't show it, but you could tell. They take off Friday morning. Around four Alaina gets a call here at the bar. I'm sitting there by the door, and I can hear someone screaming at her and she's behind the bar. She told me it went bad but she didn't say they were dead. I just assumed they'd been busted or something."

"You think she didn't know?"

"Hard to say. She was subdued, but she didn't like failure. She wasn't too broken up."

"She hid it well if she was," said Jason.

"Like I said before, she was done with them. They got the jobs that no one really wanted. I mean come on, who tries to kill a cop?"

"Who indeed."

Jim was perched on the edge of the tub, trying to decide how to get in. His left arm was still in the sling, and he needed to keep his right leg out of the water. Marianne was leaning on the sink, wearing her favorite torn jeans and a t shirt that read, "Boss Lady" on the front.

"Alright, I give up. Lend me a hand, will you?"

"I wish you wouldn't fight me on this. You know you're going to need my help, why not just let me," Marianne said. She took two steps and was standing by his side.

"I don't like thinking of myself as helpless," he said.

"Oh sweetie," she said, "you are anything but."

She took his arm as he eased his left leg into the tub, then slid backwards until he was sitting in the water, his right leg extended over the side. He took the sling off and Marianne hung it over the towel rack. Jim leaned back in the water, carefully keeping his shoulders out. Marianne slid a towel under his right leg.

"Thanks honey."

She smiled, and said, "would you like me to wash your back?"

"Sure," Jim said and leaned forward as much as he could. When she was done, he leaned back and she carefully washed his hair. When he was done, he let the water out and with Mariannes help, managed to sit on the edge of the tub. He stood carefully and Marianne helped him dry off and slip carefully into a set of silk pajamas.

"I hate this thing," he said as she slipped the sling over his head.

"If it helps you get better I'm ok with it."

"I know. But it's part of what makes me feel helpless."

She helped him back to bed. "You're moving better."

"It doesn't hurt much anymore. Still a little stiff."

Jim sat on the edge of the bed and carefully swung his feet up, with Mariannes help. He was resting on a forty five degree tilt.

"Are you tired at all," asked Marianne.

"Not really," Jim replied.

"You know we're all alone for now."

"Dad's still here, but he's asleep."

Marianne went to the door and closed it. She turned around with a mischievous look on her face.

"What are you thinking?"

Marianne took hold of the bottom of her t shirt and lifted it over her head.

"Let me do the work for once," she said.

1pm

Marianne lay still in bed for a long time afterwards. When Jim had fallen asleep, she had tried to nap but couldn't. Finally, with Jim sleeping soundly she slid out of bed. She slipped her clothes back on, then saw Jim's phone blink. She thought for a minute, then picked it up. It was a text from Jason, but she couldn't read it.

"Why can't they leave him alone," she thought, "he needs to rest."

Marianne set the phone back down, then went downstairs. Paul was sipping at a can of coke while seated at the counter.

"Good afternoon," Paul said, a twinkle in his eye.

"Hi Paul, did you eat anything?"

"I found some leftovers in the kitchen about an hour ago. How's your day going?" There was laughter in his tone.

Marianne looked at him and squared her shoulders.

"Better than expected, Paul."

Paul let out a chuckle, but didn't say anything. Marianne felt her face go red.

In the kitchen Marianne put together a salad. She took two pieces of the leftover bacon and crumbled them onto the top, then layered on some blue cheese dressing.

She sat at the counter next to Paul to eat.

"You slept late," she said.

Paul smiled and said, "well I was up late last night. I rolled around with Lloyd and Ross and didn't realize how late it was when I got home. How's our boy doing?"

"He's better. He thinks he's helpless so he has to prove to himself that he's not."

"He's not. Did he ever tell you about Iraq?"

"The first I knew he had been in the military was when he ran into the guy that was his Air Force liaison. Or whatever that's called."

"He had a chest full of ribbons from his time there. Silver star, bronze star. A Purple Heart. He probably could have had a career if he wanted it."

"Why didn't he?"

"Jim is very good at knowing when to bend or break the rules. But the army tends to frown on that sort of thing. Even if they recognize that you were right, they'll find a way to punish you in the end."

"Like the police department?"

"The PD can't hold a candle to the military. The army can send you anywhere and make you do darn near anything. Jim knew he could end up in east Burning Stump at a mess kit repair facility once the war was over. And that's not how he's wired."

"No I suppose not. Can I ask you something?"

"Of course. You're family now, in fact if not in name."

Marianne smiled, then plowed ahead. "Neither one of you has mentioned his mother. What's the story there?"

Paul grew serious. "Jim doesn't ask because he already knows. She's still alive, but her mind is gone."

"Dementia?"

"Alzheimer's," Paul confirmed, "she's a year younger than me. We've been married for forty years but every time I go to see her I have to tell her who I am. It's fifty-fifty that she believes me."

"Will I be able to meet her?"

Paul shrugged. "Don't know why not. She'll be happy to meet you. Just know she won't remember you."

"I know. But I'd like to know her. She's a part of Jim too."

"OK. I might be able to spring her for the wedding. Have you set a date yet?"

"With everything going on we haven't. We talked about it. I told him to have a judge come and marry us today, but he wants to walk down the aisle."

"It's a pride thing. I'm surprised you can't do it online."

"I'm sure it's coming. But I checked. It takes three days to get the license in this state. He's not going anywhere so I guess we can wait."

"Is there a computer in this house?"

"There's a bunch."

"Where?"

"Upstairs, in Jims office."

They climbed upstairs. When they walked in, Marianne noticed Jim had added some photos.

"Look at this," said Paul, "you are all over the place."

"Jim takes a lot of photos. Some we've used in promotions. These are from the last tour. This one is Jacksonville," she pointed to one of herself wearing a fringed jacket and holding a guitar. "This one is Savannah," she was holding the microphone over her head towards the crowd. "This one is a hunting trip last year," she said pointing to a picture of her carrying a Henry rifle and wearing a plaid jacket.

"You photograph very well," said Paul, "I can see the energy you bring to a performance."

"Oh, you're very sweet," she said.

"Let me figure this thing out," Paul said, turning on the computer. In a moment it came on, then blinked for a password.

"What does he use as a password?"

"I don't know."

Paul typed 'Marianne.' The computer rejected it.

"That's disappointing."

"What are you two up to," said a voice from the doorway.

Jim was leaning on a crutch watching them.

"Jim," started Marianne.

"It's my fault," said Paul, "I wasn't trying to intrude. I wanted to see if we could get a marriage license online."

Jim waved a hand, "It's ok. Marianne knows the password. I have two books I'm working on in there, but they're encrypted with their own password. But don't bother, I already checked. We have to go in person to the courthouse. Then we wait three days, but no longer than ninety days to get married."

Paul stood. "You checked?"

"Marianne said something the other day. The more I thought about it I the more I thought I'd look into it. Honey I do want this for us. But I don't want you to feel rushed."

Marianne nodded.

"Let's do this one right," he said.

Marianne carefully hugged him and said, "you need to sit down. You've spent far to much time on your feet today."

Jim nodded, and sat carefully in a client chair. "First things first, we should talk about tomorrow."

Marianne leaned over the keyboard and typed "Griffin." The screen opened up and the desktop displayed before her.

"Tom," said Gretchen, "we've done all we can here. It's time to go."

Tom nodded, and for maybe the twentieth time pulled his Beretta from a shoulder holster and checked to make sure it was loaded.

"Ok, I'm ready."

"I hope so. You keep checking that thing and it makes me nervous."

"You have your way I have mine," said Tom, "Where are we going?"

"I'll tell you on the way."

"I'll miss this place," he said.

"We'll be back."

"When?"

"I'm not sure. Couple weeks. Maybe a few months. We just need to let things cool off. We've cut all the ties except one, and by then he won't care. If we have to we have someone to throw under the bus."

Tom lifted a pair of suitcases and placed them into the trunk of the Buick. Gretchen got in the passenger seat as Tom got the rest of the luggage, including the rest of the pistols. She might need one later on she had reflected, there was no sense in abandoning them. She wished he didn't like that shoulder holster so much. It seemed as though it was too obvious. She shrugged, soon it wouldn't matter anyway.

"What did you do with her car," she asked.

"I parked it a block away, on the street with the keys in the ignition. By the time I walked back and got my car, and drove by where I parked it, it was gone."

"Smart." She was impressed. When the cops find the car they might waste time looking for the little thieves that stole it.

"See, that's why I like you, Tom," she said, "you thought of everything."

She didn't mean it, but he was like a puppy. A pat on the head went a long way.

111

Chapter 16

Jason and Ted were working their way northbound on I-5, fighting rush hour traffic when they heard the radio broadcasting a pursuit on the south radio frequency. Out of idle curiosity, Jason switched the radio over to listen.

When he heard the dispatcher repeat the description of the car, Jason said, "You hear that?"

"Sounds like Miller's car," said Ted.

Jason dug out his notebook and flipped back to his notes from Saturday. "Yep, that's it."

Ted reached under the dash and flipped a switch, turning on the lights in the grill of their car and causing the four way lights to flash. Jason pushed the button to activate the siren, and cars slowly started to react. Jason had learned a long time ago that people reacted differently to emergency equipment on cars. They typically took a while to get out of the way, and even longer in a plain car.

Ted moved into the left lane, forcing some cars to move over, passing others on the shoulder. The dispatcher was broadcasting the pursuit north on Rainier avenue. The pursuit had just passed South Graham street, still on Rainier when Jason broadcast that the car was stolen during a homicide.

"Two Sam, copy that," Sergeant Walsh's voice was calm and quiet through the radio. Jason could picture him rolling the toothpick around in his mouth.

"Where do you think they're going," asked Ted.

"A bunch of different choices. But if they're trying to make the freeway, really only two. South Alaska and Dearborn."

"Where do we go?"

"We are a long way out of position, Ted. And really only one road. Just drive for now."

A moment later they heard an officer say, "still north past Alaska."

"Dearborn," they both said. Ted was pushing it, and Jason could see his face flushed with excitement.

"Ted," said Jason, "we are so far behind this thing I'm sure it'll all be over before we get anywhere close."

Ted didn't say anything but did come off the accelerator a little. They heard officers say he was turning north on King Way, which Jason realized meant Martin Luther King Jr Way.

"Maybe he's not going to the freeway," said Ted.

"Just wait," said Jason.

A moment later the pursuit hung a left on South Walker and then a right on Rainier again. Ted was just approaching Columbia Way when they heard a broadcast, "west on Massachusetts."

"Shit, take the exit," shouted Jason.

Ted forced his way across four lanes of traffic, causing tires to squeal, but he made it. Jason directed him up the hill to Spokane street, and then north on fifteenth. The traffic was still heavy, but they could make better time.

"If we can get to McClellan we can cut him off at seventeenth," Jason said.

Ted took the turn on McClellan and they could see someone else had the same idea. A patrol car was parked around the corner, it's trunk and drivers door open. The officer was positioned behind a parked car with a string of sticks in his hand.

"What is that," asked Ted.

"Stop sticks. He's going to try to throw them in front of the car. If the car hits them, they should deflate his tires. But he's in a bad spot."

Just as Jason finished speaking, the officer flung the stop sticks into the road, then gave a quick yank on the string. A black Ford Taurus drove directly over the sticks and kept going.

"He didn't stop," said Ted.

"It doesn't happen right away. Hold up a minute."

The first police car went by and Jason said, "back up. Get back out to Beacon."

Ted put the car in reverse and backed up to Beacon Avenue just in time to see the Taurus flash by.

"Stop! Stop," Jason shouted. Ted stopped.

The first police car roared past, lights going and siren blaring. Then another. And another. Ted stopped counting at twelve. Finally the last car went by and Ted backed carefully out onto Beacon Avenue.

"He's either going north on fourteenth, or down the hill into the flatlands," said Jason. The Flatlands are a mostly industrial area in the south of Seattle.

An officer broke in on radio, "he's turning north on fourteenth, hold on, back westbound and he's crashed."

What Jason and Ted didn't know was that when he changed his mind and tried to go back to the west, he clipped a car coming northbound, then drove over the curb on flattened tires, destroying the rims, before it crashed into a fire hydrant. The drivers door popped open and a young black man fell out. He rolled to his feet and began sprinting down the street as the first two cars rolled to a stop. The first officer, a young guy in his early twenties, leapt from his car and began sprinting after the driver. The second officer put his car into gear, telling the third officer to cover the car. He was an older officer, in his late thirties. He drove past the first officer before driving over the curb in front of the suspect. The suspect was unable to stop his forward momentum, and bounced off the front fender in time to get tackled from behind by the first officer. His new momentum carried him back into the fender, and as his head hit the hood of the car, it left a significant dent. Frantically he started to dig into his waistband when the second officer came around the front of the patrol car and fired his taser. The young man screamed and fell to the ground.

"See, if they're running on the street, there's no reason to leave your car," the older officer said.

Jason and Ted pulled up to the crash scene. Looking down the street they could see the driver being taken into custody. Officers were trying to talk the passenger out of the car.

Jason found Sergeant Walsh and asked, "what's the problem?"

"The guy says his door won't open and he thinks his leg is broken. We're putting together a team now."

Walsh popped the trunk of his car and pulled out a long shield before assembling a team of four officers. Jason and Ted watched from the back of the formation as the team moved up on the drivers side of the car. At the door, the team pivoted so that the shield was in the front of the formation and they were at a right angle to the door. The lead officer directed the passenger to put his hands on the dash. When he did so, they had one officer cover the passenger while another reached in and took hold of his wrist. Carefully, he helped the young man pivot until the officer could get his hands under the passengers armpits. Carefully they pulled him out over the drivers seat. Gently, they laid him on the ground and rolled him over to handcuff and search him.

"What started this," Ted asked Peter Walsh.

"There was a 911 call of a drive by shooting of some kids by Rainier Beach high school. The complaint described this car, and said there were two kids shooting at other kids. No one was hit, so far as we know."

Jason nodded. It was not unusual in that part of town for victims to leave the scene and show up hours later at a hospital, needing treatment for a gunshot wound. He pulled out his phone and called Lloyd, while Ted and Peter chatted.

Lloyd answered on the third ring.

"Lloyd, we got Alaina Millers car. They have two in custody, but the passenger is going to the hospital. Do you want the driver brought to you?"

"Yes, and have the car sent to the processing room. We'll do a warrant on it later."

Jason disconnected and found Sergeant Walsh. He gave Walsh, Lloyd's directions and Peter said he would handle it. Jason and Ted walked down the hill to where the driver was leaning against a patrol car. Jason looked at the senior officer and shook his head to one side. That officer said to his partner, "keep an eye on him," and he and Jason stepped off about twenty feet.

Jason eyed the officers name tag. It read M.D. Yamada.

"Tell me what happened, Yamada."

"When he crashed he ran down the hill. My partner chased him on foot, so I took the car and cut him off. He was reaching for something in his waistband. I thought it might be a weapon so I used my taser to subdue him."

"What was he reaching for?"

Yamada reached behind him and said, "this." He produced an Airsoft pistol in the shape of a Colt .45.

"He's damn lucky you didn't shoot him."

"Hell yeah. He said he was gonna toss it, but you never know. It would have been bad either way."

"I'm glad it worked out. Great job. Can you take him straight to the Homicide office? Detective Murray wants to talk to him."

"No sweat."

They walked back to the small knot of people gathering around the car.

"Put him in the car, I'll drive him to Homicide," said Officer Yamada.

"Homicide," exclaimed the kid, "I didn't kill no one!"

Jason looked at him. "What's your name, son?"

"Adedayo Simon, sir."

"What do your friends call you?"

"Day. Why am I going to Homicide? I'm not a killer man, it was all a joke!"

"Hell of a joke son. No, I don't think you killed anyone. But you might help us figure out who did."

"Will I see my mom?"

"When we get down there, I'll see what I can do. Go with these guys and cooperate ok?"

"Anything man. I didn't kill nobody."

Yamada and his partner put the kid in the car, just as Walsh was walking up.

"I need to do a use of force interview with him."

"I know you do, Pete. Can you do it at Homicide? I really want to get him downtown."

Walsh nodded and said he would. Jason made a 'move out' motion with his hand to Yamada and he and Ted headed back up the hill.

"Let's get to the office," he said. Ted nodded as they got to their car, got in and eased into the flow of traffic.

Twenty minutes later they were back in the office, briefing Lloyd on the events. Ten minutes later, Lloyd walked into interrogation, where the young man sat, a tear running down his face. Lloyd handed him a bottle of water and said, "if you want something else, I can send out for it. But this is what I got right now."

Day nodded and took the bottle, cracking the top open with his free hand and drank greedily. Lloyd opened a file and began looking at it, pretending he was seeing it for the first time.

"Day, I'm looking at your file. There's almost nothing. You're like a single A ball player that plays in his first major league game and hits a home run. Do you have any idea what you're facing?"

Day shook his head.

Lloyd pulled a card from his pocket, then said, "do you mind if this is all recorded?" Day said "no." Lloyd then read from the card. When he was done, he said, "do you understand your Miranda rights?"

Day had tears streaming down his face. "Yes."

"Day, will you talk to me?"

Day nodded his head, "yes sir."

Lloyd said, "ok. Where did you find the car?"

"Let's see. Sunday night. We were hanging out in the flats. I like to go down there to watch The airplanes sometimes. Someday I want to be a pilot."

Lloyd nodded.

"Anyway, Grover and I were hanging out, and we walked past the Airplane. We kept walking south, and I was like man we need to catch the bus home. Grover, he sees this car parked kinda funny, and sees the keys in the ignition. And he's like, lets just drive home. So we got in the car, and he took me to my house, then stashed the car someplace close to his place."

"What happened today?"

"Well, we were walking home and we walked past the car. Grover gets this idea and grabs his brothers airsoft pistol and a pack of firecrackers. So we drive past some kids, I point the gun out the window and Grover lights the firecrackers and tosses them. Man you shoulda seen those kids run!"

"What happened next?"

"Next thing I know, the cops are chasing us. I'm driving around and they won't stop. I thought you guys couldn't chase no more?"

"A widely held misconception. What else?"

"Well, the tires blew and then I had a hard time steering it and somehow crashed into the fire hydrant. I panicked and tried to run, but that one cop cut me off. Then the other cop tackled me and I remembered that airsoft gun in my pants. So I was gonna show it to the cop so he'd know it wasn't real, but then he tased me."

"Ok. Did you take anything from the car?"

"No man. There wasn't anything. Look I know it was stupid. But we're just kids."

"How long have you known Grover?"

"Couple weeks."

"Tell me something. Where did you find the car?"

"You know where the gas station is?"

Lloyd nodded.

"You go past the hotel, there's an alley. Just past that is this huge parking lot for that airport right there."

"Boeing field?"

"Yeah. Anyway this car is parked at an angle right by the exit. Like it was dumped there."

"Did you see anyone around?"

"Not really. Well there was this one guy."

"What did he look like?"

"He was a white guy, wearing khakis. And one of those jackets people used to wear way back in the eighties."

"What was he doing?"

"He had his head down. Looking straight ahead. Like he didn't even see us. He almost ran into Grover but he just kept going. I thought it was weird but Grover didn't. He said the guy was probably on something."

"The jacket, was it like a members only jacket?"

Day snapped the fingers on his free hand. "Yeah, one of them."

"OK. If I put you with an artist, do you think you could help us draw a sketch of him?"

"Maybe. Yeah, ok."

There was a knock at the door. Lloyd looked annoyed for a moment, then said, "hang on a second."

He opened the door. Lieutenant Naes stood at the door with a worried black woman and a guy that looked like he was fresh out of high school, except that he was wearing a suit and carrying a briefcase.

"This is Day's mother, Mrs. Simon. And this is his public defender, Andras Stewart."

"Hi Andy. Mrs. Simon. Can I have a word with both of you please?"

"Lloyd. I'd like to speak to my client."

"Let me tell you what's going on first," Lloyd said, "after all he hasn't asked for you so I don't have to let you in the room."

"I am his mother," Mrs Simon said, "and my boy needs an attorney."

"I have no doubt he does ma'am. But let me talk to you both first."

Andras said, "Mrs. Simon, I think we should hear the detective out."

"Thank you," said Lloyd, "here's what we are looking at." Lloyd gave them an abbreviated version of events, explaining carefully that even though he was driving a murder victims car, Lloyd didn't think Day was responsible for the murder, that Day had just made a series of bad choices that became exponentially worse.

When he was done, Andras said, "what's next?"

"I'd like to put him with a sketch artist. The guy he saw might be the one that dumped the car. As long as everything pans out, I really don't care what sort of arrangement you make with the juvenile court. To my mind, he just seems like a good kid that made some dumb choices, the kind of things kids do all the time."

"How would you feel about a deferred prosecution?"

"Like I said, if what he says pans out, I'm good with that."

"What's a deferred prosecution," asked Mrs. Simon.

Andras said, "we go to juvenile on auto theft and harassment charges. If the prosecution agrees then the judge will likely put some conditions on him. Something along the lines of no more criminal charges, stays in school, maybe some kind of counseling. If he does all that, in probably a year we go back into court and the judge dismisses the charges. If he can't comply, then the judge reads the report and decides if he's guilty based on that."

"I don't know."

"Mrs Simon," said Lloyd, "is there a Mister Simon?"

She nodded. "He's been deployed with the Air Force for the last three months. He doesn't know about any of this."

"What's he do?"

"He's a pilot."

Lloyd nodded. "It's not my place to tell you this, but it's a hell of a deal. Plus if he cooperates and the information pans out, I'll go talk to the judge."

Mrs. Simon looked at Lloyd square in the face. "Why do you care what happens to my son?"

Lloyd looked back at her for a long moment. Andras started to say something, then changed his mind. Finally Lloyd spoke.

"I have a number of reasons. The people that committed this murder probably tried to have my boss killed. That's number one. Number two is, maybe when I was a stupid young teenager, someone cut me a break, and that, maybe, helped me to get where I am today."

"Your boss is the police man from Friday?"

Lloyd nodded his head.

"OK. He'll take it."

"Andy, let me introduce you, then I'll get the sketch artist up here."

8pm.

Jim and Marianne were laying in bed. At Marianne's insistence, Jim had taken a Vicodin. He was half asleep when Marianne said, "are you ready for tomorrow?"

"Sure." Jim struggled not to slur his words.

"Are you sure? You're about to be famous."

Jim opened his eyes. "I'm already famous."

"Jim, honey, not like this. You are famous as TW Griffin."

"I've been on TV."

"This won't be like that. I'm not talking about you doing a press conference and your friends give you a hard time. I'm talking about press camped out in your driveway and going through your garbage. Every time you go out, having someone take your picture and putting it in the newspaper. You can't get away from it."

"Maybe it'll improve book sales."

"I'm serious. It's going to be bad."

"How do you handle it?"

"You know how I handled it before we met. It isn't easy. I'd go for a jog or have dinner with friends and there would be fifty photographers taking my picture."

Before he could answer, his personal phone went off. Jim instinctively rolled onto his left side and winced. He lay back on the bed and said to Marianne, "You're worth it." A moment later, his phone still ringing, Marianne realized Jim was asleep.

119

Jason hung up the phone.

"He doesn't answer," he told Lloyd.

"Naes told me to put it on email. We'll try for Jim again in the morning, but I'll put it out department wide."

"CSI is searching the Taurus. Maybe they'll find something. Be nice to put a bow on this," Jason said.

"Amen to that," said Ross.

Jason was going back through his notes. "Maybe we should go back and talk to this guy, Gil. You said that kid, Day?" Lloyd nodded and Jason went on, "Day said something about that guy wearing a Members Only jacket."

"It's a tenuous connection, but why don't you call him?"

Jason checked his notes, then dialed a number. Gil answered on the second ring.

"Gil, this is detective King. Do you remember me?"

"Yeah, sure." Jason thought he sounded high.

"We have a description of someone that I was wondering might be part of your little social club down there."

"My what?"

"That gang you got down there. This guy would be around six feet, long brown hair parted in the middle. Favors a Members Only jacket. I don't remember seeing him in Quinns, but I was wondering if you knew him."

"Sounds a little like Tom. He used to hang out down here, but he met some chick. He was following her around like a bitch in heat man, it was bad."

"Do you remember Tom's last name?"

"No man. We called him Moocher, but he hasn't been around in months."

"What about his girlfriend?"

"Don't know nothing about her man. Never met the chick."

"Any idea where she lives?"

"Not really. Someplace like Kent or Federal Way. I understand she has a decent place, just don't know where."

"Ok, thanks Gil. You're a big help."

Gil sounded oddly proud. "Hey no problem. Call anytime."

Jason hung up. "Possible name of Tom or Moocher. They lost touch with him a few months ago when he started dating a woman from Kent or Federal Way."

"OK, update number one." Lloyd went back to his computer to add the information to the bulletin.

Ted pushed back from his desk. "Jason, do you mind if I take off? I gotta deal with that reporter, Sorensen, tomorrow, and I figure I better look pretty."

"It's too late for that," said Jason, "but go ahead. I'm not sure what there's left to do at this point."

"OK, I'll see you in the morning then." Ted slid into his coat and headed for the door.

Ross stood as well. "I'll walk out with you," he said, and joined Ted at the door. Lloyd and Jason were left in the bullpen. Lieutenant Naes was in her office, and Sergeant Worthy had left for the day. Lloyd glanced over at Naes' closed door.

"How's he doing?"

Jason looked up from his computer and leaned back in his chair.

"He stood up to the captain when it was time to interview him. So that's good. During the pursuit yesterday I had to give him directions, but that was ok. Did I mention how he had my back at Quinn's? He took out two of those assholes and they barely laid a finger on him."

"How's his drinking?"

"Haven't really noticed. He seems to like Mountain Dew but I won't hold that against him."

"OK."

"Lloyd, I know he had a problem. If I thought he still had a problem I'd be all over him. But you gotta admit he's done alright."

"I know. I'm just asking. What's the deal with this reporter?"

"She slipped him her number. He was gonna ignore it, but she called him," Jason said.

"That's all," Lloyd asked.

"Lloyd, he tried like hell to blow her off. She wouldn't do it. He got stuck."

"Well, I hope Jim figures something out."

"Me too."

Ross followed Ted out to the parking lot. When they got to Teds car, he turned to say goodnight to Ross.

"Let me ask you something," Ross said.

"Ask away."

"Did you give it up to the reporter?"

"No, she already had it figured out," said Ted.

"Because if you did ..." Ross left it unsaid.

"If I did what? You're going to kick my ass? What could you possibly do that would put me in a worse bind than I am right now?"

Ross was mute, he simply stared at Ted with a deadpan look in his eyes.

"I tell you what, if that's what it is, you better bring a lunch because it'll be an all day effort. Get the fuck out of my way so I can go home."

Ross didn't budge. "He saved your career, you know."

"I am aware of that. The chief wanted to fire me, and he talked the chief out of it. I had to transfer and he got me into media relations, somehow. I know all that."

"Then why are you making him do this interview?"

"Ross, it's not like that." Ted sighed, then said, "She knows about Marianne. You guys haven't done that great a job keeping it a secret, half the department knows." Ross looked stricken. "But it wasn't anyone from the job. She recognized Marianne walking Jim out of the hospital. If they don't do the interview and get in front of it, Sorensen goes with what she has. If she has gaps in the story, she or her producers will make shit up."

"That's despicable," said Ross.

"It's the modern news media. Jim knows it. I know it. Almost everyone but you knows it. She did me a courtesy by calling me. So I'm going to go home, eat a frozen dinner, and call her to make sure we're still on for tomorrow."

"When you're done, call me. Lloyd and Jason are gonna work this thing out. You're going to ride with me. Oh, when you see Jim, give him this." Ross pulled the sketch out of his pocket and handed it to Ted.

Ted looked at the sketch, smiled, and held up his briefcase. "Got it in here. I planned to see if he recognizes this guy. I'll see you tomorrow."

Ted got into his car. Ross stepped away and let him back out. He waved as Ted drove down the ramp to the exit, then he went to his own car, got in and followed Ted down the ramp.

9PM

Ted lived alone in a two story townhouse on the edge of Bellevue's city limits. In spite of what he'd told Ross, he dumped tomato soup into a pan and warmed it on his stove. While he did that, he placed cheddar cheese, a spicy deli mustard and a few pickles between two slices of wheat bread, then grilled it in a frying pan. When it was done, he put the soup in a bowl and cut his sandwich into two pieces. He carried them into his dining area, and turned on Sportscenter to watch while he ate.

When he had finished, he pulled his phone out, and laid Maria Sorensen's card on the table. Ted's phone had two bars on the battery. He dialed the number, and let it ring. Maria picked up on the third ring.

"Hello Ted," she purred. He had to admit, it was a nice voice.

"Just checking in with you. Are we still on for tomorrow morning?"

"Oh good," she said, "for a minute I thought you were going to cancel on me."

"No, but this is a huge favor I'm doing for you."

"What do you mean?"

"I mean this is a temporary spot that I'd like to make permanent. If this doesn't go well tomorrow, I may be back in uniform walking a beat someplace."

"I'll do my best," she said, "I don't want anyone to get hurt. I just think this makes a great story."

"So do I," Ted admitted, "but this is huge."

"How about I owe you Ted," said Maria, "you know I'm good for it."

Ted felt his palms getting sweaty. "Where will you be coming from?"

"I'm at home in Kirkland and I recorded a bit for the morning news so I don't have to go in to the station until after the interview."

"OK. Do you know where the Park and Ride is? The one just off of 520?"

"Sure. It's right on my way to work."

"You don't take the bus?"

"I used to. But people started recognizing me from Television, so I drive in now."

Ted smiled, the irony not lost on him. "I'll meet you there. Say, ten AM. I'll be in a black Crown Victoria."

"Is that a city car? I don't picture you in a Ford."

"What do you think I drive?"

"I'm not sure. Maybe a BMW."

Ted smiled. His BMW sat in the garage when he had a company car.

"Good guess. Anyway, I'll pick you up in the Crown Vic. If I'm there before you, I'll take a spot, and we can switch when you get there. What are you driving?"

"I've got a Volkswagen Atlas, Black."

"That's an SUV, right? You better tie a ribbon on the antenna, or something."

"How about a red ribbon? Then you can pick me out in a crowd."

There was something about her voice that made it hard to breath. Ted swallowed hard before responding.

"Sounds good. I'm gonna get some sleep. I'm looking forward to seeing you tomorrow."

"Thanks Ted. And I mean it, I owe you. I promise I'll pay you back."

Ted rang off, then looked at the ceiling and said to no one in particular, "how the hell am I supposed to sleep?"

On the other end of the line, Maria laid her phone back on the nightstand and smiled to herself.

In the hotel, Gretchen lay staring at the ceiling. Beside her, Tom lay sleeping, like he always did after. For a man, he wasn't half bad, and he was useful in other ways too. But she knew at some point she would have to cut this tie as well.

Were there any other ties? Jim was the only one. She'd made a half hearted attempt to seduce him, but he'd clearly not been interested. Those idiots had forced that on her. There were times she missed Fred, but the money she'd got wasn't half bad. She had help with that one, and was grateful for it. She calculated again how much she'd made so far. It wasn't Microsoft money, but it was decent. They'd be comfortable when they could finally be together.

Chapter 17

Ray had finished searching the car around midnight. There hadn't been much. He'd found some prints, about where he'd expect to find them. Steering wheel, seat adjustment lever, rear view mirror and the headlight switch. He matched prints on the wheel to both Grover and Day. The prints he found on the drivers seat adjust and on the headlight switch, came back to Day. There were prints from the first two fingers of someone's right hand on the right side of the mirror, where someone would have put their fingers to adjust the rear view mirror. Those prints did not match Grover or Day. Ray asked for, and got, a set of prints from the owner of the car, Alaina Miller. The prints did not match. So Ray started off his day preparing the prints and entering them into a computer program known as the "Automated Fingerprint Identification System." In spite of the fancy name, Ray knew it would be all day before it returned a match, so he moved on to one of his other cases.

Ross came into the bullpen, carrying a cardboard tray with four coffees on it. One he dropped off in the lieutenants office, then gave the rest to Jason and Lloyd, keeping one for himself. Lieutenant Naes came out of her office and asked for an update.

"Ted is gearing up for this interview with the captain and that reporter," Lloyd said, "when he gets back he and Ross are going to run some things down. In the meantime, Jason and I are going to noodle this out. Hopefully we can get a better name on him."

Jason said, "We got a first name of 'Tom' and a street name of Moocher last night. But no one really knows who he is."

Rebekah nodded to herself, and looked across the room at the overflowing mailbox that belonged to Captain Churchill, the admin typing quietly into her computer.

"Ok," she said. "It seems like every time you peel off a layer, you find two more. Are all your cases like this?"

"Not all of them. Last year we had one that was pretty rocky for a while, but we got that one put to bed finally."

"SAU could be like this from time to time. But this has a certain level of, I don't know, sophistication?"

"Most homicides," replied Lloyd, "are crimes of spontaneity. They don't usually involve a lot of planning. This case, I think, involves some planning with an end goal in mind. Once we know the strategy, we'll know who."

Something was circling around the edges of Rebekah's mind but she couldn't pin it down. Finally she said, "Ok. It may be a homicide, but it's still detective work. Keep at it."

She left them there and went to the captains mailbox.

"Dionne, until he comes back, why don't you just bring his mail to me?"

Dionne smiled and nodded. Rebekah carried the pile back to her office and sorted through it. Department mail she set off to one side, to look at later. Anything that was sealed she put in her briefcase to deliver to Jim later.

Ted was dressed. He'd had coffee, but was too nervous to eat. He had dug out his best suit from Men's Wearhouse, a pinstripe affair with a shirt white as snow and a red necktie. He looked at the clock for maybe the fiftieth time, wondering why he was looking forward to this meeting with both dread and excitement.

He sipped his coffee again. Then he forced himself to sit down at his breakfast table and go over his notes. He and Jason had watched the interrogation yesterday. Ted was intrigued at this mystery man that had walked away from…not the car, but the area of the car. So he was a person of interest. But Jason seemed to think he might be involved with the Tacoma crew that Alaina had apparently led. Which circled back around and made him a suspect again. Then he thought about the pursuit. He hadn't known the area that well, but he'd listened to Jason and they'd been there to help at the end.

Ted looked at his watch and saw it was time to go. He slipped into his jacket and trench coat, and stepped outside. The forecast was partly cloudy, and the overcast sky verified the forecast. He climbed into the full size Ford and drove to the park and ride, about five minutes away. He drove through it once and saw a Forester parked with a red ribbon on it's roof rack. Then he realized it was an Atlas, and pulled in behind it. Maria popped the rear hatch as she got out of the drivers seat.

"You're early," she said.

"Well, I didn't want to be late," he said lamely.

Maria smiled and shook his hand. Ted found it soft and warm.

"Let me help," he said as he reached for her camera. There was a large microphone on top, and a large tripod. "It's not as big as I thought."

Maria smiled, "everything is digital these days. I'll record it onto an SD card and pop it into a computer for editing. No muss, no fuss, no worries about broken tapes."

"Nice. Anything else you're going to need?"

"No, that's pretty much it." She closed the hatch with the push of a button, then hit her alarm. The car beeped back at them, and Ted held the front door of his car for her as Maria climbed in.

Once in the front seat, Ted said to her, "I need to impress upon you the importance of privacy. Do not give any indication as to address or location when you broadcast this."

Maria looked at him out of the corner of her eye. "Should I wear a blindfold?"

"Like in the movies? No, that won't be necessary," said Ted.

"Too bad. Maybe later than."

"Oh God," thought Ted, "is she serious?"

Ted didn't give her a blindfold, but he took a ten minute drive and made it close to thirty before they pulled up to the gate at the entrance to Jim's neighborhood. They explained to the guard that they were expected, and he disappeared into his shack to make a phone call.

"Nice neighborhood," said Maria.

"Not bad."

The guard came out a minute later. "They're expecting you," he said. The guard pushed a button and the gate raised. Ted drove through as the guard tipped his hat to Maria.

Ted took a right and drove past Sheridan and Janes house before pulling into the driveway of Jims house. He hit the trunk release and came around the back of the car to let Maria out. She thanked him and he retrieved her equipment from the trunk.

"Do you think I could get some exterior shots?"

"Might be best not to," Ted replied, "you can ask, but he's serious about his privacy."

They approached the front door and Ted rang the doorbell. Rosa greeted them.

"Hello mister Ted. Miss?"

"Sorensen. Call me Maria."

"Miss Maria. Come in."

They followed Rosa into the living room. Jim was sitting up in the recliner, his arm in a sling and his feet in the air. He was dressed casually in a pair of Levis and a flannel shirt. Marianne was wearing an electric blue dress with a high neck. She stood and smiled warmly at Maria. Jim lowered the footrest and shook hands with Maria before looking back and forth between Ted and Maria with interest, before he spoke.

"Pardon me if I don't stand," he said.

"That's quite alright Mister Churchill," said Maria.

"Call me Jim," he said.

Marianne gestured to a chair and Maria said, "if it's ok with you, I'd like to get the camera set up."

"Sure, go ahead," said Jim, "do you want coffee? Tea, water?"

"Water if you have it," said Maria.

"Rosa, could you bring her some water? Coffee for the rest of us?"

"Right away, Mr. Churchill," said Rosa, a gleam in her eye.

Maria mounted the camera on the tripod, and said to Ted, "could you make sure that doesn't fall off of there?"

Ted nodded.

Maria sat down, and pulled a recorder out of her purse, setting a microphone between them.

"Before we get started, could I get some preliminaries out of the way?"

Jim and Marianne nodded.

"Can you talk about the, uh, incident?"

"I can talk around it. But not about the actual incident itself," replied Jim.

"Is there anything else that's off limits?"

Jim looked at Marianne.

"I would prefer not to discuss my ex husband."

"Understood," Maria smiled.

Rosa came in a moment later with a bottle of water and a glass. Miguel behind her carrying a tray. Neither one said anything until Maria said, "thank you," to Rosa. She smiled and Rosa and Miguel disappeared.

"Do you have any questions for me before we start?" Maria was curious.

"What do you get out of this," asked Jim.

"To be honest, I'll get national exposure, which in my business is never a bad thing. I will have an exclusive and breaking story. And it's a great human interest piece."

"When will this air?"

"Hopefully I can have it edited and on the five o clock news. Which likely means five forty five...ish. The interview could take anywhere from five minutes to a couple hours, but when it's all done the segment itself will run around two, maybe two and a half minutes."

"Honey, you got anything?"

"I've done this sort of thing before, I think I know what to expect," said Marianne.

"Alright then, lets get started," said Maria.

It was about eleven thirty when Maria stood and turned off the camera and her recorder. Jim had lost interest after the first few minutes and spent most of the time watching Marianne. He noticed her eyes brighten but her voice remained soft as she spoke with a lilt. She had a glow like she did when she performed.

"Would you like to stay for lunch," asked Marianne.

Maria glanced at her watch, then said, "as long as Ted can get me back to my car on a straight shot, and not drive twenty minutes out of our way, sure."

Ted's face flushed.

Rosa came in carrying a tray with four covered plates. Miguel following with a pitcher of lemonade. Rosa set her tray down and then placed each plate on the table, removed the covers and went back to the kitchen. Lunch was buffet style. Each plate held an entrée and everyone took what they wanted.

"Sit wherever you like," said Marianne. Jim slowly stood and limped to the table. When he sat Maria was on his left, Marianne brought him a plate and sat on his right.

They no sooner started eating when Ted's phone rang. He left the room to answer it. Jim waited until he was out of earshot, turned to Maria and said, "are you two dating yet?"

Maria almost choked on a piece of chicken. "No. Why do you ask?"

"A word of advice. You'll need to make the first move."

Maria adopted a conspiratorial tone. "Not that I would, but why is that?"

"Ted's a good guy. Don't tell him I said that. But he's a bit gun shy around women."

Maria nodded as Ted came back into the room.

"What was that about," asked Jim.

"Jason with a reminder. I have something to show you when we're done."

"Why not now? Let me see it."

Ted shrugged, "OK."

Ted picked up his briefcase and pulled a manila folder from inside. He checked the label and slid it across the table to Jim. He opened the folder and looked at the sketch that Day had helped develop.

"I know this guy."

"How so? Like an arrest or something?"

"No. Uh. Is this related to the case?" Jim glanced at Maria.

Maria said, "I'm interested. But if it's supposed to be confidential I can leave the room."

Jim and Ted looked at each other. Finally Ted shrugged and said, "your call."

Jim turned to Maria. "You've been honest with us so far. Can I trust you to keep anything you hear under your hat unless I tell you that you can use it?"

Maria pondered that for a minute. "Can I use what I hear to look at it from a different angle?"

"Like what?"

"If I hear a name, can I go at it from a different direction, knowing it will bring me to the same name?"

"Like how," Jim asked.

"Fred kills Wilma. Can I ask Barney about Fred."

Jim looked at Ted. Again Ted shrugged.

"Only if you clear it with Ted before it airs. We cannot afford to have an investigation compromised."

"That means Ted will have to keep a close eye on me," she said.

"You up for that Ted?"

"Yes," Ted said thickly.

"Deal?" Jim extended his hand.

"Deal," said Maria.

Jim turned to Marianne, "Honey, look at this and tell me who this is."

Marianne looked at the sketch, then leaned back and thought for a long minute.

"Tom. Tom something." She opened her eyes and sat up. "Tom Meeker. He was with Gretchen at the wake. You told me later you thought there was something between them."

Jim snapped his fingers, "You're right. Ted, this is Tom Meeker, he's Gretchen Hendersons boyfriend."

"OK. He's a person of interest. Does he have any reason to come after you?"

"Nothing concrete. I've been waiting on some information from the state."

"What sort of information?"

"Maria, this is the part that gets really dicey. If you for any reason think you cannot keep what I'm about to say off the air, you might want to leave the room."

Ted jumped in, "Maria, he's serious. If you don't think you can keep your promise you have got to let us know now."

Maria looked from one to the other, then at Marianne.

"Who would it hurt if I do air it?"

Jim said, "it could drive a killer into the ground. It could cause them to panic and lash out. It might hurt a lot of people."

"Ted, is he serious?"

"As a heart attack."

"Then I won't air it until you give me the go ahead or someone else does. But I want the exclusive."

"Ted will be your contact."

"OK," Maria said.

"Ted, I think Gretchen poisoned Fred Henderson. I had the ME test his blood and I'm waiting for the results. They should have been in by now and I would have called on Monday if this hadn't happened."

"Did she know you suspected her?"

"I don't know how but I think her and Tom hired those two idiots to attack me and when that didn't work she started cutting her connections with the crime. Have you talked to Tacoma about their case?"

"Not yet. I'll call Jason and have them fax up their sketch."

"Jason knows Gretchen. He should look at the sketch. Call the crime lab about the test results from Fred."

"Yes sir."

Maria's plate was empty. "I don't mean to be impolite..."

"Maria," said Jim, "as soon as we can, you'll be the first call we make."

"I'll hold you to that," she said as she and Ted stood. "Who is Fred Henderson?"

Jim said, "Fred was a homicide detective that died from a heart attack."

"I'll wait out in the foyer. I feel like if I learn anything else I'll explode," said Maria. She left the living room.

"Anything else, captain?"

"Not at the moment. We need to find them, until we do no one is safe."

Marianne walked with Ted to the foyer and whispered in his ear. Ted nodded, then picked up Marias camera equipment, took her by the arm and walked her outside.

"What did she say to you," Maria asked, once they got in the car.

"She thanked me. She said he hasn't had that kind of light in his eye since he woke up in the hospital."

Maria nodded. "You certainly piqued his interest. Now, if this story pans out, I'll owe you a lot. I owe you a bunch anyway, but that's a huge story."

They were driving out of the neighborhood as Ted said, "You could start paying me back tonight."

"How so," Maria turned in the seat to look directly at him.

"What time do you get off work?"

"The evening news goes off at six. I'm off then."

"Have dinner with me tonight. I'll pick you up at your station."

131

"OK. But make it eight, and come to my condo. I'll cook." She explained, "If I go out, especially right after a story like this, I get mobbed. Dinner. That's all I'll promise."

"Works for me," Ted replied, "just give me your address."

It was just past three when Ted walked into the bullpen.

Ross glanced at his watch, "about time you showed up."

"This thing took longer than I thought," Ted replied, "and then they asked us to stay for lunch."

"Well lucky you. Keep your coat on, we're going to Tacoma."

Ted followed Ross out to the parking garage. Ross squeezed his bulk into a Toyota Prius. Ted shrugged and got in the other side.

"We could take my car, it's bigger."

"Naw, this car is great. They're the wave of the future. In ten years we're gonna be driving all electric cars. Gas stations will be replaced with battery chargers."

"OK. Just thought we'd be more comfortable."

"I'm good," said Ross.

"Where are we going?"

"We're going to pick up Danny White, and then go over and talk to Gil Tuller. I want to show him the picture and see if they know Meeker."

"We got a photo montage?"

"No, just gonna use the sketch."

The freeway was packed at that time of day, with commuters trying to get home. With two of them in a city car, Ross saved a little time in the car pool lane, but it wasn't much. Well over an hour later they met with Danny in the parking lot of the electric supply.

"I guess we're gonna show off our sketch artists."

"Man, I don't know. I always feel like we get lucky when someone gets recognized."

"Yeah, and then it's like how did that happen," said Danny.

Ted checked his watch. "Is he alone in there?"

"I think so," said Danny, "at least all I see is his bike and no cars."

"We waiting on anybody," asked Ted.

"No. Why?"

"Let's get this over with."

Ross looked at Danny and shrugged.

"We'll go in together," said Ross, "you go first."

Danny agreed, and they piled into their cars.

"Why are you in such a hurry?"

Ted shrugged. He didn't want to say he had a date, so he said, "I don't know. Just a vibe I'm getting."

Ross was quiet as he made the turn onto the street, then said, "What's the vibe telling you?"

"Every time we talk to someone on this case, they end up dead."

"You noticed that too? OK, here's what we're doing. All our notes are going into thumb drives and we're not saving them to the computer. We were talking about it while you were gone. We think there's a leak in the office."

Ted sat up. "You can't be serious."

Ross didn't answer because they were in the parking lot. They got out and joined Danny at the front door. Danny pushed through and they located Gil behind the bar. He was the only one in the front.

"Hey," said Gil.

"Hey," said Ted, "who else is here?"

"No one man," he said but his eyes flicked towards the back room.

Ted moved around behind the counter and pulled aside the curtain. A members only jacket sat on the back of a chair. The back door was just swinging closed. Ted looked around the room and saw that no one was there. He strode around the table and looked out the door. One of the three from Saturday was sprinting down the alley behind the bar. Ted shrugged and went back.

"One guy, took off out the back and left his jacket behind."

Gil shrugged. "I was told to stall you."

"Did they know we were coming," Ross asked.

"No, they were going to vote someone to take over. Personally I think they're done. They got no enforcers, the boss is dead. No one is gonna pay attention to them now."

"I suppose not," said Danny, "Gil are you still cooperating?"

"Yeah, sure."

"You ever see her before?" Danny placed a sketch on the bar. It was a pretty woman, wearing a nurses scrubs and a surgical hat.

"Maybe. Tom might have brought her by once, but she never got out of the car. Come to think of it, that was the last time Moocher was here."

"When was that?"

"Maybe five, six weeks ago? Yeah, five. He never said nothing after that, just didn't come around. Larry said he called a few times, but he didn't say what they talked about."

"OK, thanks. Ross?"

"Take a look at this." Ross laid the sketch of Tom Meeker on the bar.

"Yeah, that's Tom alright. Or Moocher."

"Why Moocher?"

"He was the guy, you go out to eat, ya know? And he'd get like a steak or something expensive. Then he'd say he forgot his wallet."

"I know the type. What's he into?"

"A little of this, a little of that. Nothing big."

"One more thing," Ross said and laid a picture of a pistol on the bar. "That's a Walther P22. You ever see that before?"

Gil paused before he spoke.

"So they provide protection on the docks, right?"

Ross nodded.

"Sometimes shipping containers get washed overboard and the contents get reported as lost, so the owner collects insurance money. But the container gets unloaded here and they'd pick up the contents. Like all those members only jackets."

"I wondered about that," said Ross.

"So Larry talks to someone and they get a container. Inside was a bunch of stuff, but there was a crate full of those little .22 pistols. Moocher took the crate and I never saw it again. There were probably twenty of those pistols inside."

"Thanks man. Watch your back, ok?"

"You got it."

The three cops stepped back outside to the parking lot. Ross touched Danny's elbow and said, "let me see that sketch again."

Danny laid the sketch on the hood of his car.

"Shit," said Ross, "we got problems."

"What do you mean?" Even Ted looked quizzical.

Ross looked at Ted and said, "you ever meet Gretchen Henderson?"

Ted shook his head.

Gretchen had been a nurse at Swedish hospital. She had met Fred Henderson when he went there to interview a prisoner. Fred had been smitten right away, and Gretchen strung him along. She had moved into Freds house within a few weeks of the meeting and had married him a few weeks after that. They had been married for about five years, during which time Gretchen had quit her job and went to work for the health department. When the marriage started to go south, Ross had talked to his own wife, who still worked at Swedish. She had a friend in Human Resources. She had told Lisa Nolan that they couldn't prove it, but Gretchen had quit Swedish shortly after an investigation into the theft of narcotics. Fred had recently died of a heart attack but by then they were separated. Fred had been talking about a reconciliation but Ross didn't know if that had happened.

When he was done, Danny said, "What kind of narcotics were taken?"

Ross replied, "Lisa wasn't sure."

"No sweat. I can get that when I do a background on her. Sounds like she had her hooks in your guy."

"She did, but that's not the problem."

"That's a hell of a thing to not be a problem," said Danny.

"We've got a leak in our office," said Ross, "Jason hasn't told anyone but Lloyd, Ted and me about Gil here. Because every time we put a new witness in our notes, they end up dead."

"Well shit. What are you gonna do?"

"We gotta have a meeting. Just those of us on the case. But we can't do it at work. I don't trust the lieutenant. I barely trust Ted here."

"Thanks a lot," said Ted.

"No offense."

"None taken," Ted said unconvincingly.

"You guys got any suggestions?"

"We could meet here," said Danny.

"That's no good. Four of us headed to Tacoma at the same time. Whoever the leak is would know we were on to them."

"I got an idea," said Ted, "when I was there earlier, Marianne told me that Jim got, I dunno, energized or something when I showed him Meeker's picture. Like he had his spark back. We could set up a meeting at his place. Jim's good friends with the three of you, so it wouldn't be strange for you to head over to check on him."

"I like this. Danny, I think you should be in on it, if you're ok with that."

"Hell yeah. If you're right, she killed a prisoner we were supposed to safeguard," said Danny.

"I'll call Jim," said Ted, reaching for his phone.

"Hell yeah. It's your idea, you sell it to him."

It turned out to be an easy sale. Ted laid out the problem for Jim, and that they needed a brainstorming session in a safe place.

"We should bring Lieutenant Naes in on this," Jim said, "she is your commander until I return."

"That's part of the problem," said Ted, "we think she might be the leak."

"Ah well I see where that could be a problem. OK, I'll have Rosa put some coffee on. What time will you be here?"

Ted looked at his watch, then at Ross. "Say, what, six thirty?" Ross nodded.

"Six thirty it is," said Jim.

Ted rang off. "We better get moving, four oh five is gonna be packed." I405 was the freeway that went around the east side of Lake Washington and was a way to bypass Seattle proper.

Ross said to Danny, "do you know where Hunts Point is?"

Danny nodded. Ross gave him Jims address so Danny plugged it into the GPS on his smart phone.

135

"I'm right behind you," he said.

Jim got off the phone with Ted and said, "They think Lieutenant Naes is the leak."

"The hell you say," said Lieutenant Naes.

It was just after six thirty when Lloyd and Jason pulled into the driveway. Ross and Ted were parked on the left, Danny White's car was parked on the right. Jason pulled into the middle. Mike Worthy pulled in behind them, parking between Jason and Danny.

"Every time I come here, I marvel at this house," said Lloyd, "I ought to write a book."

"What's going to happen," asked Jason.

"Amidst all the wailing and gnashing of teeth, I think we'll get our point across. Then we'll work out a strategy and come to some conclusions. If we're right, Lieutenant Naes had a hand in Jim's shooting."

"I just find the whole thing hard to believe. She's got a solid history with the department, and she was tough as nails in SAU."

"Yeah that part bugs me too. So maybe Jim can show us how we're wrong."

They walked to the front door and were greeted by Rosa. Lloyd hugged her and asked, "how is he?"

"Better. He's on his feet more. But he's hurting."

"Where's Marianne?"

"She won't leave his side. She is worried he's going to hurt himself."

"How long are you and Miguel staying?"

"Miguel will stay as long as I do. I'm not leaving until Marianne says we can. Anyway, there's pizza on the table if you are hungry and a cooler of beer."

They nodded and found their way in.

As they walked into the living room, Lloyd saw Jim and said, "How're they hanging, boss."

Then he stopped dead in his tracks. Seated at the head of the table was Jim Churchill, but on his left was Lieutenant Naes. On Jims right was Marianne. Seated at the table and looking glum were Ross and Ted. Rebekah had her arms crossed. Danny White was standing off to the side, selecting a beer from the cooler. Mike Worthy came in behind them, said, "hi boss," then went to the cooler and picked out a Budweiser. Lloyd and Jason took seats at the table and Lloyd finally broke the ice.

"Why do I feel like we're all about to have a bunch of egg on our faces?"

Mike plopped down next to Lloyd and said, "You guys are half right. There's definitely a leak in the unit."

Finally Jim spoke. "Lloyd, you're senior. Ted is the newest guy in the unit, but Jason has the least seniority. I want clear uncolored opinions as to why Lieutenant Naes is the leak. Everyone else at this table has a lot to lose. You've always been straight with me and I don't want to put anyone on the spot but this needs to be aired out."

"Jim," Lloyd started, then stopped. "Captain Churchill, I started having some concerns when I saw how they had to have picked you up coming out of headquarters. Your Explorer is department issue, and there are many like it with the same paint scheme. If they didn't know when you were coming out they'd never have known how to find you. Then we start making connections, and what's his name, Benvenuti gets killed. Ross and I end up taking a homicide and find out she's another connection to Tacoma. Danny here," Lloyd pointed to Danny White, who nodded and took a sip of his beer, "could have been a leak, but he knew we were talking to Gil. Lieutenant Naes didn't, because Jason and I intentionally did not put it into our follow ups."

Jim nodded. He looked around the room and said, "anyone else want to add anything?" He eased his left arm as he looked around the room again.

Danny White took another sip of beer and said, "why shouldn't I be under suspicion?"

"Another reason is that Miller didn't call you. She called someone else, and that person called whoever killed her, or did it themselves," said Jim.

Danny nodded.

"Rebekah, your turn."

"Jim recruited me to this unit because of my reputation. What you are alleging, conspiracy to commit murder of a police officer, conspiracy to commit aggravated murder in the first degree, those are serious charges. I'm outraged that any of you would think that of me, but I can understand why you'd think it. I'll say it now, so there is no doubt. I am not the leak."

She looked around the room.

"The leak has been going around for a while. You never wondered how certain members of the press would report a story with information no one else had?"

No one said anything.

"Jim wanted me to plug the leak, but it's taken a while to figure it out. We were discussing who it was when Ted called. By the way Ted, why did you call?"

Ted looked up. "Ross was driving."

"Did you think I was the leak?"

"You got me here. I owe you that. If I have to go back because of this, so be it. I thought we were doing the right thing."

Jim stood. "No one is going anywhere. Ted, Rebekah brought you in because you finally started to act like a cop. You've shown good instincts and everyone say's you're learning a lot. But," Jim looked around the table again, "I didn't just bring Rebekah in to plug a leak. I needed someone who could run this unit when I'm gone. I am on the departments sick, lame and lazy list right now. Rebekah is running the show. Lloyd and Ross, you two are the most senior in the unit. Do I have to express my disappointment?"

Lloyd shook his head, "sir with all due respect we had every reason to think…"

"Lloyd," Jim interrupted, "it's water under the bridge. You four did the right thing by coming to me, and if you had done so earlier I could have explained it. Now it's time to move on. Your commander has a few things to say."

"Thank you captain," said Rebekah, "first off I understand why you would have thought what you did. I couldn't tell you about the leak because I didn't know who it was and Jim wanted a fresh pair of eyes on it. So, no hard feelings. Lloyd, you were exactly right. There was a phone call made to Ms Henderson as Jim was leaving the building. I think Lazzari had a phone that Henderson called and that the phones were taken after Lazzari was killed. When Jason had the fight with Benvenuti there was another phone call made to Henderson. I believe that Miller called Henderson or Meeker and met with them thinking she was going to get more money and a way out."

Rebekah checked her notes.

"Jim had Jason put his hospital gown in for analysis after he spilled water on it that Henderson poured for him. She had laced it with Lidocaine. Quite a lot of Lidocaine actually."

She looked at her notes again.

"Jim had to call the state lab to get back the results of the blood test he asked for on Detective Henderson. He had three times the safe amount in his bloodstream. The medical examiner has confirmed that this would have resulted in increased levels of potassium in his system and a major heart attack. Let's not forget, Ray found Tom Meeker's fingerprints on the rear view mirror of Alaina Miller's car."

She looked around the room.

"This woman and her boyfriend are responsible for the deaths of a police detective and four other people, and the attempted murder of Captain Churchill. Now does anyone know where the hell they are?"

Jason said, "we've been out to the house. The car is gone and the house is closed up. No way to know if it's temporary or permanent."

"Anybody have an idea as to where they might have gone?"

Jim said, "didn't Fred have a place in Kalispell?"

"Montana," replied Jason, "yeah, he had a cabin near the Flathead river."

"Then we should ask the sheriff out there to check it. That's an all day drive, so they could be there by now. Maybe, and this is just a suggestion, your unit commander will have to authorize it, the sheriff out there could check it in the morning. If she's there with her boyfriend this could all be solved by tomorrow."

"Do we agree there's probable cause," asked Rebekah.

The detectives all nodded their assent.

"The trouble is, how do we get a warrant out knowing we have a leak in the office? She'll be on the phone ten seconds later."

"I can handle that," said Danny, "your case is primary, but we have one count of murder and one count of conspiracy to commit murder in Pierce County. I can get drivers license photos and put together an affidavit. I'll have it emailed to me and forward it to Flathead county."

"Do it," said Rebekah.

Danny stepped out and was on the phone talking to his partner.

"I'd like to fly out there and be there if she's picked up," said Lloyd.

"No. This is a hunch. If she's there, you and Jason can get her and bring them back."

"Fair enough. Thank you."

Danny came back in the room. "I told him enough to convince him to type up the warrant. It'll be here in probably fifteen minutes."

Jim gestured towards the sideboard with his good hand. "That pizza isn't going to eat itself. Dig in guys."

The only one that didn't immediately go for a slice was Ted. He checked his watch when he stood and glanced towards the door.

"Hot date, Ted?" Jim had a sly smile.

"Sort of," Ted said.

"Maria?"

"She said she owed me one. I suggested we could have dinner tonight. I'm supposed to meet her at her place at eight."

Jim checked his phone for the time. It was seven thirty.

"Where does she live," he asked.

"Kirkland. I think it's one of those condos on Lake Washington boulevard."

"You should go. That's about ten minutes away. Pick up some nice flowers or something."

"You sure?"

"Hey Ross," Jim shouted across the room, "can you catch a ride with Jason and Lloyd?"

"I ain't riding in the back seat," said Ross, "but yeah."

"Give Ted your keys, he's on a mission."

Ross tossed his keys to Ted. "Don't scratch it."

"I'll be kind," then to Jim, "thank you."

Ted went out the door, and a moment later drove off in Ross' Prius.

Jason was talking to Marianne.

"Is Jenny around? I was sort of hoping I'd see her."

"She went up to the Johnston's when we started setting this up. Jim didn't think she should be party to it."

"Why are you here?"

"Jim said the same thing to me. I told him I was going to make sure he didn't stay on his feet too long and no way was I leaving. Why don't you run up to the Johnstons and say hello," suggested Marianne.

"I'll wait until we hear back about the warrant."

"Your funeral," she said.

Lloyd and Ross were talking to Sergeant Worthy.

"You knew about this?"

"It was a tough call, but Lieutenant Naes was clear, no one else could know," Worthy said.

"Mike, we could have helped."

"Rebekah was clear, no one that did not absolutely need to know. She had to figure it out first. She would have clued you in eventually, but no one expected the attack on Jim."

"I guess not. But damn it."

"I know, I know. In the end though it was worth it."

"Really? Our captain a cripple, five people dead? Was it really worth that?"

"Honestly, no, but no one thought that would happen," said Worthy.

Danny came into the room. "Where's Ted?"

"He had another meeting," said Jim, "you have the warrant?"

"Yep. If you have a printer I can print it out for you."

"Go to air printer and select Jims printer."

He did, and Marianne went upstairs to Jims office, returning a moment later with a piece of paper. She handed it to Jim, who looked at it and passed it around the room.

"Take a look at this. If anyone has a problem with it, say so now."

Rebekah was the last one to look, then handed it to Jim. "Unless anyone objects, it looks good to me."

Jim said, "it's your call Rebekah."

"Let's do it," she said.

Danny picked up his phone and pushed a button. The others could only hear his side of the conversation as he spoke to someone on the other end.

When he was done, he said, "Flathead county is going to send out a couple detectives first thing in the morning. I explained as much as I could without giving away the farm, but they know to call me or Jason once they have made contact."

"I think that's all we can do for now," said Rebekah, "Jim thank you for allowing us to use your house."

"Hopefully the next time will be a social occasion," Jim replied.

As they filed out through the foyer, Jason said, "you guys go ahead," to Lloyd and Ross, "I'll catch an Uber later."

They nodded and left. Jason walked up the street and waved as Lloyd and Ross' car drove by, followed by Danny. He knocked on the Johnstons door and Jenny opened it a moment later.

"I'm sorry I didn't call first," said Jason.

Jenny stepped through the doorway and kissed him, then led him inside by his tie.

8pm.

Ted followed his GPS around Lake Washington Boulevard until he found the condominium he was looking for. Marias was settled in with a number of other toney units. He parked on the curb in front, then adjusted his tie in the mirror and smoothed his hair. Ted started to get out, then ducked back and opened the glove box. He found a nearly empty container of Tic Tacs and popped the last one in his mouth. Then he took a deep breath and walked up to the front door. While she had referred to it as a condo, he realized it was really a townhouse. Ted rang the doorbell and waited a moment. The place was dark and he realized it had an empty feel to it. He checked his phone, but there were no messages. He shrugged and started back to his car when he saw headlights turn into the lot off the street. He recognized the Volkswagen Atlas as it pulled into the driveway and the garage door started to come up. When she saw him on the sidewalk, Maria smiled and waved before pulling into the garage.

Maria stepped out of the car and said, "come give me a hand."

Ted stepped up and realized she had three to go boxes in the back seat of her car. He picked them up as Maria grabbed her purse and a bottle of wine, before following her inside. Maria hit a switch on the wall and the garage door wound down. He followed her through a door into a small foyer that led to a set of stairs. They went up to the first floor, which contained a kitchen and a living/dining area.

"I apologize. I moved in three months ago and I just haven't had time to go furniture shopping," Maria said.

Ted looked around the living room. There was a couch against one wall with some artwork behind it. The couch faced a large television and a coffee table. The dining room was devoid of tables and chairs, but the

141

kitchen had a breakfast counter and three barstools. Ted set the food there and said, "it's really nice. You've got a great view."

She did, as he could see across Lake Washington with a view of Magnuson Park in Seattle.

"Thanks," she said, "after I split from my ex, I lived with my parents in Bellevue until I could afford my own place."

She had been wearing a black raincoat, but she took it off and hung it in a closet. She had on a black wool skirt with a red silk top and a jacket that matched the skirt. Ted shed his trench coat and helped Maria set up two places on the counter.

"Can you open the wine, please?" Something about the way she said it that made Ted think he'd do anything she asked.

"Sure," he said, "do you have a cork screw?"

"Oh no. I didn't think of that."

"No problem," said Ted, "just bear with me."

He reached down and took off one shoe. Maria looked at him, not understanding. Ted looked around the room, then limped to the doorway from the stairs. He rapped it with his knuckles and nodded to himself. Ted put the bottom of the bottle in the heel of his shoe, then using both hands swung them together into the doorframe. The cork came out about an inch, so Ted swung it again. About an inch and a half of the cork was sticking out of the neck. Ted dropped his shoe on the floor and slipped his foot back into it, then grasped the cork and twisted it out of the bottle. When it came free, he held it up proudly.

"If nothing else, you can at least drink," he said.

"Genius," Maria said, "I don't think I've ever seen anyone do that before."

Ted shrugged, and Maria got out two glasses. Ted poured one for her, then asked, "do you have like a coke or something?"

"Oh god, you don't drink!"

"Just not alcohol. Actually, water's fine."

"Just a second," Maria said, opening her refrigerator. "How about orange juice?"

"Excellent. And no, it won't bother me."

Maria raised an eyebrow at him.

"If you have a glass of wine."

She smiled, and poured a measure of orange juice into his glass.

"I hope you're not a vegetarian as well," she said, "I got us a couple of Cuban sandwiches from the Beachcomber."

"That is one thing I am not," Ted grinned.

She placed a large sandwich on each plate, then opened another container and scooped salad for each of them.

Ted sat against the wall. Maria shed her jacket and hung it over the back of her barstool. Ted took a bite of his sandwich, swallowed and said, "can I ask you something?"

Maria had taken a bite, but Ted wasn't sure from where. She swallowed and said, "sure."

"I'd like to talk with you about something, but how can I be sure it won't end up on the news?"

Maria nodded. "I suppose I should be offended, but I know you guys tend to think of us as the enemy. We're not."

Ted agreed, "Remember I worked in media relations for a long time. But I need to know…"

Maria took another micro bite and said, "I don't know how I can convince you. There is a recorder in my purse, but it's off. You could search me to make sure I'm not wearing a wire." As she said it she held her arms out to her side.

Ted blushed, and managed to stammer, "I don't think that's necessary."

Maria relaxed and said, "Ted here's the thing. I promise you that I won't use anything you say on the news. I reserve the right to think of it as background but I won't use it. If I do, I'll ask you about it first."

"I know guys that have spoken off the record to reporters and have gotten burned."

"Ted, all I can say is you can trust me. If you don't then don't tell me."

Ted took a sip of orange juice, then asked, "Have you ever heard of someone leaking information from the homicide unit?"

Maria laughed, "Of course! It happens all the time."

Ted looked shocked. "What do you mean?"

"Your captain can be a bit of a martinet at times. He'll hold a press conference and if it suits his purpose he'll hold back information. Then mysteriously someone will drop a dime to a reporter."

"Why does he do that?"

"My theory is that it's something he wants in the press for some reason, but if he releases it in a press conference it could get lost in all the other information. So he gets someone to release it, usually one of the secondary detectives. That way the reporter thinks he has a scoop and works harder to get it on the air."

Ted was impressed. "How did you come to this conclusion?"

"It's not hard. I noticed a pattern and when I thought about it, the information that was presented didn't hurt the case and often resulted in information coming back to the detectives."

"OK. Here's the thing. We think someone in the unit is feeding information to a couple of homicide suspects. Have you heard anything like that?"

143

Maria propped her elbow on the counter and leaned her head on her hand. She looked at him sideways and said, "dammit. No, and I promised you I wouldn't use anything."

Ted nodded, "you can see why I asked."

Ted had finished eating. Maria left most of her sandwich on the counter. They took their glasses and moved to the sofa. Ted followed her and she turned and said, "take your coat off and be comfortable."

Ted draped his jacket over the back of his barstool, then sat on the end of the couch. Maria sat in the middle, after kicking off her shoes and tucked her legs under her.

She gestured towards Teds hip, and said, "Have you ever shot anyone with that thing?"

"No," he said, "I've been lucky."

"I thought you guys were in shootouts like every day."

"That's what you see in the movies, but it's not like that. On average an officer fires his gun in the line of duty once every nine years. Some units, like SWAT or canine might have a higher rate, but other units, like detectives and admin types, not so much."

"Really? How about your handcuffs?"

Ted laughed, "I didn't even wear them when I was in media. But policy does require it for on duty officers. When I got drafted to Homicide I had to dig them out. Honestly, I haven't used them in four or five years."

"But you did?"

"I was in auto theft at the time. My last day in the unit, we did a stake out on a stolen car. We took down two that day. We found them sleeping in the car."

Maria nodded.

"What about you," Ted asked, "what's your story?"

"Well, lets see. I studied broadcast journalism at the U Dub, where I met my ex. I graduated and got a job in Spokane. My husband followed me out there, but he was bored. He did IT work, so he had plenty to do, but he also had a lot of free time and a problem keeping his pants on."

"I'm sorry."

"It's not your fault. Anyway, I got offered a job in Portland, so I went there for a year while the divorce was finalized. Then I came up here."

"You ever thought about going national?"

"You've got to get noticed. I know I'm good enough, which is why I grabbed onto this interview with Marianne. A chance like that doesn't come along every day."

Ted nodded as she continued, "I'm hoping I get noticed and the network picks me up, but the timing has to be perfect even then."

Ted enjoyed listening to her talk. Then she asked, "what did they think of the interview?"

"I don't think they've seen it yet. This thing broke this afternoon, and we had the meeting at his house. I doubt they had time."

"Too bad, maybe they'll see it at eleven."

They chatted a little longer. Ted realized that somehow Maria had edged closer to him. He checked his watch and saw that it was after eleven.

"Wow, I had no idea it was getting this late," he said.

"Do you have to go?"

Ted was reluctant but said, "I do have to get up early. Theres' an operation in Montana that could affect us."

Maria leaned in and put a hand on Teds chest.

"Are you in a rush?"

Teds voice was thick.

"No."

She leaned in and they kissed.

1128pm

Jim and Marianne were sitting up in bed, having just watched themselves being interviewed on television. Or, as Jim had pointed out, Marianne being interviewed with Jim more of an afterthought. Which was fine with Jim.

"I could have sworn she talked to you more than that," said Marianne.

"She did. But I imagine they had to edit it for the three minutes it was on TV."

"Still, it doesn't seem fair."

"I'm okay with you getting the spotlight."

Marianne smiled and kissed him lightly on the mouth.

"Honey," Marianne said, "you know I love you, right?"

"Yeah honey, I do."

"Then I have to tell you. You need to see someone."

"Honey, what are you talking about?"

"Rosa and I keep finding guns in every room of the house. She found one in the bar this morning when she was cleaning. There's one in your office desk. I found one in the gym downstairs. Hell, I found your forty five in the nightstand."

"Why were you looking?"

"Because I keep finding them. Honey I get that you're paranoid by nature. But you've never kept guns in every room of the house before."

Jim was quiet, so Marianne went on.

"I don't mind it so much. Even Rosa is matter of fact about it. But when Jane has her baby, I'm hoping to babysit for her and we can't have guns where little hands can find them."

145

Jim nodded. He was quiet for a minute, then said, "You're right, I can't leave them laying around like that. I'll put them away in the morning."

"Well, maybe not the one in the nightstand for now," Marianne said, "but the others, yes. And what the hell were you doing in the gym anyway?"

"One armed curls and leg lifts. It's about all I can do without Sheridan yelling at me. Nothing more than five pounds, right?"

Chapter 18

Thursday
5am, local time.

Gretchen had decided that now was the time to cut this tie. She had grown sick of his complaining as they drove away from Seattle. It had been non stop until they got here. Tom was in the living room watching television. Gretchen dabbed some Chanel between her breasts as she undid the two top buttons of the shirt she was wearing. She slid her jeans off but kept her underwear on. She stepped to the doorway of the bedroom and leaned against the frame.

Tom sat in an overstuffed chair, a glum look on his face. Gretchen thought maybe he was just tired from the long drive. As she leaned against the door frame she called his name. When Tom looked up, Gretchen ran a finger down between her breasts.

"Why don't you come over here, baby," she cooed at him.

She hated that she had to talk to him like a child. Soon she wouldn't have to deal with that again.

Tom looked up. She thought he seemed to come to some sort of conclusion. Tom smiled, and stood. Gretchen smiled and turned to go into the bedroom. She was almost to the bed, when he came into the room. Gretchen turned.

"How do you want it sugar," Gretchen asked, smiling.

"Like this," Tom said as he stepped closer.

Gretchen didn't see the fist until it was too late. She didn't feel any pain, just a flash of light and then darkness. She was conscious of being lifted off the rug and then flung onto the bed. Her blouse was torn open and buttons clattered across the wooden floor. Gretchen tried to move, but her body didn't respond. She felt something cold and metallic against the skin on her hip, then the material of her panties parted and they were gone. Gretchen tried to speak but words weren't coming. She tried to lift her arms but they barely moved. Then he was on top of her and she couldn't

147

breath. Air simply wasn't coming and it was a moment before Gretchen realized that Tom's hands were around her throat. Just as she was about to pass out again, Tom finished. He lay on top of her for a moment longer. Then he got to his knees and slapped her across the face, hard. It seemed to clear her mind and she was able to open her eyes. Her wrists were lashed together with plastic ties and he held his knife at her throat. A syringe in his other hand.

"Don't think I don't know what you were going to do, bitch."

Gretchen shook her head emphatically. She was petrified.

"You were going to kill me with this, weren't you?"

She shook her head again.

"Don't fuckin' lie to me, bitch," he said calmly, before placing the tip of the knife blade in the hollow of her throat.

Gretchen didn't dare move.

"I'll ask again, were you planning to kill me?"

She thought over her options, and then carefully nodded in the affirmative.

Tom took the knife away.

"What the fuck am I going to do with you now?"

"Why is this happening? I'd never hurt you," Gretchen croaked.

"All right. I need to finish this thing. The way I figure it, is I got three choices. I can leave you here for the locals to find. You'll probably bat your eyes and shake your ass and they'll buy whatever you sell them. I could kill you right now." To emphasize his point he placed the point of the knife against her throat again, and held it there. "Or, I can take you back as my play toy. Which means I've got to watch you like a fucking hawk."

He pushed a little on the point and she was afraid he was going to cut her. Then he backed off.

"What the fuck are you trying to say?"

"I would never hurt you."

"Really? I find that hard to believe. You had a syringe loaded and ready to go."

"I've had that all along. It was for if we got caught and there was no way out. I was going to take that instead of going to jail. Can you imagine me in jail, I'd be fresh meat in there."

"You would at that. But I think you're lying to me again." This time he held the knife over her naked breast. "Maybe if I think you're lying to me I should cut off a nipple."

"Nooo," she wailed, "I'm not lying! Please don't cut me.."

Something inside her broke. She cried for a minute as he held the knife against her breast.

"I'll do anything you want," she said finally, "I promise."

"Anything?"

"Yes. Whatever you want."

Tom pulled the knife back and tossed it in the air, reversing the grip. Then he plunged it into the pillow next to her head.

"You better fuckin' believe it."

Richard "Dick" Moss was the Chief of Detectives for the Flathead County Sheriffs department. He had been tasked by the sheriff himself to assist Tacoma PD in locating and arresting two murder suspects that were supposed to be holed up in a cabin by the Flathead river. They went out Montana 35 and turned off on a dirt road just west of the river. He had ten deputies and detectives following in four Explorers. As they approached the river he called a halt about a mile short of the cabin. Two deputies stayed with the cars while the other eight put on tactical vests and Kevlar helmets. Of the eight, four were armed with rifles and two were armed with shotguns. The other two carried tasers. They split into two teams, two rifles, one shotgun and one taser apiece. After checking their radios, they moved out on foot, one team in front of the other. Dick was a little concerned about radio transmissions but he made sure that each team had a cellular phone as a backup.

Dick waited patiently in his makeshift command post. They moved slowly and Dick listened to what little chatter there was. He listened impatiently for almost thirty minutes before the two teams had set up a perimeter around the cabin. One of the teams said there was a black Buick in the car port. They held their positions while Dick made a phone call to the judge.

"The car is there," he said.

"I'm adding that in the affidavit," he said, "I'll fax it over right away but it's legal to execute anytime."

Dick hung up and got on the radio. "The warrant's signed, move in."

The team in the lead moved up to the front door. One of the riflemen slung his rifle and helped the taser officer with a battering ram, affectionately known as 'the door key,' to force open the front door. As soon as it was open, the team went in. The cabin was relatively small and they cleared each room carefully. There was no basement, but there was a loft. They had to access it by a narrow set of stairs. Two deputies climbed the stairs until they were just below the edge of the loft. One of the rifle deputies was doing his best to cover the entrance but there was only so much he could do from down below. They had debated on calling in the other team, but they did not feel it would do any good.

The fourth team member took a flash bang grenade off his tactical vest. He pulled the pin, while holding the spoon down. He looked at the rest of his team and got a nod from the number two deputy on the stairs. He took a deep breath, then took two steps out into the living room, turned and threw the grenade over the edge of the loft. He heard it crash into something before he stepped back under the loft as the flash bang went off with a loud thump and a brilliant flash of light. The two deputies on the stairs scrambled up, rifles at the ready, as they crossed over the threshold.

"Clear," called out one deputy.

"Clear," called out the other.

"Comin' down," he said as he slid back down the stairs.

"Chief, the house is clear," said the team leader into his radio, "but we broke a chandelier."

"Well shit," Dick said, "that's coming out of somebodies pocket."

Danny was in his office when he got the call. After Dick explained what had happened, Danny asked, "were you able to verify the car?"

"By the vehicle identification number. It was registered to Fred Henderson in Federal Way, Washington."

"Is there any way for you to check if he had a car registered in Montana?"

"That requires a hand search in Helena. Not impossible but it could take a while."

"Who would I talk to over there?"

"Hell, I'll ask. It's an ongoing investigation, right? So no worries. By the way, who's gonna pay for the chandelier?"

"Send the bill to Seattle Homicide, care of Captain Churchill."

He left her tied to the bed while he went out. He walked the two blocks to McDonalds just off highway 26 and bought two big meals. It had been a mad dash into Kalispell, switching vehicles and then down to his grandparents place in Riverton Wyoming. They'd been on the road most of the last couple days, and this morning had been a huge release for him. He had to admit he liked this truck, a Ford F-150 with a crew cab. On the way back, he was a block from the house when he saw another Ford F-150 in a neighbors driveway. It didn't have a crew cab, but he didn't think that would matter.

He took the Leatherman tool off his waist, and looked around carefully. The house was dark and the street was deserted. He eased around the far side of the truck to the front, and squatted in the gap between the garage door and the bumper. It only took a moment to unscrew the Wyoming plate from the bumper and to drop the plate and the bolts into the McDonalds bag. Then he slid around to the back of the truck and got the rear plate off in a matter of moments, dropping it with the other one into his McDonalds bag. Tom walked quickly out to the street, but strolled slowly to the far end, making sure he wasn't being followed. At the back of their house was the neighbor of the house he had stolen the plates from.

Tom walked into their house and pulled the plates out of the bag, setting them by the door to the garage. The house was tiny, just one floor with two bedrooms. He went back to the master where Gretchen was still tied to the bed.

He cut the ties on her wrists and snarled, "get up. You got ten minutes."

Gretchen didn't say anything. Her head was still swimming as she rubbed her wrists for a minute, then slowly stood before walking unsteadily towards the bathroom. As she started to pass Tom, he grabbed her by the throat and pushed her into the wall.

"If you even think of doing something stupid, I will fuck you up." His tone was conversational.

Gretchen struggled to breathe until Tom let up on his grip. He let her go and she went into the bathroom and turned on the shower. She turned and saw that he was watching her from the doorway. She looked away and stepped under the water. When she looked next, he was gone.

Gretchen stepped out of the shower, leaving the water on, and quickly dried off. She didn't bother to dress and didn't touch her hair. He wasn't in the bedroom. She tiptoed to her bag. The Lidocaine was missing. She was afraid of that. She remembered seeing a pair of marble wedge bookends in the living room. She slipped down the hall, still naked, and found them, covered in dust on the book shelves. Gretchen hefted one in her hand. The only place he could be now was the garage. She went to the door, and saw him wedged in the space in front of the truck, his back to her, screwing something onto the front. She puzzled it out for a moment, before she realized he was putting on new plates. Her bare feet were silent on the concrete of the garage as she eased up behind him. Tom tightened the last bolt and straightened up, still on his knees. Gretchen brought the bookend down hard on the back of Tom's head. He pitched forward, hitting his forehead on the bumper. She stepped between his legs, and could still hear him moaning. Gretchen hit him again, then again, and again. She lost count of the number of times she'd struck Tom, only stopping when her arms got tired. She leaned back, gasping, her body covered in blood and brains. The bumper of the truck was bloody too. Furious, she spit on him for good measure.

Gretchen turned and went back into the house. The shower was running cold now, but she climbed in and cleaned as much as she could. When she stepped out of the shower, her skin was blue and she was shivering. She found the McDonalds big meals where Tom had left them and warmed one up in the microwave. She ate it more for the warmth than the nourishment, while wrapped in a large towel.

Tom had told her it had been his grandparents house until they died, but that his parents still paid the utilities on it, although they were almost never there. She waited a solid thirty minutes, then tried the shower again. The hot water tank had done it's job and after showering again and scrubbing her hair out, she returned to the bedroom where she brushed out her hair and put on her makeup, finally dressing in a mid thigh woolen dress and tall leather boots. Gretchen propped a mirror on the dresser and checked the bruising along her jaw. Touching it sent a wave of pain through her head. Gritting her teeth she used her foundation makeup to cover the bruise that was starting to form. Gretchen packed her bags, then went through Toms until she found the guns. There were three .22's. The small guns were Walther brand, inexpensive but they had proven to be functional. She loaded one and stashed it in her purse, dropping the rest in her luggage.

When she was dressed, she went out to the garage and opened the door. She thought for a minute, then checked the rear bumper. A Wyoming plate that matched the one on the front, adorned the chrome bumper. In the bed of the truck was a five gallon can of gas strapped to the wall. She took it out and set it by Tom's body before backing the truck out. She shut off the truck and went back into the garage, hitting the switch to close the door.

Gretchen walked through the house, making certain that any trace of her presence was gone. She wiped down doorknobs and light switches. She picked up the various items that Tom had used on her. Everything went into a garbage bag that she dropped into the bed of the truck. Once that was done, she went back out to the garage. She used about two gallons of gas on Tom's body, then ran a trail of gas out to the front door. The fumes were starting to make her eyes water, but she carefully placed the can next to the front door, and stepped outside. When she was certain no one was around, she dug in her purse for a matchbook. Gretchen reached in and pulled the gas can out onto the porch. Then she struck a match and dropped it on the gas trail, making certain that the flame caught before jogging off the porch, her head hurting with every step.

Gretchen tossed the gas can into the back of the truck, jumped into the cab and started it up, before backing out of the driveway. As she put it into drive she saw smoke curling from under the garage door. She found highway 26 and drove north about two miles before she found a car wash. She pulled into one of the bays and dropped some coins into the machine. Then she used the hose to clean off the front of the truck. She made sure that every drop of blood and tissue was gone before she hung up the hose. The humidity didn't do her hair any good, but she could fix that later. The garbage bag she dropped into a trash can by the vacuums.

She drove back through town. When she got to Pershing she looked down the street and could see a police car blocking the intersection at 10th, where the house had been. Gretchen felt no emotion, she simply followed 26 out of town as it rambled west past the airport. She wasn't sure where she would go, she just started heading west as much as she could.

Chapter 19

Thursday
8am

Ted woke up to the sound of his phoning ringing, from a long way away. He looked around and saw Maria, sitting at a makeup table, wearing a kimono style robe and applying makeup.

"Good morning sleepyhead," she said.

"I think I overslept," he said.

"Well, we were up late. Your phone keeps ringing downstairs."

Just then Maria's doorbell rang. Maria picked up her phone and punched in an app.

Then she spoke into the phone, "Hi Marianne, just a minute."

She stood, stepped into a pair of slippers, and said, "I'll be right back. Wouldn't pay to leave Marianne Wilson waiting."

When she left, Ted said, "Shit." He rolled out of bed and stepped into his pants, tugged on his shirt and went into the bathroom to use the mirror to comb his hair. When he came out, Jason King was standing in the doorway.

"I know, I'm late. Am I fired?"

"Shut up," said Jason, "and listen. You and I have been talking on the phone all morning. You were going to pick me up but you had a flat."

"Um, ok."

"I was using Jim's computer this morning, and Googled Tom Meeker. Anyway, he was quite the athlete in Riverton Wyoming."

"He's from Wyoming?"

"Very good, first try. I've been talking to Lloyd, and he's going to call out there as soon as we get into the office to compare notes. I'm betting he was a little hooligan and the local police there will be more than happy to help out."

"OK. I'm sorry…"

Jason cut him off, "Never apologize. No one is gonna believe it anyway, we all knew you had a date last night. Looks like it went pretty well."

Ted nodded, "Better than I expected."

"You got lucky," Jason said, "Flathead county hit Freds cabin by the Flathead river. It was empty but her car was still there."

"How does that make us lucky? Now we don't know what they're driving and we don't know where they are."

"I didn't say we. I said you. But you're right. Danny's working on whether or not there was another car at the cabin."

Downstairs Maria and Marianne were chatting over coffee.

"Are you two going to see each other again," Marianne asked.

Maria smiled, "I hope so."

Jason and Ted came downstairs and into the living room.

"Marianne, Ted is giving me a ride to work, can you make it back by yourself?"

"I'm sure I can find the way, Jason. I'm glad everything is okay." She sipped her coffee and said, "Go without the tie, Ted."

Ted nodded and folded his tie into an inside pocket as they headed downstairs.

"How do you feel about him," Marianne asked.

"He's more complicated than I thought. He knows how to open a wine bottle without a corkscrew but he doesn't drink," Maria said.

"Did you talk about work?"

"Some," Maria replied, "but he swore me to secrecy and I intend to honor my promise."

"Good. Do you remember where the house is?"

"I'm not blind. I could find it in the dark, blindfolded." When she realized what she had said her face turned red beneath her makeup. Marianne pretended not to notice.

"Lunch is at twelve. You're invited if you'd care to join us."

"I'd love that. I'll see you then."

Marianne set her cup in the sink and said goodbye before heading out to Jim's Subaru.

Gretchen turned south on highway 191 at Moran and drove into Jackson. She stopped for gas and breakfast and then headed out highway 22 towards Wilson. She stopped again for gas, then kept going, not stopping until she was in Idaho. She didn't think much about where she was going, she just wanted to keep moving.

10AM

Lloyd got off the phone with the Riverton Police department.

"They said a detective is going to call us back. Something's up though."

"Why do you say that," asked Ted.

"Lover boy speaks. I don't know, something in the tone of voice I guess. They seemed overly interested in what I had to say."

"Lover boy? Hey, I had a flat."

"That doesn't explain why you're wearing the same suit you had on last night."

She found herself in a town called Idaho Falls. Looking at her smart phone she found a few cheap motels, and picked one at random. Money wasn't a problem yet, but she'd better start thinking about it. Gretchen paid cash for two nights and signed the register, "Ann Arbor." The room was on the ground floor, so she parked the truck in front and went inside.

The room was spartan, but it had a bed, a shower and a microwave. There was a coffee maker and motel room coffee. The lobby offered a continental breakfast. She flipped on the television and scrolled through the menu until she found a news station. They were far enough away so that the fire in Riverton wouldn't be the lead story, but it would be in the top half of the hour. When it came on they didn't really say much. They knew the fire had been set, and they'd found a body but he hadn't been identified yet. The fire was mostly in the front of the house and the garage, which had really gone up, and the reporter referred to investigators locating a quantity of narcotics, but he didn't go into detail. Gretchen knew it had to have been her stash of Lidocaine. She shrugged. He must have hid it in the garage because she'd looked everywhere else.

Then a reporter for a Seattle news station came on. After she was introduced, she said, "Marianne Wilson disappeared from the public eye last Friday night, after her concert in Charlotte North Carolina. She hasn't been seen by the public since then until now. She reached out to me and allowed us into the home she shares with her fiancé, Captain Jim Churchill of the SPD. Marianne, why did you suddenly disappear after your concert?"

Gretchen sat bolt upright and suddenly started paying attention.

"Hi Maria. After the concert was over two very nice gentlemen from the Charlotte police department approached me and asked me to call one of our very good friends here at home. I knew right away it was going to be bad, and I am so thankful the news wasn't worse."

"They told you Jim had been injured, right?"

"They told me he was in surgery. I knew there was no way I was going to be able to play Roanoke. Jim and I have always believed that family comes first."

"What was that like, hearing that someone you love was in trouble?"

Gretchen was looking at Jim. The reporter asked him maybe two questions during the three minute segment. She thought about what she had just learned. The confirmed bachelor, Jim Churchill, was engaged to be married to none other than Marianne Wilson. She smiled at the thought. Then she reached for her phone.

11 am

Lloyd's cell phone rang. He looked at the number and saw it was from Wyoming.

He pushed the button and said, "Detective Murray."

"Chief Denzel, Riverton police department. I heard you called about Tom Meeker this morning."

"I did. We understand he has roots in Riverton."

"Well he did. What do you want him for?"

"He's the primary suspect in at least one murder, possibly two others, and he is a 'person of interest' in an attempted murder for hire."

"He hasn't changed much. Well, getting an interview with him is gonna be kind of tough."

"Why is that? Do you have him in custody?"

"Sort of. There was a fire in his grandparents house this morning. I've been out at the scene all day. Fire went in to put it out, and found a body in the garage."

"Is it Meeker?" This would be bad luck.

"It's hard to tell. Basically the body was the seat of the fire. But we found some paperwork in the bedroom that makes us think it was him."

"Do you know how he died?"

"You know how coroners are. He won't say for sure, but he thinks it could have been blunt force trauma to the head."

"Chief, I looked online. You're out in the middle of nowhere. Please don't take offense, but are you guys equipped to handle this?"

"No offense taken. I've got twenty eight officers and there's other calls besides this one. The State Police are taking over. What can you tell me about this guy?"

"We believe he was traveling with a woman named Gretchen Henderson. Any sign of her?" Lloyd described her as best he could over the phone.

"No, although it looks like someone cleaned up the place before pulling out."

"What about fingerprints or DNA?"

"What burned was mostly in the living room and garage. The other parts of the house are intact with maybe some smoke damage. I'll talk to the troopers when they get here, they might be able to turn something up."

"I might come out there. I've got to get my boss to approve it first and she's been penny pinching lately."

"You got my number. Let me know."

Lloyd hung up and went to Lieutenant Naes office. He rapped on the door as she looked up from her computer.

"I just got off the phone with Riverton Wyoming. They went to a fire there this morning on property owned by the Meeker family. When they broke in they found a body had been torched in the garage."

"Is it your suspect?"

"Burned beyond recognition but sounds like it. I'd like to get out there."

"We can't be sure it's him."

"No, but I'd say there's an eighty per cent probability it's him. I wouldn't ask if I didn't think it was important."

"When would you leave?"

"There's a flight out of Sea-Tac to Denver. I'd have to switch planes there, but I could be there by tonight."

"What would Jim say?"

"Why don't you ask him?" Lloyd was irritated.

She reached for her phone, then stopped.

"How many people have they killed?"

"At least four, maybe five by now. Lieutenant..." Rebekah waved a hand.

"Go. Call when you get there."

"Will do," Lloyd said and left the room before she could change her mind.

Noon

Jim was sitting in the recliner on Mariannes orders, with his feet up. Rosa and Marianne were in the kitchen putting together lunch. Sheridan and Jane were sitting in the living room, Jane taking up most of the couch. Maria was sitting in another recliner and Sheridan was sitting on the arm of the couch. Maria and Jane were talking about the pregnancy. Sheridan was telling Jim about the excitement of impending fatherhood. While Jim was thinking he and Marianne would have a family someday, he was hoping for a distraction. When it came it was not quite what he expected.

Jim looked at the phone and saw the call was from a blocked number. He shrugged and answered it.

"Hi Jim." The voice was low and breathy and sounded like sex.

"Gretchen? I would have thought you'd call sooner." Jim made eye contact with Sheridan and motioned towards the kitchen. Sheridan got an arm under Jim's shoulder and got him to his feet.

"What are you doing?" He heard promises that couldn't be kept.

"We're about to eat lunch," said Jim as he stepped into the kitchen. When he sat at the breakfast bar he rapped his knuckles on the counter to get Marianne's attention. She turned with a look of annoyance on her face, then a question.

Sheridan said, "He's on the phone with someone named Gretchen and he wanted you."

Marianne came around the bar and took Jims other phone out of his hip pocket.

"That's a shame," Gretchen said to Jim, "I was hoping to have some time to chat with you."

"I've got time," said Jim as he scrolled through the contacts on his personal phone until he got to Ruben Pemberton. He slid that phone to Marianne and she hit send.

"I hear you're engaged now."

"You must have seen the interview. Does that mean you're still in town?"

"You aren't going to get me that easy, Jimmy."

"I had to try."

"Oh I know. You know, you and I could get together. One last fling before you're tied to the ol' ball and chain."

"You already tried to kill me once."

"You know that wasn't my idea, right? Tom knew how I felt about you and he wanted to get rid of the competition."

"But you went along with it, right?"

"I just thought he was going to have them scare you. You know, like beat you up or something. I had no idea what was going to happen."

"How does Tom feel about you calling me?"

"Oh don't worry about Tom."

Jim was quiet for a minute, long enough for Marianne to mouth, "Is she gone?"

Jim shook his head and said, "What happened to Tom."

Gretchen had thought about how to answer this question and had chosen a moment of silence, then worked a sob into her voice.

"He raped me, Jim. He abused me and raped me and I had nowhere to turn."

"Where are you? I'll send someone."

"I can't Jim. No one will believe me."

"Gretchen, you can use this. If you come in, I'll talk to the prosecutor."

"Can I turn myself in to you?"

"I'm out for another couple of weeks, but Lloyd would take good care of you."

"I only want you, Jim. I'll wait until you're healthy, then I'll let you take me."

Jim caught the innuendo.

"Gretchen, I don't know about that. We need to know you're safe."

"No one but you, Jim. I want you to handcuff me and search me."

"Gretchen, come in. Come to headquarters, I know you know how to get there. Tell the desk officer you're there to see Detective Murray. I'll make sure he's there."

"Sorry Jim, I'll only come in for you. And not at headquarters."

"OK, tell me where and when."

"I'll call you, Jim. I'll let you know."

"Gretchen, we can work this out." No answer. "Gretchen?" Still nothing. Jim looked at his phone and saw they had been disconnected. Marianne held out the other phone. Jim dropped his work phone and took the one from Marianne.

"Ruben, did you get it?"

"It wasn't her phone Jim, at least not the one she owns."

"What can you tell me?" Jim knew it had been too much to hope for.

"It's a prepaid phone. She probably picked it up in Idaho. At least that's what the prefix shows. Anyway, it hit off a cell tower in Idaho Falls. The closest I can get you is somewhere near the airport. Idaho Falls Regional Airport."

"So she could be on her way to anywhere by now."

"It's a regional airport, hold on." Jim could hear computer keys clicking on a keyboard. "Looks like the second busiest airport in Idaho."

"So where does it serve?"

There were a few more clicks of the computer. "You could catch a connecting flight to Denver, and from there anywhere. You could fly to a lot of other regional airports, and go to some other hubs."

"Thanks Ruben. You've been a big help." Jim closed his phone.

Marianne and Sheridan were looking at him with concern.

"I'm pretty sure she killed Tom Meeker," Jim said.

"How so," Sheridan asked.

"She referred to him in the past tense, and when I asked how he felt about her calling me, she said I didn't have to worry about him." Jim picked up his work phone again and said, "I better call Lloyd."

Jim called Lloyd, but got no answer. He left a voice mail, then decided to call Rebekah Naes.

"Hello Jim, I hope you're enjoying your vacation."

"Very funny. I'm calling because I just got a phone call from Gretchen Henderson."

Rosa signaled that lunch was ready. Jim waved her on.

"How long ago?"

"Maybe five minutes. I called Ruben while I was on the phone with her. He puts her somewhere near the airport in Idaho Falls."

"I'll call the PD out there and I'll send Lloyd an email. He's on his way to Riverton Wyoming. Seems the Meeker family homestead burned and there's a body inside."

"I bet that's Tom. Gretchen implied she'd killed him after Tom had raped her."

Jim checked his watch. "When is his flight?"

"He should be in the air soon. There's no direct flight so he has to make a connection someplace."

"OK. Can you send a bulletin to Idaho Springs? I think she's a safety hazard and I don't trust she's going to ever come in peacefully."

"Consider it done. We are going to have to go nationwide with this. She could literally be anywhere."

4pm local time

Lloyd deplaned in Idaho Springs. He had found out at the airport that no one flew directly to Riverton and this was as close as he was going to get for now. He immediately went to the ticket counter and learned there were no more flights to Riverton for the day.

"How long to get there by car?"

"If you left right away, you could be there by ten tonight." The girl at the counter was young and pretty, and reminded Lloyd of his wife at that age. She gave him directions to the car rentals, and he found one that could rent him a car without a reservation.

"How big a car do you need?" The agent was a burly black man.

"Maybe a midsize. Something that gets decent mileage."

Lloyd rented a Chevy Malibu with GPS. He got in the car and plugged in his phone, allowing it to start up. It started flashing at him right away, so before he pulled out of the lot he checked his voice mail. Jim Churchill had left a message that Gretchen had called him and he thought she had killed Tom Meeker. Lloyd silently agreed, and considered calling Jim back, but decided he might as well get started. No matter what, he would still need to get to Riverton.

Lloyd pulled out of the parking lot with the GPS directing him to the highway, Marianne Wilson singing from his playlist on the cars speakers. He'd gone just a few blocks when he spotted a Starbucks.

"Jeez, they're everywhere," he said to no one in particular.

Lloyd pulled into the parking lot, and went inside. He purchased a large metal thermos and a travel mug and asked the barista to fill them with coffee. He picked up a panini sandwich and a cheese danish for the road. He went back to his car and got in. Out of the corner of his eye he noticed a large black pickup, maybe the third one he'd seen since he'd left the airport. Lloyd unwrapped the sandwich and took a sip of his coffee before carefully pulling out and heading for the highway. He eventually found the Swan Valley highway and headed towards the Snake river.

Gretchen had just parked in the lot when she saw the Malibu pull in. She glanced at the driver and immediately recognized him and simply laid down in the front seat. She tugged her purse from under her torso and found the grip of the little .22. She managed to get down onto the floor and backed up to the passenger door. After a few minutes, she peeked over the dash and spotted the Malibu, empty, almost directly across from her. She ducked down, feeling her heart pounding in her chest. She weighed her options. She knew what she looked like, and she had an idea that they didn't know about Tacoma yet. Maybe if she surrendered she could get a jury of men. For sure she could get an acquittal then. A few more minutes went by, and she chanced another peek. She saw Lloyd getting into his car again, and ducked back down. She felt a little more confident. Lloyd didn't seem to recognize the truck and he hadn't seen her. While she sat, she pulled the sleeves of her dress up and massaged the welts on her wrists. The dress had a high neck, which effectively hid the handprint on her throat. Makeup effectively covered the bruise on her jaw. In a week or so she would be almost as good as new.

When Gretchen peeked again, the car was gone. She tugged her sleeves back into place, then sat up. A half dozen cars were in the lot. Gretchen slid the pistol back into her purse, got out of the truck and went inside. She ordered a latte and bought a salad. When the coffee was made she went back to the truck and drove to the hotel.

When she'd spoke to Jim, she remembered he had said something about how Tom's assault could help her. She went into her room and casually removed her boots and stripped to her underwear. Fred had spoken once about using the camera to document injuries, so she used her phone to take selfies, then closeups of her neck in the mirror and the bruising on her wrists and ankles. She considered sending them to Jim, then decided against it. She'd used a burner phone when she'd called, but she wasn't sure if she took her own phone off airplane mode if they'd be able to track her.

Gretchen ate her food, then dressed again, this time in jeans and a sweater. She packed her bags and carried them to the truck, dropping them in the backseat. She had another night, but she didn't think she had that much time.

Gretchen got into the truck and drove towards I-84, headed for Oregon.

6pm

It was a little before the hour when Lloyd pulled into Jackson. As he passed the city limits his cell phone rang. Lloyd picked up the phone and saw it was Danny White from Tacoma.

"Hey Danny, how's things?"

"Not bad. I have the results of that hand search."

"Hang on." Lloyd found a spot on the shoulder and pulled out his notebook. "OK, go ahead."

"There's a new Ford F-150 crew cab registered to a Fred Henderson at the cabin in Kalispell." Danny recited the plate and gave the vehicle identification number for good measure.

"Thanks Danny. I'm currently on my way to Riverton. We think one of our suspects may have bought the farm there."

"Too bad for him."

"Couldn't happen to a nicer guy if it's true."

They exchanged pleasantries and Lloyd rang off, then called Lieutenant Naes.

"Hey Lloyd, we've been trying to get hold of you."

"It's like a massive dead zone over here for cell phones. Hey, Gretchen might be in a truck now." He passed the description to lieutenant Naes.

"Thanks. Are you anywhere near Idaho Springs?"

"The plane dropped me there about two hours ago. I'm in a car driving to Riverton. Why?"

"Jim got a call from Gretchen. TESU pinged the phone and it's somewhere near the airport in Idaho Springs."

"Damn. What did she say to Jim?"

"Jason debriefed him. Basically Jim said she referred to Tom in the past sense, and claimed she left him after he attacked Gretchen. Also, she says she'll turn herself in only to him."

"What do we have in the way of protection for Jim and Marianne?"

"Jim doesn't want anyone. He thinks she doesn't know where he lives and he's probably not wrong."

"But?"

"But SWAT put a Yukon with two officers outside the gate to his neighborhood."

Lloyd smiled. Naes seemed to be thinking of everything.

"OK, I'll call again as soon as I know something," Lloyd said.

"I know you will," Naes said and hung up.

Chapter 20

Thursday 8pm

Gretchen found a truck stop along the highway. She parked in the back as far as she could from the door, but near the on ramp back to the freeway. She got out and stretched by the truck, taking her purse. She walked through the lot, casually looking into other cars, trying to find one with the keys inside. As she walked along she suddenly got hit with a spotlight. The light was blinding, and she immediately froze.

"Good evening ma'am. What are you doing here?" The speaker was an Oregon State Police officer.

"I'm here to get something to eat," she said, turning up the wattage on her smile.

The officer approached her, flashlight in hand. "Do you have any ID?"

Gretchen opened her purse and briefly thought about the gun in there, but said, "oh shoot. I left my wallet in my truck."

"Forgive me if I'm wrong ma'am, but it looked like you were peeking into the cars around here. What's your name?"

"Ann Arbor," said Gretchen.

The officer looked at her, shrugged and wrote it down along with the birthdate she gave him. It dawned on Gretchen that he may have thought she was a lot lizard.

"Well, if you're here to eat, you'd better go get your wallet," said the officer.

"Yes sir, I will," said Gretchen.

She went back to the truck and made a show of looking for her wallet, then when the officer finally drove off she started the truck and pulled out of the lot. She carefully eased onto the freeway and as soon as she was out of sight of the truck stop she set the cruise control to seventy five, ignoring the grumbling in her stomach.

Jim was exhausted. Lunch had run long, then just as it was finishing up, Jason had called to discuss Gretchen's phone call. Jason was worried that Gretchen might show up at Jims house, but Jim did not think she knew where he lived. Now Jim was laying in bed trying to sleep, but Marianne was strangely silent.

"Honey," he asked, "what's bugging you?"

"It's nothing."

Jim knew this was dangerous territory but pushed ahead. "Seriously, what's on your mind?"

Marianne put down her hairbrush and turned in her chair.

"Jim, did you have a thing with Gretchen?"

"No honey."

"She didn't seem to think so."

"Marianne,.."

"Just be straight with me." Her green eyes were boring holes right through him.

Jim said, "Marianne, you are the love of my life. No way would I even look at another woman."

Marianne nodded for a minute before turning back to her mirror.

"You'd better not. If you did, she would be the least of your worries."

Jim got up and limped up behind her. He put his good hand on her shoulder and said very quietly, "I want to spend the rest of my life with you. I'd never do anything to screw that up."

Marianne stood, smiled and kissed him before saying, "I should hope not. Now get back in bed, you've been on your feet enough today."

10pm local time

Lloyd rolled into Riverton a little ahead of the hour and decided to drive to the scene. His GPS took him to Pershing, then to tenth. As soon as he turned the corner, he could see a Wyoming Highway Patrol car parked in front, along with a Riverton police car. He pulled to the curb in front of the house, taking his ID and badge out of his pocket before stepping out of the car. Lloyd held the ID in front of him as he approached the cars from in front.

The door popped open on the Riverton car and a tall angular man stepped out. Lloyd noticed two stars on his collar points, and the name tag that read, "Denzel."

"Good evening Chief," said Lloyd, "I spoke with you on the phone this morning."

"Detective Murray, good to meet you," said Karl, "how was the drive?"

"Gorgeous until it got dark, than mostly a series of heart attacks after that."

"Glad you made it. Do you want to see the house?"

"Sure, if it's not a bother. I can wait until daytime if you'd rather."

"The power is off, but if you have a flashlight I can give you an overview."

Lloyd returned to his car and got a flashlight out of his bag. The trooper and Chief Denzel were waiting for him, and led the way to the front door. Denzel opened the door, and the three of them played their flashlights over the scene. Lloyd let his light follow the charred trail across the carpet in the front room, to the open garage door. The wall and ceiling around the doorway were charred and the smell of smoke was everywhere.

"The body was in there," asked Lloyd.

"Yep," said Karl, "he kind of looked like he was boxing."

"Sort of like this?" Lloyd crouched down and brought his fists up in front of him.

"Pretty much exactly," said Karl.

"That's normal. The heat from the fire causes the muscles to contract and you end up in a 'boxers stance.'"

"So he might not have been trying to protect himself?"

"I'd say there was a reasonable chance he was dead when he was set on fire."

"The coroner should be able to figure that out, I guess," said Karl.

"Pretty easy to tell, really. If he was dead there won't be any smoke in his lungs."

The trooper excused himself and went outside. Lloyd could hear him retching.

"How safe is it in here," asked Lloyd.

"Safe enough."

"How much work has been done?"

"Not a ton. The body got taken out about four hours ago. They got a ton of pictures I guess. They said they'd be back around nine tomorrow."

"OK, lets go outside a minute."

They stepped outside and Lloyd told Karl about the phone call from Gretchen to Jim.

"Sounds like she's our main suspect," said Karl.

"I agree, but I think they'll need to check for DNA. Did the ME give a cause of death?"

"What's an ME?"

"In Seattle that's the Medical Examiner. I guess you call him a coroner."

"Oh, yeah. He said it was preliminary, but he thought blunt force to the back of the skull."

"Did you see the bookends in the living room?"

"What about them," asked Karl.

"If a woman wanted to use one to smack a guy over the head, they'd be almost perfect. Marble, wide base, and tapered for an easy grip." Lloyd mimed holding them in his hands. "You could hold it like this, and lift it up over your head and bring it down hard." Lloyd demonstrated the motion. "You might want to ask the lab guys to check them for DNA and fingerprints."

Karl nodded. "How many of these have you investigated?"

"A lot," said Lloyd, "more than my share."

"How often have you had one involving fire?"

"It's not rare. Usually to cover up evidence, although in this case if what Gretchen told my boss is true it could be anger. Like she knew he was dead but still wanted him to suffer."

"Tell you what, why don't we come back to this in the morning. State will be here and you'll probably be able to look around better."

"Sounds good to me. What do you recommend for a motel?"

"We got a bunch, but you can stay with my wife and I. Don't even think about saying no, my wife heard a big shot detective was coming and made up the guest room."

Lloyd couldn't argue, he was exhausted. He followed Karl the six blocks to his house. Karl's wife was pleasant enough and showed him to his room. Lloyd took off his jacket, then sat on the bed to take off his shoes. The next thing he saw was the sun streaming through the window and birds chirping outside.

Chapter 21

Friday

6am

Lloyd sat up and stretched, feeling his back pop back into place. His pants and shirt were wrinkled from being slept in. Lloyd found his suitcase and got his Dopp kit. The bedroom was attached to a bathroom, so Lloyd shaved in the sink and brushed his teeth. When he was done he changed into a polo shirt and a pair of pants with cargo pockets. He clipped his gun to the waistband next to his badge and wondered how much longer he would be doing that.

He made his way out to the kitchen and found Karl and his wife Marge. Karl was still wearing his chiefs uniform, but it showed every indication of being freshly laundered that morning.

"They let you guys sleep in, in Seattle?"

"Good morning Karl, Marge. I haven't slept like that in ages."

Marge set a plate of bacon, eggs and toast in front of Lloyd along with a steaming mug of coffee. Lloyd thanked her and set to work on the eggs.

"What exactly is your interest in our case," asked Karl.

"There's still some work to do on our end, but it looks like your crispy critter and his girlfriend took out a hit out on our captain. We found a witness, but when we weren't looking we think Tom there killed her. The woman is wanted for a murder in Tacoma but they're hanging together so we're looking at conspiracy charges too."

"Why would they go after your captain?" Marge was pouring coffee.

"I'm not sure yet. Jim plays his cards close to his vest sometimes, and he hasn't said anything yet," Lloyd deferred.

"Maybe he doesn't know," said Karl.

"He might not. She called him yesterday. I'm wondering why."

Karl leaned back in his chair, chewing a piece of bacon.

"Did he have a thing with her?"

"No," Lloyd said, "I seriously doubt that."

"Maybe she has one for him. I once had a secretary that got obsessed with me. She'd call me all the time and at work she was always coming in and spending time with me."

"How did you handle it?"

"We came to the mutual conclusion that it was affecting our working relationship and that it had to stop."

"She quit?"

"No."

"You fired her."

"No, I married her," Karl laughed, "and she quit when we had our first kid."

Lloyd laughed out loud. Marge smiled and turned red.

"I don't think that's Jims problem. For one thing he's engaged to...a wonderful woman."

"If you say so," said Karl, "you about ready to head out?"

Lloyd drained his coffee cup. "Let's go."

7am

Lloyd parked behind Karl's cruiser in front of the house. A fresh faced trooper was sitting in his car in front. An unmarked cruiser was parked in front of the marked car, blocking the driveway. A tall lanky blonde woman was standing by the front door. She was wearing a silk shirt and black pants with a big Glock clipped to her waist alongside a round badge.

Lloyd and Karl got out of their respective cars and Karl said to Lloyd, "watch out for her. That's Vivian Janson and she's a bit of a ball buster."

They walked up together and as they approached Karl said, "Hello Vivian. This is Lloyd Murray, he's a detective from Seattle."

"What's Seattles interest in our little homicide here?"

Lloyd laid it out for her. When he was done she shrugged. "I saw a bulletin on her this morning. You think she killed him?"

"I do. I was here last night and I noticed the bookends inside. They'd be perfect blunt instruments."

Vivian glared at Karl and said, "you went into my scene?"

"I kind of insisted," said Lloyd, "I wanted to get a feel for it."

"Karl you know better. You've been a chief for thirty years."

"Vivian," Karl started, but Lloyd interrupted.

"It's really my fault," said Lloyd, "Karl didn't want me to go in, but I was persistent."

She glared at Karl, then at Lloyd. Finally she said, "Well the damage is done. You might as well come in."

She turned and as they went inside Karl nodded at Lloyd.

"We spent most of our time with the body, yesterday. So what would you do in Seattle?"

"She claimed Tom raped her. I guess I'd start in the bedrooms and look for evidence of that."

Vivian led the way into the back bedroom. The bed was unmade and two suitcases lay open on the floor. Vivian pulled a black light out of her kit and peeled back the covers.

"I assume you photographed everything already," asked Lloyd.

"Yep."

A power cord snaked across the floor, from a generator and powered a light mounted on a stand. Vivian turned out the light and shined the black light over the sheets. They could clearly see stains covering the bedding.

"I'm guessing they had an active night," said Vivian.

Lloyd crouched down by the bedposts. "Look at this," he said.

Vivian looked where Lloyd shone his flashlight. There was a rub mark on the wood.

"What are you thinking?"

"Someone was tied to the bed," said Lloyd.

Vivian nodded, and turned the lights back on.

"Anything else?"

"Did you check out the bookends?"

They marched back into the living room. Vivian looked closely at the bookends. The one closest to the bedroom sat on the shelf slightly cockeyed. Vivian, using gloved hands, picked it up and looked at the bottom. Lloyd could see blood underneath.

"You're right twice. Anything else?"

"Have you found any Lidocaine yet?"

"In the closet in the spare bedroom. We haven't touched it yet."

"If it's not too much to ask, could you print the box it's in and the bottles? Also could you get the lot number for me?"

Vivian pulled out her notebook and flipped back a half dozen pages, then read the lot number to Lloyd.

"What's the significance of the Lidocaine?"

"If you take too much it increases the level of potassium in your system and induces a heart attack. She's killed two people with it and tried for a third."

"Why didn't she use it on Meeker?"

"Dunno. When I find her I'll ask her."

Gretchen was moving slowly, trying not to attract attention to herself. When she got to Pendleton she opted for another motel, paying cash and using the name Ann Arbor. She didn't want to do it, but she got out a pair of scissors and cut her hair back to shoulder length. Then she got into her truck and found the Safeway in the heart of town. She parked in the middle of the lot, went in and bought a box of red hair dye. When she came out she found another truck identical to hers except for the color, with Oregon plates. She found a screwdriver behind the back seat and went to work stealing the plates, fighting the dizziness radiating from her jawline.

Lloyd was watching Vivian work. He had to admit she was thorough and was probably as experienced as anyone in Wyoming would be. Her crime scene people had showed up and she was directing them as to what areas needed special attention.

Lloyd asked Karl, "did anyone talk to the neighbors?"

"No one was home on either side. Across the street is empty. We checked the houses in back but no one noticed anything."

"What about the body? Was there anything unusual?"

Karl said, "he had a gun on him. It was pretty badly damaged from the fire but he had it in a shoulder holster."

"What kind of gun," Lloyd asked.

"Beretta. A nine millimeter."

"Any chance of ballistics?"

"Maybe. It was pretty badly damaged," said Karl.

Lloyd shrugged.

"Were there any other guns? We're looking specifically for twenty two's."

Vivian barely looked up and said, "not so far."

It didn't feel like there was much for Lloyd to do.

"Vivian," Lloyd said, "unless you think I can be useful I'm going to take off."

"Thanks for your help," she said.

Lloyd said goodbye to Karl and drove to the Riverton airport. There was a commuter flight to Idaho Falls that morning that would connect him with a flight to Seattle. He could be home by that evening. Lloyd turned in his car and spent the wait going through his emails on his phone and catching up his notes. At ten they called for his flight. He shut everything down and boarded the plane.

By ten Gretchen had managed to turn her hair mostly red. She checked it out in the mirror and liked what she saw, mostly. It would take a while to get used to having it that short.

She got dressed again and had lunch in the restaurant. In the lobby was a pay phone. After she had paid her tab she decided to make a call. The phone rang and then went to voice mail.

"Hey baby, I'm in Pendleton. Don't worry I'm ok, I'm coming your way. See you soon."

She closed the line and thought about calling Jim, but decided that was too big of a chance. She did not want to drive the truck, and there really wasn't much to do in the desert. She went back to her room, passing the swimming pool along the way. There was a family playing, with a teenage daughter and a young boy, and an older man and woman. Gretchen shrugged and when she got to her room, changed into a modest one piece swim suit. Then she returned to poolside and sat in one of the lounge chairs. She was pretending to sleep and pretended not to notice the husband looking at her.

After she'd laid there for about a half hour, she stood and stretched, making sure she pushed her chest out, then turned and jumped into the water. She swam a couple laps, making sure the husband was still watching. She climbed out of the pool and let the cool air wash over her pretending not to notice the effect it had. Out of the corner of her eye she noticed the teenager watching her, and decided that was too much. She wrapped herself in her towel and went back to her room, being sure to smile at the husband when she walked past him.

"Wiggle your fingers," said Sheridan.

In response, Jim held up his left hand and wiggled all five fingers.

Sheridan put two of his fingers in the palm of Jims hand and said, "squeeze my fingers."

Jim did.

"There doesn't seem to be any nerve damage. You should start doing some physical therapy to get your range of motion and strength back. Same with your leg. You're going to limp for a while but it should get to a hundred percent eventually."

"When can I get back to work, doc?"

"Maybe in about ten days. And I want you to start on light duty. No field work. I can't have you chasing bad guys," Sheridan said.

"I'm a captain, for crying out loud. That's not what we do."

"You are a captain but that didn't stop this from happening in the first place," said Marianne. She had been off to the side watching.

"That's a one off, honey," said Jim, "the odds of that happening again are worse than winning the lottery."

"I won't feel like that's true until that woman is behind bars."

Sheridan was packing up his bag. "Keep doing what you're doing. I think you should take the stairs more and work on your grip strength. No weights heavier than five pounds. If you have any problems, call me."

"How's Jane," asked Marianne.

Sheridan sat down and looked between them. "Frankly I'm a little worried. She had a good time yesterday, but it exhausted her. She's not that young and I'm worried about her and the baby."

"Ten fingers, ten toes," said Jim.

Sheridan looked confused.

"That's all that matters. That the baby is healthy. She's doing what she needs to do. You know better than anyone the advances that medicine has made. She's going to be fine and so is the baby."

"Thanks Jim. I hope you're right."

"I am. You should go check on her."

Sheridan nodded and said, "come by later. I'm ordering a pizza because she insists. And I also know she won't eat hardly any of it."

"We'll be by. Go home."

Sheridan shook Jims hand, and hugged Marianne, then left them in the living room.

"There you go," said Jim, "I'm darn near good as new."

"That's not quite what he said honey," said Marianne.

Jim waved a hand. "I know you're worried about me, but seriously I'm all right."

"He doesn't sleep with you."

Jim looked at her with a question on his face. She sat on the arm of his chair and took his good hand.

"You don't sleep, at least not much. Unless you take something. When you do sleep, you're restless. You didn't use to be."

Jim spoke softly. "I can't help that. It'll get better."

"Jim, I want to spend the rest of my life with you and have your babies and raise our family, but you have to take care of yourself too. What's it going to take?"

Jim paused. "When Gretchen is caught. I'm not worried about me. But I am about those around me and what she might do."

"Let your guys do their job. You don't need to worry about that, they'll find her."

Lieutenant Naes hung up the phone and went out into the bullpen. Jason and Ted were at their desks, Jason was helping Ted look up a Rap sheet on the computer.

"Gentlemen, I need to see you two in my office."

Ted stood. They followed Rebekah into her office and closed the door.

"We need to do something to flush Gretchen out of hiding."

"We've got bulletins out everywhere. But we still haven't plugged the leak. Maybe we could use that to our advantage," said Jason.

"How?"

"She was fixated on Captain Churchill. Could we use him as bait?"

"I don't like the idea of putting him in danger. What I'm thinking is arresting the leak."

"Do we have enough?"

Rebekah had been holding a Manila folder. She slid it across the desk. It was transcripts from a wiretap warrant. It contained phone calls from someone identified as Gretchen Henderson. Jason pored over the document.

"Holy shit," he said, "can we use this?"

"Silver Platter doctrine," said Naes, "the feds started an investigation for the interstate flight to avoid prosecution charges. They got the wiretap without us asking for it, and they're sharing it with us. I just got off the phone with a prosecutor and she said it's good to go. She's applying for the warrant. But look at the last two sections."

Jason flipped through and saw what she meant.

"When do you want to do this?"

"No time like the present," Naes said.

Jason handed the file to Ted and he flipped through it. "I see what you mean."

Jason looked out into the bullpen, his face hard. They made a hasty plan, then filed out of the office.

Dionne Barrone was sitting at her desk and looked up to see Jason and Ted come out of the lieutenants office. She went back to her typing.

"Dionne."

She looked up. Lieutenant Naes was standing in front of her. Ted and Jason were on either side of the desk.

"What can I do for you, Lieutenant?"

"You can stand up," she said.

"What?"

"Stand the fuck up," Naes said conversationally.

"What's going on," Dionne said, "I'm really kind of busy."

Jason said, "you've been hiding things from us, Dionne. You were good at it, it took us a while to figure it out. But you're getting phone calls from a murder suspect and you've been talking about her crimes. You're under arrest for conspiracy to commit murder and harboring a fugitive."

Dionne reached for her desk drawer, but Ted grabbed her arm and jerked her out of her seat. Jason grabbed the other arm and bent it behind her back, forcing Dionne onto her toes. Jason reached behind him and took a pair of handcuffs off his belt. Dionne was starting to yell, and trying to pull away, but Ted and Jason had locked her down. Jason got the handcuffs on, and they walked her to the front of the desk. Rebekah conducted a quick but thorough search. Ted opened the top drawer of Dionnes desk and said, "shit."

Dionne seemed to shrink into herself and went limp. Jason was holding her up, and looked at Ted. He was putting on a pair of surgical gloves, then reached into the drawer and pulled out a small twenty two caliber pistol.

"Let's put her in interrogation," said Rebekah.

11am

Jason finally walked into the interrogation room, carrying a Manila folder. He was reading a page, and flipped it over. Finally he closed the file and dropped it on the table across from Dionne. He sat in the chair across from her, staring, unblinking.

Dionnes wrists were chained to the ring in the middle of the table. She realized how little she knew about Jason, and wished they'd sent in Lloyd.

"What?"

Jason looked at her a moment longer, and then said, "You are in a lot of trouble."

"You don't have a thing on me," she said.

"You haven't worked here that long, but you've been here long enough. Do you think you'd be sitting there if we didn't?"

"I haven't done anything!"

"Then talk to me. Maybe I can fix this."

"There's nothing to fix. When I get out of here, I'm going to sue you, and Naes. You all just made me a rich woman."

"Ok. You have the right to remain silent..." It took a couple minutes to recite the Miranda warnings. When he was done, Jason said, "By the way you are being recorded."

"I didn't do anything. I don't care. Ask me anything."

Jason shrugged. "OK. How long have you worked for the city?"

"Four years. First in public health, then for the police department."

"What's your current assignment?"

"You know that I'm the administrative assistant to the captain of Homicide," she said, proudly.

"Who hired you in that capacity?"

"Captain Daniels was my first boss. When he got transferred Captain Churchill asked me to stay."

"So you pick up the captains mail, type up his notes, track his schedule and take care of the unit, correct?"

"Among other things, yes."

"Do you socialize with any of the detectives?"

"I've had drinks with a couple."

"Have you ever had drinks with Captain Churchill?"

"No, strictly professional with Captain Churchill."

"Did you ever socialize with a detective named Fred Henderson?"

"I've known his wife since my days in Public Health. I'd have dinner with them sometimes. I liked Fred."

"How well did you know his wife," Jason looked at his notes for effect, "Gretchen."

"I got to know her pretty well in my public health days. She was a friend."

Jason nodded. He picked up the file and flipped through the pages until he got to the one he wanted.

"It's done. We're rid of him. Response: When will you be home? Answer, soon. We'll never have to be alone again." Jason looked at Dionne. "Sounds like more than a friend to me."

"We were plan..."

Jason cut her off. "There's more. Do you want to hear it?"

"How did you get that? You can't use it, that's illegal!"

"Ever hear of the 'Silver Platter Doctrine?'"

Dionne shook her head.

"If one jurisdiction, in this case the feds, can obtain evidence legally and choose to share it with another jurisdiction that could not otherwise obtain it legally."

"That's a thing?"

"It is," said Jason, "and I would say that you are screwed, blued and tattooed. Right now I am your only option to set things right. So tell me now, what is your relationship to Gretchen Henderson."

Dionne looked at Jason for a long moment before her face crumbled.

"We met two years ago when I worked at public health. She had been married about three years by then. We started going out to lunch together, then dinner, and one night we had a few drinks and wound up in bed together."

"When did you hear from her last?"

"She left a message on my voice mail. She's on her way back to Seattle but I don't know how long it's going to take."

"Where is she now?"

"I don't know. She and Tom went to Montana. But they left pretty quickly. She wouldn't tell me where they were going."

"Doesn't it make you jealous that she had a boyfriend?"

"She's bisexual. We aren't exclusive, but we love each other. When we're ready to be exclusive we'll know it."

"How did Fred die?"

Dionne shrugged.

"We know about the lidocaine. How did she administer it?"

Dionne shook her head a moment, then she looked straight at Jason.

"She didn't."

Jason sat back and waited.

Finally Dionne spoke. "Gretchen gave me a vial of what she called medicine, and told me what to do. When Fred was away from his desk I put it in his coffee."

"Did you know what was going to happen? Did you know it would kill him?"

"Gretchen told me how much to use. She said she just wanted to give him a scare."

"Did you know it would kill him?"

Dionne nodded. "I wasn't sure. But I had a feeling."

"What's the story with Tom?"

"Meeker? He told Gretchen he had money. Turns out he's just a low life gangster. She started with him because he told her he could get things done. Illegal things."

"Why did she want Captain Churchill killed?"

"He didn't believe Fred died of natural causes. He had the medical examiner draw blood and sent it off to be tested. When I told her about that, she freaked. I guess she didn't think they'd test Fred."

"What happened to the test results?"

"I pick up the mail. They were sent to Jim but I intercepted them."

"When did that happen?"

"Friday morning. I told Gretchen, I don't know what she did after that."

"Did you read them?"

"No. I shoved them in my desk. I never looked."

177

"Dionne, did you tell anyone when Captain Churchill left the building last Friday?" Jason leaned in, intent.

"I sent her a text message. I don't know why she wanted to know that and I don't know what she did with the information."

In the observation room, Rebekah said, "she gives lesbians a bad name."

Gretchen was working her way west along the Columbia river. She mainly stuck to side roads and was taking her time. When she got to White Salmon, Gretchen located a pay phone in front of the Ace Hardware. She stopped and tried calling Dionne again, but got no answer. Gretchen decided to spend the night. She got directions from the clerk inside to a decent motel that had it's own restaurant. She had a salad with chunks of chicken cut into it, then went back to her room and took a shower. When she was done, she went down to the lobby and called Dionne again.

A male voice answered. "Hello?"

Gretchen hung up and checked the number. She had it right. She went back to her room and packed. She took the key with her and dropped it in the trash can outside. Then she got in the truck and started driving north on highway 141. As she left the motel, she saw a Klickitat county sheriffs car drive by her. Gretchen forced herself to be calm and keep the speedometer down. It took almost forty five minutes to make the drive. As she drove, Gretchen found makeup wipes in her purse and used them to wipe the makeup off of her face. She saw a sign for a bed and breakfast and turned in the driveway.

Gretchen knocked on the door and a woman in her mid forties answered the door.

"I hate to trouble you ma'am, but I just left my husband and I'm trying to get to relatives in Seattle. Do you have a room for me tonight?"

"Well sure, I suppose. How long are you planning to stay?"

"Just tonight ma'am." She made a show of looking over her shoulder. "Is there a way I could park my truck in back? I don't want him to find it."

"What did he do to you, dear?"

Gretchen hooked a finger in the neck of her sweater and pulled it down enough to for the woman to see Tom's handprint. The bruise on her jaw was vivid and angry.

"I don't know if you can see that still, but that was just for starters." Gretchen knew the marks on her neck would be visible, she had been working them all the way from White Salmon.

It had the desired effect.

"You poor thing. Park the truck in the garage, I'm the only one using it. I'll meet you by the back door and I'll put you in the room in the back."

"Oh thank you, you're too kind."

Gretchen pulled up the short driveway and pulled into the open garage. She grabbed one of her suitcases and tugged it after her. True to her word, her host met her at the back door.

"Don't worry about the rent for tonight dear. This is a slow time and I'm happy to have the company."

"Oh thank you," said Gretchen as the woman showed her to her room. It had a bathroom attached and as soon as she was alone, Gretchen drew a bath and climbed into it. She let the warmth soak into her muscles, making them relax. She lay in the bath for about twenty minutes, then took inventory of her bruises. The ones on her wrists and ankles were a deep purple, as well as the ones on her thighs. She scrubbed herself as thoroughly as she could and finally stepped out of the bath feeling somewhat better. She dressed in her yoga pants and a t shirt and turned on the television. She found a news channel but did not see anything about White Salmon. Probably just being paranoid. She tried not to dwell on the past, but she wished she had not fallen in with Tom. That had been a disaster. He didn't know about Dionne, but it had been his idea to kill Fred. After that, things just kept happening and she couldn't stop them. She had thought she had it under control until that night in Riverton when he had found her out. She took the pistol out of her bag and placed the barrel in her mouth. Then she pulled it out and dropped the gun back in her handbag. She couldn't do that, not yet. But she thought she knew who could do it for her.

Chapter 22

One week later. Friday noon.

Jim and Marianne were waiting patiently at the bottom of the steps to the Gulfstream while Jenny and Jason were saying goodby.

"I wish you could come with us," Jenny said.

"Me too."

And then they would kiss. Jason finally handed Jenny a small box.

"Open this on the plane."

"I can hardly wait," she said.

And then they kissed. Again.

"Good thing you're not the first act. I think we're going to be late," said Jim.

"Don't be like that. We're as bad as they are."

"Yeah, but we're an engaged couple."

Finally Jim turned to Jason and said, "Turn her loose. They've got a show to get to."

Reluctantly Jason kissed Jenny one last time and she went up the steps. Marianne hugged Jason and then went into the plane. Jim shook Jason's hand and said, "see you on Monday," before limping up the stairs.

Jason remembered Jim telling him once how he felt when Marianne went away. Now Jason understood. He waited while the plane rolled out to the runway and watched it roll faster and faster until it lifted into the sky. Once it was safely in the air, Jason walked slowly back to the car and climbed into the passenger seat.

"And you called me lover boy," said Ted.

"That was Lloyd. We should get back to work."

"Ok, where to?"

"The office. I want to go over every inch of that file to see if we missed anything. That woman can't just disappear."

"You got it."

They pulled into the parking garage twenty minutes later, and went into the bullpen. Ross and Lloyd were at their desks, shirtsleeves rolled up.

"You guys got anything," Jason asked.

"Hemorrhoids from all this sitting," said Ross, "but otherwise no. How important is it we find her?"

"Eight will get you ten she makes another run at Jim. But she's got to be running out of money. Motels are expensive."

"So she's staying at a dive. Did you call the US Marshals," asked Lloyd.

"Right after you got back from Wyoming," said Jason.

"She'll turn up," said Ted, "she has to."

8:30pm, Jefferson center, Roanoke VA.

Jim was enjoying watching Marianne get ready. She had someone doing her hair while someone else was working on her makeup. Tonight she was wearing a sequined dress and every time she moved she seemed to shimmy. Jim liked the effect. She was smiling, but Jim recognized it as her 'game face.' She had been practicing all week, since she got the phone call from Hank that he'd set the dates for her tour. The rest of the band had shown up on Tuesday. Rosa and Miguel had managed to find room for everyone. Jim had actually enjoyed the distraction of the music. When they got together he could see how well they worked.

Marianne caught his eye. "Are you ready for this?"

"I'd better be," he said.

"How's the leg holding up?"

"Sheridan's a miracle worker. "

"Time for the meet and greet," Marianne said.

Jim stood and limped after Marianne as she followed an usher to a roped off area behind a temporary wall. A line of fans stretched down the hall. Jim figured maybe a few hundred had paid for the privilege of having their picture taken with his fiancé.

Jim was wearing a black suit made from silk, with a white cotton shirt and no tie. He stood off to one side, watching the crowd and watching Marianne as she interacted with the fans. They came up in singles, pairs and the occasional trio. She really beamed when she had a picture taken with a kid, and twice she got to hold infants, cooing at them as the moms stood nervously.

Finally, the last one came through and Marianne thanked him. She came out of the roped off enclosure and said, "I have just enough time for warm ups."

Jim kissed her quickly and said, "break a leg."

"You're going to be backstage, right?"

"I wouldn't miss this for the world."

Marianne smiled, then he followed her to a practice room. The band was stretching and warming up. Marianne went through her scales, then

181

she and Jenny ran through a couple of songs. Finally, it was time. Everyone from the band stood around Marianne as she uttered a prayer. Then they all stuck a hand in the middle and gave a quiet cheer. As they exited the room, one of the other acts stuck his head in and said, "Good crowd tonight."

"Thanks, Jon." And then they were off. The band walked in from the side of the stage and took their spots. Then they started playing. Marianne looked sideways at Jim, then went out on stage and started singing. The crowd roared when they saw her and Jim could see some were already singing along with the music. The energy was unbelievable.

When the song ended, Marianne went up to the microphone and spoke.

"Hello Roanoke! How is everybody tonight?"

The crowd roared their appreciation.

"I just wanted to thank all of you for your kindness over the last two weeks, and I'm so happy you all decided to come back and spend some time with us."

Again the crowd roared.

"Y'all know that a few weeks ago I was supposed to be right here on this stage, but I got word that my boyfriend had been hurt pretty good. I flew back to check on him, and y'all know what he did? He said he had something he wanted to ask me in Roanoke!" The crowd roared. Jim said, "aw shit." He'd been using a cane all night, but now he leaned it against the wall. One of the stagehands said, "sorry about that buddy."

"You knew about this?"

"I found out when you did. Man she's full of surprises."

From on stage, Marianne was saying, "now I'd like y'all to meet the man that stole my heart. Can y'all help me call him out?"

The crowd was now chanting, "Jim, Jim, Jim,"

Jim took a deep breath and strode to the stage, trying not to limp. Walking on stage was a shock. He'd never been on this side of the lights before. He walked to Marianne and kissed her. For a moment, the lights, the crowd and the band all melted away. Marianne took Jims hand and palmed something into it, winking at him. Jim finally stepped back and said into the microphone, "thank you Roanoke. I hope you all get some good memories from tonight. But I get to go home with her!"

The crowd laughed in appreciation. Jim turned back to Marianne, who was beaming. He hugged Marianne and whispered, "I'm going to get you for this."

Jim said into the microphone, "Marianne Wilson, you are the love of my life. Will you marry me?"

The stadium went quiet as Marianne smiled and nodded and said, "Yes!" Jim slipped the ring on her finger and Marianne kissed him.

They hugged again and then turned to the crowd. Jim raised his hand, with Mariannes, then said, "Y'all are invited." The crowd roared its approval.

Jim turned and waved at the crowd as he walked back to his cane. He looked to the stagehand and said, "Find me a chair."

"You got it," he said as Marianne launched into a love song.

When the show was over, Jim and Marianne climbed into a remodeled motor home, along with Jenny, while the rest of the band climbed into a second RV. The stage hands went on another bus, and the equipment went into a semi-truck. The buses pulled out around two in the morning. By then, most people were asleep in their bunks. Marianne was no exception. The concert had energized her but Jim knew that she left everything on the stage. He lay in the narrow bunk with her and watched her in the ambient light from the window until the dark and motion helped him to drift off.

Saturday found them at the Colonial Life Arena. The afternoon was spent on rehearsals and sound checks. There were two other acts opening for Marianne, one a four person group, and the other a single act with a band in support. Jim thought they all sounded pretty good and enjoyed rehearsals, sitting arm in arm with Marianne until it was her turn. She went onstage that night at ten, and followed the same routine, bringing Jim out before the second song.

This time Jim told the crowd, "Y'all can borrow her for the next couple hours, but I want her back." The crowd cheered and applauded and before he left the stage, Jim kissed Marianne again and told her he loved her.

After the concert they followed a similar routine. Marianne was exhausted and fell right to sleep. Jim watched her until he fell asleep himself, and he did not wake up until after they had arrived at Capital One arena.

Marianne shook him awake, saying "get up sleepyhead." Jim thought it was ironic, as she was laying on top of him. She seemed to realize it at the same time as she said, "oh no, am I hurting you?"

Jim gave her a squeeze and said, "no honey, I'm fine."

"We gotta get ready. Are you up for this?"

"I could eat first."

She rolled off of Jim, and he slid out of bed, landing awkwardly on his bad leg.

Marianne stuck her head through the curtains and said, "You sure you're ok? I'm pretty sure they heard that inside the arena."

"I just landed funny, I'm good," Jim said. He pivoted on his good leg and stepped into the bathroom. He stuck his head out of the door and said, "Think anyone cares if I shower?"

183

"Go ahead, I'll be next."

Jim was in and out of the shower in three minutes. When he slid back the curtain, Marianne was leaning against the sink.

"Let me see," she said.

He stuck his right leg out in front. Marianne bent and looked at the scar on top of his thigh.

"It looks good. Now the shoulder."

Obediently he let her look at his left shoulder.

"Sheridan made me promise that I'd look after you," she said by way of explanation.

"I don't mind," said Jim.

"I can see that," she said.

A few minutes later Jim came out, dressed in a t-shirt and shorts. He went to the galley and brewed a pot of coffee. He looked for something to make for breakfast, when Marianne joined him.

"It looks like we're out of a lot of stuff," he said.

Marianne found oatmeal and milk, and shooed Jim out of the kitchen. Jim sat in a booth and was a little surprised when Jenny slid in across from him.

"Good morning, sunshine."

"Shut up," said Jenny pleasantly while sipping her coffee.

Jim smiled. "Still not a morning person."

Marianne brought out two bowls and placed one in front of Jim, the other in front of Jenny. She went back into the galley and came out a moment later with another bowl and slid in next to Jim.

"Are you awake yet," Marianne asked of Jenny.

"I miss Jason," she said, "I might be a bit jealous."

"I'm sorry honey," said Marianne.

"He's working his case," said Jim, "I know what it feels like when you have unfinished business in this job."

"Honey, you wouldn't have met Jason if it wasn't for Jim," said Marianne.

"I know. I don't resent what you have. I just wish he was here."

"I know he wishes he could be here too," said Jim, "and next tour I promise he'll make it."

Marianne said, "When can we get in for a sound check?"

"In about an hour," said Jenny.

"It's Sunday. You should call him while you have the chance."

"Do you think so? Isn't it like five in the morning there?"

"Trust me," said Jim, "he's up. He's probably in the office."

Jim was half right. Jason was up and dressed, wearing a polo shirt and khaki pants trying to make sense of the file. His finger traced the route to

Idaho Falls from Riverton on a map on his dining room table. Then he tracked along I-84 through Pendleton and Hermiston until he got to White Salmon, where the call he had answered came from. He thought about that again. They'd served a search warrant on Dionnes house. In the bedroom they'd seen pictures of Dionne and Gretchen. Then the phone had rung and on a whim he answered it. There had been no conversation. Just a moment of silence and then a dial tone. They'd traced the number to a pay phone in White Salmon but by the time the Klickitat county sheriff's department had gotten the word she was gone. The hotel didn't recognize her picture from the bulletin. So where the hell would she go?

Jason didn't think she'd stay on I-84. That left crossing back into Oregon or going north. Jason traced route 141 to Trout lake, and noticed it had an airfield. He looked it up on the internet. The airfield was likely closed, and probably was mostly for sightseeing. He rejected that idea, but began looking at the map again. He traced out two routes through the Gifford Pinchot National Forest, that led out to Swift Creek. On a whim, he called a forest service information line and learned both routes were open.

"Jesus, if she's in there she could be anywhere," he said to no one in particular.

Jason's phone abruptly rang. He looked at the screen, and smiled to himself.

"Hi honey," he said.

"Hey baby. Miss me yet?" Jenny's voice sounded good in his ear.

"Every minute."

"Are you any closer to catching this woman?"

"Maybe. I think I've narrowed it down to about a quarter of the state."

Jenny laughed, then he asked her how the concerts had been.

9pm

Marianne had been onstage for about an hour when Jim noticed the woman. There was an area in front of the stage reserved for those Jim termed, "high rollers." There was no seating but it was roped off and people could dance and move around. One woman had ducked under the ropes and was standing right by the stage. Jim couldn't see her face but she was tall and thin. Jim started to get up when the stage manager put a hand on his shoulder.

"Marianne told me to keep you back here. She said to let security do their job."

Sure enough two burly security guards in black t shirts had moved in and were trying to convince her to leave. She started to get agitated as Marianne kept on singing. The woman swung an open hand at one of the security

185

guards but he simply backed up. When her hand went by, the guard stepped in and wrapped her up in his arms. The other guard grabbed the woman's legs. They carried her off towards stage right, opposite where Jim was.

"Where are they taking her," Jim asked the stagehand.

"Security has a room over there."

Jim got directions to the security office and made his way around, leaning on his mahogany cane. He knocked on the door and when it opened he showed his badge to the young woman inside.

"Can I talk to her?"

"Sure," the guard said, "why not?"

Jim stepped in and took one look at her. He was disappointed, he had no idea who she was.

"Where's she from?"

"She says Maryland," the guard said, "but we have no idea if that's true or not."

"I'd like to ask her a couple questions."

"Go ahead."

Jim sat down across from her. His leg ached and felt stiff. Jim stared at her a moment.

Finally, he said, "Do you know who I am?"

She looked at him, bleary eyed and red faced and said, "You are the boyfriend." She was trying to be precise.

"How do you know that?"

"Shit, she introduced you."

"You didn't hear about me before the concert?"

"You were on TMZ."

"Do you know a woman named Gretchen?"

"Yeah."

Jim's heart raced. "How do you know her?"

"She's my ex husbands new wife. The bitch."

Jim was disappointed. He got her name from the guard. It was Betsy Rhyman. He thanked the guard and left.

He made it back to his seat on stage left just as the concert was ending. Marianne and the band came off the stage and then went back for the encore. Jim texted Betsy Rhyman's information to Jason and Lloyd and waited until Marianne came off the stage for the last time.

She was the last one to come past the curtain. Marianne was brimming with energy and her eyes glowed. She kissed Jim and they walked together to the dressing rooms. When they got to her room, they went in and closed the door. Marianne immediately pushed Jim up against the door and kissed him passionately.

When she came up for air he said, "best concert yet."

Marianne was all smiles. "Did you see that woman at the front of the stage?"

"I did, what was her problem?"

"I think she was high," Marianne said, "she just stood there for the longest time, swaying to the music. She never said anything. Finally I gave security the signal to move in and they did."

"Yeah, I think she was just a drunk fan," Jim said.

The band and crew had a small party in the hallway by the dressing rooms. Beer and champagne flowed freely and someone had provided trays of crackers with meat and cheese. They hung out for an hour or so, making plans. Marianne asked Jenny if she wanted to fly back with them.

"If you don't mind," she said.

"It's no problem," said Marianne, "we'd love to have you."

"We're planning to leave from Ronald Reagan airport at midnight. We're taking the Gulfstream," said Jim

"I'll kick in my share for a cab."

"I'm hoping to get in with enough time to take a nap before work," said Jim.

"You're working tomorrow? Bless your heart," said Jenny.

"We should meet for lunch," said Jim, "I'll make sure Jason is available."

Chapter 23

Monday

3am Seattle time

Marianne was driving back from the airport. Jim was stretched out on the passenger side and Jenny was asleep in the back seat.

"Jim, are you awake," Marianne asked quietly.

Jim grunted the affirmative.

"It really bothers me that that woman called you."

"I don't have an answer to that, honey."

"Are you sure there isn't something?"

"I tend to think the worst of people, so when I meet someone socially I have to consider that. But when I met Gretchen I did not like her from the start."

"Why is that?"

"Looking back, there wasn't any one thing I could put my finger on," said Jim, "but I think it was just the way she seemed to be coming on to everyone. Men, women, didn't matter. She was a huge flirt but Fred thought she was the best thing since sliced bread."

"So why did she get fixated on you?"

"Could be a couple things. I was her husbands boss, so maybe I represent power. But this is what I think." Jim paused for a minute. "When Fred died, I asked the ME to send blood and tissue samples to the lab. I'd been waiting for results. But I looked into health records. Fred was overweight but he was a bit of a hypochondriac. He went to the doc every time he had the sniffles, but his Doc said other than being heavy there was nothing wrong with him."

"You think Fred was murdered?"

"I'd bet a paycheck on it."

"Is she the one that set those two on you?"

"Probably her and Tom Meeker. Jason and Ted made the connection to a mob in Tacoma. Tom was a part of that and together they worked to eliminate that connection."

Marianne was locked into the road ahead. "Is that why you spoke to that woman last night?"

Jim nodded, "yes, I wanted to see if there was a connection. Jason hasn't had a chance to check yet, but it doesn't appear there is. Would have been a hell of a long shot."

"OK, so she targets you because she thinks you can prove she killed her husband. When are they going to get her?"

"Honestly? I think I'm going to have to bait her."

"Jim, you are in no shape for that."

"Don't worry, I have a plan."

"You always do."

5am

Jason thought he would be the only one in the office when he walked in the door. Ted was sitting at his desk tapping on a computer. Lloyd was in his shirtsleeves looking over his file.

"Lloyd, you are here first again. How is that possible?"

"Early bird gets the worm? I think I pulled Ted away from a night of earthly delights."

"Bastard. We were almost done with dessert," said Ted.

"Ah, the old sorry I have to go to work ploy. Don't worry just wait until next time," said Jason.

189

"You better be right. Anyway, Lloyd caught a case and Ross has a doctors appointment, so he called me."

"You could have called me," said Jason, "I wasn't doing anything."

"I had to get Ted out of the clutches of that woman," said Lloyd.

"What was the case," asked Jason.

"Guy calls 911," started Ted, "and tells the operator he killed his wife. Patrol goes out, the husband comes out onto the porch, kneels down and shoots himself in the head. He was dead right there."

"Where was the wife?"

"He'd strangled her in her bed. Patrol is clearing the house and find her in the bedroom. They think she's dead. Ted and I are downstairs while CSI is videotaping the scene. That was when she sat up. Scared the crap out of Ray. Two kids, asleep in their beds, didn't hear a thing," said Lloyd.

"Incredible," said Jason. "Did you find anything on that name that Jim sent us?"

"Betsy Rhyman from Maryland. Aged 42. Divorced. No kids. Prince Georges county has a couple DV reports with her as a victim and a crisis report. She's not really on their radar and there's no criminal history."

"What's the crisis?"

"Her husband called because she threatened suicide. She told the officer it was an empty threat but they sent her to the hospital anyway."

"Jim said she wouldn't leave a prohibited area and assaulted security."

"I'll contact DC later and see if they did a report."

Ted said, "Jim will be in later today. What do we tell him?"

"We're no closer to finding her than we were when he left. But we sent flyers out nationwide just in case."

"He's not going to like that," said Ted.

"That's why you are going to tell him," said Lloyd.

9am

Jim rolled out of bed and sat up. He flexed the fingers of his left hand and raised his arm. It hurt, but it was bearable. His leg was stiff but after he bent it a couple times it felt better. Marianne was not in bed so Jim limped to the bathroom and stepped in the shower. He shaved under the running water and rinsed off. When he stepped out he could smell coffee coming from the bedroom.

As he stepped through the door, wearing only a towel, he said, "this is why I love you."

Marianne smiled as she handed him a mug.

"Drink it in good health," she said.

Marianne was wearing a purple dress with roses embroidered on the front.

"You're all dressed up, I thought you'd sleep in this morning."

"I'm going to go see Jane after you leave, then I'm going to collect Jenny and we are going to meet you and Jason for lunch."

Jim sipped his coffee and then started getting dressed. He managed to slide into a pair of dark slacks and a pale blue shirt, leaving the collar open. His Glock was still sitting in evidence, so he found a holster for his Colt and clipped that to his waistband, next to his badge. He had a pouch for a spare magazine that he wore on his opposite hip, but he hadn't replaced the flashlight yet. He slid into a jacket that matched the pants.

"No tie," Marianne asked.

"Not today."

He looped the sling around his neck and tucked his arm inside. Jim went into his closet for a moment, then came back out.

"If we're meeting for lunch, I probably shouldn't eat," said Jim.

"I asked Rosa to make you a smoothie," said Marianne, "it'll be good for you."

"It's a little early for tequila."

Marianne gave him a withering look, then they went downstairs. Rosa handed him a glass filled with something green. Jim looked at Marianne, looked at Rosa and then looked at the glass.

"What is this?"

"Seaweed, kale, stuff to keep you healthy."

"Oh damn."

Jim took a sip, grimaced, then drained the glass.

"That had better be good for me," Jim said.

"I hope you stay in the office," Marianne said, "Even Sheridan says you're not ready."

"He said I'd be ok with light duty, so long as I take it easy."

"We'll see you for lunch," she said and kissed him as he limped out to the garage.

When he was gone, Marianne sat at the counter.

"What's bothering you, miss," Rosa asked.

"I have a bad feeling. I really hope I'm wrong, but I feel like something bad is going to happen."

Rosa made a show of wiping off the counter. "Miss, he's going back to work for the first time. He was bad hurt the last time he went to work. Could this just be you being worried about him?"

Marianne looked thoughtful for a moment. "You could be right. I hope so."

Jim drove his new Explorer across the floating bridge towards the city. His leg ached but it was under control. The cane that Marianne had given

191

him rested on the passenger seat. The bridge was crowded but the traffic was flowing smoothly if slowly. The drive was uneventful and he pulled into the parking garage about fifteen minutes late. As he stepped out of the car his phone rang. Jim ignored it and using his cane, made his way to the building entrance.

Jim came into the bullpen and found Lloyd at his desk. He was sitting across from Ross and next to Jason and Ted.

"Which one of you tried to call me just now," Jim said.

"Hey boss, welcome back," said Lloyd.

"Good to be here. Who called me?"

The four of them looked around and shrugged.

"Well if it's important they'll call back," Jim said, "Jason, you have a lunch date today."

"Excellent," he said.

Jim went into his office, eased into his chair and looked at his phone. The call had come from a blocked number.

"Dammit," he said in his empty office. He called the Telephone and Electronic Surveillance Unit and spoke to Ruben, knowing the answer before he made the phone call.

"I'm sorry Jim, but with a blocked number there is no way to know who that is. I wouldn't be able to get a judge to sign off on a warrant and no prosecutor would touch it."

"Thank's Ruben, no worries. If it's who I think it is she'll call back."

"If she does, I might be able to do something then." Ruben hung up.

Jim stumped back to the bullpen.

"Guys, I think Gretchen Henderson tried to call me."

He had the attention of his detectives.

"If she calls back, I'll signal you guys. Call Rueben Pemberton in TESU and he'll try to get a trace on her."

"Got it boss," said Lloyd as Jim went back into his office.

Jim was wading through his backed up email for about twenty minutes before the phone rang again.

Jim stepped to the door and waved at Lloyd as he answered the phone. "Hello?"

"Hi Jim," the voice was breathy.

"Hi Gretchen, where are you?"

"I'm not telling you that. But I tell you what."

Jim stuck a thumb in the air and said to the phone, "what's that?"

"I'll turn myself in, but only to you."

"Hey Gretchen, you put me on light duty. I'm not supposed to leave the building."

"Not even to arrest me? Come to Einstein Bagels in city hall and I'll turn myself in to you there."

"Why don't you just come to the lobby here at headquarters?"

"No. The bagel place. I'll give you fifteen minutes because I know you're slow. And Jim?"

"What is it?"

"Come alone."

"Gretchen, come on. I'll meet you in the lobby." But it was too late. She'd hung up.

Lloyd looked up from his phone, "Ruben couldn't get an accurate fix but he thinks she's nearby."

Jim looked at his watch.

"I got fifteen minutes to get to Einsteins on fourth avenue. Ted and Jason, get down there as quick as you can, find someplace to watch where you won't be seen. Maybe the parking garage. Lloyd, you and Ross walk down now, same thing. Don't be seen."

"Who's going into the place?"

"I will," said Jim.

"Boss, with all due respect…"

"She's expecting me. And she knows me. We gotta move so lets go."

Lloyd and Ross grabbed their coats and headed for the elevator. Jason and Ted headed out to their car. Jim went back into his office and slid his jacket over his shoulders before adjusting his sling. Then he picked up his cane and limped to the elevator. He rode it down to the lobby shifting impatiently as people got on and off.

Finally the doors opened and Jim stepped off the elevator into the lobby. He went past the desk officer who was on the phone when Jim walked by. Jim was leaning on the cane as he crossed the street and went down the hill. The bagel shop was right on the corner and he went in without stopping. He looked around. There was a handful of people in the shop, so Jim stood in line and ordered a bagel and cream cheese. He sat at a table and watched out the window but Gretchen did not come by. He waited fifteen minutes, then pulled out his phone and made a group text.

"I think we've been had. Going back to the office."

As he came out of the restaurant he was joined on the sidewalk by Ted.

"I'm going to walk back with you," he said, "the others are going to keep an eye on this place for a little longer, just in case."

"OK."

Jim tried to focus on his breathing going back up the hill. He was grateful they had to wait for the stop light so his breathing could get under control. The light turned and they crossed the street. Ted stepped in front and grabbed the heavy door as Jim passed through. This put Ted behind by about a step.

Jim stepped into the lobby, and caught a flash of red off to his right. He glanced over and saw a red haired woman coming off the bench and walking towards him. He turned away and stepped towards the security door to the rest of the building.

"Something about the way she walks," thought Jim.

He turned back towards the woman just as Ted wrapped his arms around her and tackled her to the floor. A .22 pistol fell out of her hand and skittered across the floor to stop at Jims feet. He put his foot on top of it and yelled, "DJ!"

The officer came out from behind the security door, running towards the commotion. Gretchen was screaming now, and trying to fight Ted, but he had her in a bear hug.

"You're not going anywhere," Ted said as Gretchen screamed and bent over, trying to bite him.

The officer managed to get one wrist into handcuffs, then Ted fought the other wrist into the small of Gretchen's back so it could be handcuffed. Ted caught his breath for a minute and said to Gretchen, "are you ok?"

Gretchen let out a low, angry growl. Jim looked around at the small knot of people that had formed, pushing against the wall at the far end of the lobby. A patrol car pulled up outside, screeching to a halt, it's lights flashing and siren blaring. A male and female officer jumped out. Another car pulled to a halt behind the first and another officer jumped out. The male and female officer came in first, the third officer right behind. Jim identified himself, and told the first two officers, "search her and drive her up to the homicide office. Put her in one of our cells and sit on her. We'll meet you there."

Jim asked the third officer if he had a camera. By now two more cars had pulled up, and one officer was blocking the entrance while a sergeant walked into the lobby.

"Interview these folks. Get their information and bring it to me," said Jim.

"Yes sir," said the sergeant.

"Ted, you ok?"

"Yes sir. I thought she was Maria because of the hair. When I realized it wasn't I saw her hand coming up with a gun in it. She was going to shoot you in the back of the head."

"I believe it. Get a picture of this gun here in the lobby, then lets get upstairs."

The officer with the camera came in and handed it to Jim, who handed it to Ted, who took several pictures of the gun, and of the lobby, including perspectives from the benches and from outside. When he was done Ted took a rubber glove from his pocket and carefully picked up the gun. The desk officer that Jim knew as "DJ" gave Ted a small box to put the pistol into.

As they went into the secure area, Ted said to DJ, "I'll get your handcuffs back to you. When you get a relief, can you come upstairs and give us a statement?"

DJ nodded.

Ted and Jim got on the elevator before they noticed the Chief was already on board.

"Good morning ma'am," said Jim.

"Captain Churchill," the chief said, "aren't you out sick still?"

"Just came back to light duty chief," he said, "and detective Cysinski and I just got back from that bagel place down the street."

"Is that what you have in the box?"

"No ma'am."

"You just don't want to share?"

"There was a little altercation in the lobby. We took care of it. This is just the suspects gun."

Ted lifted the lid of the box.

"I see. Well, not bad for being on light duty," she said.

The elevator opened on their floor. Jim said good by to the chief and they headed for the office.

"Give CSI a call. They might want to see if ballistics matches with the Miller shooting."

Ted agreed and headed to his desk. Lloyd and Jason were standing by their desks.

"Where's Ross?"

"He's sitting with our suspect," said Lloyd, "how do you want to handle this?"

"We have two different cases, plus Tacomas. Maybe a tag team?"

"Let's give her a few minutes to calm down and then we'll go at it."

Jason said, "She fought all the way into the room. I'm not sure that we'll get anything out of her."

"Do we need an interview," asked Jim.

"I think we should at least try," said Lloyd.

"OK, whenever you're ready," said Jim.

Fifteen minutes later Lloyd and Jason walked into the room. Ross walked out and went into the observation room with Jim. Gretchen had worn herself out. She was handcuffed to the ring in the middle of the table. While she was normally fit and healthy looking, two weeks of road travel and bad nutrition had caught up to her. She had yelled and pulled at the ring on the table until she couldn't. Now she sat in a chair, bent over at the waist, leaning her head on the table. Jim flipped on the speaker in time to hear Jason finish reciting Miranda rights to Gretchen.

"Are you ready to talk now, Gretchen?" Jason was calm, soothing and friendly.

Jim watched Gretchen rouse herself and sit upright.

"You're Jason, right?"

"Yes ma'am," he said.

"OK, Jason. Fuck off."

Jim thought the vulgarity seemed contrived. Jason pushed on.

"Let's go back to two Fridays ago. Do you remember that?"

"Yeah. That's when Jim was shot."

"Tell me what you know about that."

"No. I wasn't there."

"That's two different things, Gretchen. Here's the thing. I can tie you to the shooters. I can show that you were afraid Jim was going to put you in prison for killing your husband. And I can show that you hired those two to kill Jim. I just want your side of the story."

Gretchen leaned forward, her elbows on the table and said, "Ok, Jason. Come here."

Involuntarily, Jason leaned forward. Gretchen jumped as far forward as she could, narrowly missing Jasons ear with her teeth. Jason jumped back and Gretchen screamed.

"Go to hell!"

The door to interrogation opened and Jim stepped inside. His left arm was still slung but he was walking without a limp.

"Everyone out," he said.

"Skipper," Jason started.

Jims eyes were black. Lloyd nodded towards the door and the two stepped outside, then stepped into the observation room. It was crowded in there with Ross.

"Jim," Gretchen purred in interrogation.

"Cut the shit, Gretchen," Jim said.

"I'm real sorry about your arm, Jimmy."

"This? It's an inconvenience. Tell me about Tom."

"Tom? I don't want to talk about him."

In observation, Jason said to Lloyd, "What's he doing?"

"Watch and learn," said Lloyd.

Jim leaned forward, "Gretchen, if I'm going to help you out, I need to know what Tom had on you."

Gretchen's eyes lit up.

"Oh Jimmy, he's not half the man you are."

"What kind of man is he?"

"He blackmailed me," she said, "he slipped me a roofie and took advantage of me. He took pictures and threatened to send them to Fred if I didn't cooperate. He had total control over me."

"Where are the pictures?"

"I'm not sure. Maybe they're still on his phone."

"Walk me through it. How did you kill Fred?"

"I didn't think it would kill him. I told Dionne to put some lidocaine in his thermos. I told her just enough to cause some chest pains. I thought maybe it'd scare him. He wasn't supposed to die."

"So Fred was an accident?"

"Of course! I loved him."

"So why did you take a hit out on me?"

"That was all Tom. He thought you were testing Fred's blood and if you found out we'd both go to prison."

"You were going to let him kill me." It wasn't a question.

"Oh Jimmy, no. They had this crate of pistols, the little ones, you know, .22's. I told him just to scare you. You weren't going to be killed."

"Who killed Fortunato?"

"That had to be Lazzari. He was the only one in the car."

"OK. Who killed Lazzari?"

"That had to be Tom. He left to pay them off. He was gone for a while, and when he came back he said they never showed. He must have killed them. Maybe he panicked."

Jim nodded. "But you were there."

"No, I would have told you if I was."

Jim skipped over the lidocaine in his water glass and didn't ask her about Benvenuti at first.

"Did Tom kill Alaina?"

Gretchen nodded. "She called him wanting more money because Jason had made the connection to them. She told him to meet her at that ratty motel. Tom said she let him in and he shot her right away."

"Did you go with him?"

"No. I stayed home. I didn't want to be anywhere near that woman, I thought she was dangerous."

"But you knew he was going to kill her."

"He took my phone and tied me to the bed. There was nothing I could do."

"Why did you leave town?"

"Tom thought it was getting a little too hot for us. He wanted to switch cars so we got Freds truck and went to Toms grandparents place in Wyoming."

"Why did you kill him there?"

197

"You wouldn't ask that if you knew what he did to me."

Jim lowered his voice. "What did he do?"

Jim sensed it was the first real emotion he got from her when her voice broke as she said, "it was brutal, Jim. He treated me worse than an animal. I was more like a thing to him."

She went into detail about that night, and how he wouldn't let her up until after he had come back with breakfast. Before he let her use the bathroom, he'd choked her.

"If you want proof," she said, "I took some pictures with my phone."

"Is that why you killed him," Jim asked quietly.

"I was afraid he was going to kill me," she said.

"How did that happen?"

"I got out of the shower," she said, "and he came after me. I tried to run and I found these bookends in the living room. I hit him once with one and he collapsed in the living room. I got dressed and got the hell out."

"How did he get into the garage?"

"He must have walked out there looking for me after he woke up."

"Gretchen, why did you set fire to him?"

"But I didn't." She was leaning forward, insistent. "When I left he was still alive."

"OK, Gretchen. Just a couple more questions."

Gretchen leaned back in her chair and nodded.

"Why Benvenuti?"

"Who?"

"Larry. The weightlifter guy. Why did you kill him?"

"I don't know what you're talking about." Jim could see she was starting to panic.

"We have a witness that puts you in the room with Benvenuti. You shot him up with Lidocaine and faked a heart attack. You tried to do the same thing with me but that didn't go so well."

"But Jim, you have to believe me!"

"Gretchen, you're going to get the needle for this. You've killed too many people. I can maybe help you with Wyoming, but with everything else…"

A look of realization came over Gretchen's face.

"Jim, please. Help me. It'll be worth your while…"

"So you can finish the job you started? Forget it."

Jim stood and headed for the door. Gretchen sat back in her chair, her arm still attached to the bolt in the table and smiled to herself.

An hour later Jim and Jason were seated across from each other in an Italian restaurant when Jenny and Marianne found them. Marianne dropped onto the bench next to Jim, kissed him and said, "you look happy."

Jim smiled, "it's been a busy morning." He then related the events of the day.

Marianne looked at him seriously.

"I thought you said you would be stashed at your desk?"

"We figured she wouldn't come in unless she saw me. So I took a chance."

"We?" Marianne raised an eyebrow.

"We had to do something. And it seemed like the thing to do at the time."

"Well, dammit, don't do that again."

"I don't have to now. She's in jail."

Marianne nodded.

Jenny said to Jason, "she tried to bite your ear?"

Jason nodded, "almost did too, but she missed."

"Is that normal?"

"Not in the least. That woman is seriously bent."

"It would seem so."

"So what happens now," Marianne asked.

Jim replied, "depends. We have a solid case but anything can happen. Even if she gets off here, Wyoming still wants her."

"Isn't she claiming self defense?"

"Her story is bullshit. But you never know. At least she puts herself in the room with him."

Marianne asked, "Jenny have you been to Nordstroms down here? I'd like to look at their wedding registry. We should go there after lunch."

3pm

Gretchen was laying on her back on a bunk in the women's section of the jail. The underwear and orange jumpsuit the jail provided her were uncomfortable and scratched. But she didn't move, she simply stared at the ceiling.

A short, stocky female guard came by and said, "Henderson, you have a visitor."

"Who is it?"

The guard shrugged and said, "get up."

Gretchen stood, slowly, and came out to the hallway. A second guard, this one a big man, stood behind the female. The woman pointed down the hall and Gretchen led the trio to another door. The door buzzed and she pushed it open, then waited for the door to close. The door on the other side then buzzed and she pushed it open, the guards following behind her.

They came into a reception area, and she was told to sit down. A moment later she was told to stand again, and taken into a small room. Gretchen looked through the glass partition that separated this room from the one next to it. She was surprised to see Marianne Wilson sitting on the other side of the glass, her blonde hair framing her face. Gretchen picked the telephone handle from the wall next to the glass and waited for Marianne to do the same.

Marianne sighed and picked up the phone.

"What do you want with me," asked Gretchen.

Marianne paused a moment, then said, "I want you to remember one thing. If you should ever get out of here, and you ever come anywhere near my family, I will hear about it and you know what will happen."

Gretchen spoke into the phone, "what would that be?"

But Marianne had already hung up the phone. She pulled a lipstick out of her purse, and ran it over her lips using her faint reflection in the window. Then Marianne put the lipstick away and wiggled her fingers at Gretchen, before turning and walking through the door on her side.

Gretchen carefully hung up the phone. She turned and walked back to the door. The guard let her out and escorted her back to her cell.

Chapter 24

Jim was leaning on his cane, staring out of his office window. Two city workers were diligently pulling weeds in the municipal garden on top of city hall. Clouds were scudding low above the Olympic mountains, which meant rain in the afternoon. For now though, the sun was shining and the air was warm.

There was a knock at the door. Jim turned to see Lloyd standing in the doorway.

"Come in, Lloyd," said Jim, motioning to a chair.

"Thank you sir," Lloyd said as he sat at the familiar round conference table.

Jim limped to a chair and sat across from him.

"Lloyd, I want to thank you for all you did on this case," Jim began.

"No problem Jim, I was happy to help."

"Well, thank you for sticking around and helping Jason to break in Ted."

"Skipper," began Lloyd, "that's my job. I decided that you need me to stick around, so I decided to give it another year."

Jim leaned back in his chair and paused a minute to let that sink in.

"Lloyd, thank you. We could really use the help around here."

"Thought you'd want to know. You guys set a date yet?"

"Turns out she wants a June wedding. Keep your calendar clear."

"Will do, skipper." Lloyd stood and they shook hands before he turned and left the office.

On his way out, Lloyd passed Ted in the doorway.

"Good luck," mouthed Lloyd.

"You wanted to see me," Ted asked Jim.

"Have a seat," said Jim.

Ted sat in the chair vacated by Lloyd.

"How are things, Ted,?"

"Well, I've been enjoying myself. Jason and Lloyd are good teachers and so is Ross. I feel like I'm starting to get my sea legs under me."

"How about personally? Are you still seeing Maria?"

"We have a date for tonight."

"How is that working out?"

"We had to make some rules. She won't use anything I tell her unless she asks me first."

"I spoke to your captain this morning," Jim said, "he said you worked your butt off in media relations."

"Sir, do I have to go back there?"

"Here's the thing, Ted. I can't send him anyone, I'm already short handed over here."

"I see." Ted looked dejected.

"But I told him you are wasting your talents in media relations and Homicide takes priority. And he agreed."

"I don't understand," Ted replied.

"Ted, you're staying here. I spoke with Naes and she really liked your work. So you and Jason will team up for now."

"Thank you sir. That's good news!"

"Welcome aboard, Ted. Don't let me down."

5pm

Jim and Marianne sat at the dining room table. Jim was twirling spaghetti onto a fork when he said, "funny thing happened today."

"What was that?"

Jim was focusing on his spaghetti. "We get a copy of the visitor log from the jail. Guess who visited Gretchen Henderson yesterday."

Marianne felt herself flushing. "Jim..."

Jim interrupted, "the log was signed by someone named Cassidy Upton."

Marianne started to speak, and caught herself. "Honey, I had to see her."

Jim smiled at her. "I know. I'd have done the same thing."

"How could you know what I said?"

"Those phones you talk through?" Marianne nodded. "Those lines are recorded. They save the records for ninety days. Ted pulled the tapes and saw you on the video." Jim got serious for a minute. "Just don't do it again. That woman is dangerous and there are people from that gang that are still out there."

Marianne nodded. "I promise. I think I made my point anyway."

"You certainly did."

Friday 4pm
Prescott AZ

Jim and Marianne pulled into the parking lot of "The Ranch," a memory care facility. Marianne was driving a rented Ford Expedition and had followed the GPS straight from the Prescott Municipal Airport. She put the selector into park but before she could shut off the motor, Jim said, "Hold on."

Marianne looked at him and cocked an eyebrow.

"Are you sure you want to do this," Jim asked, "because it's not too late to back out now."

"I know that I want to do this," Marianne said, "and it feels like I need to. She's your mother, and she might forget me fifteen minutes after we leave, but it's important to me."

Jim nodded, then he leaned across the car and kissed Marianne. She shut the car off and they got out into the late afternoon sun. Jim left his cane in the car, and Marianne came around the car and took his hand. The Ranch was a sprawling one story building, built around a courtyard. Once inside the décor was decidedly western. Jim checked at the front desk and the receptionist directed them around the corner on the right side. Jim limped down the hall. Marianne was wearing her hair down and slipped her sunglasses into her purse. They got to the room, and Jim rapped on the frame of the open door.

"Come in," said a male voice.

"Hi pop," said Jim, "we made it."

Paul Churchill stood as Jim and Marianne came through the door. He hugged his son and then took a kiss on the cheek from Marianne.

"How's the wing," Paul asked.

"Sore, but getting better all the time," Jim said.

A woman in her sixties was seated at a table in the room. She was staring at them, as if she was trying to place the two of them. Paul turned to her.

"Joann, look who's here."

"Hi Mom," said Jim, "I'd like you to meet someone."

Joann looked at Jim without comprehension.

Jim spoke softly. "Mom, it's me, Jim. Your son."

"I know who you are," said Joann, "but I feel like I should know her." Joann pointed at Marianne with her chin.

"She's my fiancé, mom. Her name is Marianne."

Marianne stepped forward and took her hand.

"I'm so happy to meet you, Joann. Jim's told me all about you."

"Have we met?"

Marianne looked around the room.

"No we haven't, but my picture is right over there." Marianne pointed to the nightstand. A picture of Jim and Marianne sat in a frame, Marianne smiling brightly.

Jim looked around the room. Pictures of Jim in army dress greens and police class A uniforms were interspersed with pictures of Jim and Paul in civilian clothes and uniform. There were pictures of Marianne as well, both with Jim and on stage. There were a lot of pictures.

"I see you've been busy, dad."

"I'd have had more pictures of your fiancé if I'd known about her sooner," Paul said.

"Both of you, don't you start now. We are here for Joann," said Marianne.

"Who are you dear," asked Joann.

"I'm Marianne. I'm your sons fiancé. We are getting married in June and I wanted to meet you first."

"Oh congratulations. I'm so excited for...my son."

Jim looked at his dad.

"This is a good day," Paul said quietly.

Jim nodded. He'd been expecting this but it was still a shock.

Marianne and Jim had dinner with Paul and Joann. Afterwards Jim, Paul and Marianne were chatting in the parking lot before heading back to Pauls house.

"I wish I had met her before," said Marianne.

"She was a wonderful woman and still is," Paul replied, "and I think she's still in there somewhere. It's just that no one knows how to let her out."

"She taught school in Seattle for years," said Jim, "and retired when dad left the department to come to Prescott."

"Do the pictures help," Marianne asked.

"Some I think. In truth it's hard to tell but it doesn't hurt."

Paul turned to Jim. "How's the investigation going?"

"Jason should be closing it out today," he said.

At that moment Jason and Todd were in the parking lot of Quinns talking to Gil Tuller.

Jason said, "we're just trying to wrap up some loose ends. We just need to know how deep this thing goes."

Gil looked at Jason, glassy eyed. "Man, the only ones that knew what was going on was Larry and Alaina. Even then I don't think Larry knew everything."

Jason nodded. "Gil, I would still like to talk with the rest of this crew."

"I got no idea where they are. That last time you were here, they took off and they ain't been back."

"Did Alaina keep any files here? We didn't find anything at the house."

"Yeah sure, she had an office here. Come on."

Gil led the way into the bar as Jason was mentally kicking himself for not thinking of this earlier. Gil led them through the bar and into the back before he took a left turn and opened a door into a tiny, cramped office. Inside was a filing cabinet that sat behind a desk. A chair sat behind it and a single client chair stood in front. There was barely room to get around the desk, in fact Gil had to turn sideways to get past it. He opened the top drawer of the cabinet and pulled out a ledger. He laid it on the desk and opened it. About six pages in he found what he wanted and turned it around for the detectives to see.

In one column were the initials G.H., followed by a telephone number, written in a spidery crawl. The next column were the initials J.C., and in another column was the numbers 50k, 30k and 10k. In spite of himself Jason let out a chuckle.

"What?"

Instead of answering Ted, Jason pointed at the first column.

"Gil, who is that?"

"I don't know man, but that looks like a telephone number."

"I'd bet money that's Gretchen Henderson. So that's the client. That column is the target," Jason was pointing to the initials 'JC,' "and the rest is money."

"How does the money work," asked Ted.

"I think fifty thousand was the agreed on price. Thirty was probably what she was paid. She gave ten each to Fortunato and Lazzari. She was supposed to get thirty grand for herself. Alaina got shorted twenty grand."

"That's why she called Gretchen. Twenty K is nothing to sneeze at."

Jason flipped back through the first six pages.

"Look at this. I bet we can solve a number of cases out of this." To Gil he said, "Are there any more ledgers?"

"Let me look," said Gil, turning back to the file cabinet.

Gil reached into the drawer and came out with a pistol. He aimed it one handed at Jason.

"Why'd you have to push it," he said, "you coulda just been satisfied nailing that bitch, but you had to keep pushing it."

Jason didn't move. The gun looked tiny in Gil's hand, and Jason knew it had to be a .22, but looking down the business end Jason thought it looked like the Mount Baker tunnel.

"Gil, it's ok. We're just trying to get some closure for the families."

"You asshole," said Gil, "my name is in these books. I drove the fucking car."

"Gil, that's ok. You don't have to do this." Jason was talking but he was trying to determine if he could leap across the small desk or not.

"You don't get it. Alaina ran things. I was her right hand."

"Gil, did you shoot Lazzeri?"

"Fuck you," Gil said and straightened his arm.

Jason saw the flash but did not hear the bang. Something smacked the side of his head and he stumbled backwards when he saw a neat round hole appear under Gils left eye. Gil's head rocked back and he fell against the cabinet and slid straight down, his body suddenly limp. A stream of gore and blood followed Gil's body to the floor.

Ted's Glock was still smoking. Jason saw Ted's lips moving but couldn't understand what he was saying.

"What?"

Ted's mouth was moving, and it took a minute before Jason realized he couldn't hear Ted. Jason pointed to his ear, and Ted understood immediately. Ted pointed to the right side of his forehead. Jason put his hand up against the left side of his head. When he pulled it away Jason's hand was slick with blood.

"Aw shit. Jenny's not going to like this."

Two hours later Lieutenant Naes and Sergeant Worthy were being briefed by Detective Danny White, Tacoma PD.

"For some reason it seems that Mr. Tueller fixated on Jason. Your man tried to keep him talking as much as he could and when it became apparent there was no other way, Detective Cysinski was able to draw and fire on the suspect."

"Where's Jason now?"

Danny pointed to the medic unit. Jason was sitting on the rear bumper, Ted was standing next to him. Rebekah walked to the back of the ambulance. Jason started to stand but Rebekah waved him down.

"How's your hearing?"

"I'm real sorry, lieutenant. I had no idea it would end like this." Jason was peering out from under a heavy bandage.

"I hear you both did real well, trying to talk him down."

"Not well enough," said Jason, bitterly.

"Don't beat yourself up," said Mike, "if Ted hadn't shot him, he would have killed both of you."

"If I'd been smart, I'd have gone behind the desk," said Jason, "and maybe we wouldn't be in this fix."

"Danny tells me that Gil's name is all over those books. He picked up the money from the clients and drove Alaina everywhere. He'd get his cut, Alaina would take hers, and the rest would be split with whoever she picked for the job. Fortunato and Lazzari probably thought they were the go to guys for the tough jobs, when the reality was that Alaina and Gil were trying to get them killed. Gil probably knew that could get him the needle if we figured that out."

"How helpful are those books," Ted was curious.

"Probably a couple dozen jobs in them. It'll take time to figure out which ones are homicides and it looks like they ran all over the Pacific Northwest. But probably at minimum four or five homicides. By the way, before we came down I called Ray. He got a match on the prints in Alaina's car."

"Let me guess," said Jason, "Gil?"

"First try too. He probably drove the car and killed Lazzari at the park and ride."

Jason asked, "Have you called the captain yet?"

"No," Rebekah said, "they're in Prescott with family. You know, if I call Captain Churchill, he's going to tell Marianne. And she's going to call Jenny."

"I don't want Jenny to find out that way."

"No, I didn't think you would."

The medic spoke up, "hey man, if you're going to call someone else get to it. I really need to get you to the hospital."

Jason nodded and pulled his phone from his pocket. He pushed the speed dial and let it ring. Rebekah and Mike stepped away, followed by Ted.

"What do I do," asked Ted.

"You're on administrative leave until we can convene a firearms review board for you."

"So who investigates?"

"Tacoma homicide. Lloyd and Ross are the liaison with them." She pointed across the parking lot where Lloyd Murray was deep in conversation with a Tacoma detective.

"Don't worry," Rebekah continued, "you're in good hands."

Ted nodded. Mike Worthy handed him a box.

"Make sure you get to the range and run some rounds through this thing. The city will want it back eventually."

Ted took the box and looked inside. A brand new Glock, still in the original packaging, lay inside.

Jason was talking to Jenny.

"So, honey, I might be a little late tonight."

"It's about damn time you called," she said, "you are all over the news. What the hell is that bandage about?"

It was almost midnight when Ted got home. The Adrenalin from the shooting was still running through his blood when he pulled into the driveway. A black Volkswagen Atlas was parked at the curb in front of his house. Maria Sorensen stepped out as Ted put the car in park.

"Hi honey," said Ted.

"I'm glad you called," she said, "I'm glad you're ok."

"Come in," he said and they headed up to the house.

"What did you think? I saw you on the perimeter but I couldn't get to you," said Ted.

Maria shivered. "Are you sure you're ok? You didn't get hurt?"

They stood in Ted's kitchen.

"At one point I stopped in front of a liquor store. But I don't want to go down that road again."

Maria touched his face. "I got some good shots of you, and Jason. How did it happen?"

Ted told her. When he was done he thought he saw tears in her eyes.

"Does this kind of thing happen often?"

Ted said, "depends. The odds are against it. But you never know."

"I don't know if I can handle this," said Maria.

"How about this," said Ted, "lets just handle tonight.

Maria nodded, as Ted stepped in and kissed her.

ABOUT THE AUTHOR

The author has over three decades in law enforcement. This is his second book.

Made in the USA
San Bernardino, CA
03 June 2020